THE PRIDE LIST

EDITED BY SANDIP ROY AND BISHAN SAMADDAR

The Pride List presents works of queer literature to the world.
An eclectic collection of books of queer stories, biographies,
histories, thoughts, ideas, experiences and explorations,
the Pride List does not focus on any specific region,
nor on any specific genre, but celebrates the great diversity
of LGBTQ+ lives across countries, languages, centuries and
identities, with the conviction that queer pride comes from its
unabashed expression.

ELEVEN-INCH

Michał Witkowski

TRANSLATED BY W. MARTIN

LONDON NEW YORK CALCUTTA

BOOK INSTITUTE

© POLAND

This book has been published with the support of the
© POLAND translation programme

Seagull Books, 2021

Originally published in Polish as *Fynf und Cfancyś*, 2019
Copyright © Michał Witkowski

This translation is published by arrangement with Społeczny Instytut
Wydawniczy Znak Sp. z o.o., Kraków, Poland.

First published in English translation by Seagull Books, 2021
English translation © W. Martin, 2021

ISBN   978 0 8574 2 891 2

British Library Cataloguing-in-Publication Data
A catalogue record for this book is available from the British Library

Typeset by Seagull Books, Calcutta, India
Printed and bound in the USA by Integrated Books International

ELEVEN-INCH

DIANKA

had cuts on her hands, she came from Bratislava:

'Only an hour's drive from Vienna!'

Her name was Milan. A gorgeous, sixteen-year-old blond with blue eyes and long lashes, just like the wholesome good boy in the kiddie cartoons. But behind the veneer of this wholesome boy lurked a fat old hag. A bit of a sloth too. She worked in the U-Bahn, at Karlsplatz station. Downstairs, in the centre of the subterranean Platz, was a round, glassed-in bar we called 'the aquarium', which had a view of the toilets. Masses of adolescent Poles, Czechs, Romanians and Russians would make the rounds—and geriatric Austrians too, of course. Some of them were unbelievably beautiful, while others were monstrously ugly. There was no middle ground down there ...

Dianka would never forget the pervasive stench of citrus-scented disinfectant, which mingled with the smell of shit from the toilets. She hated standing around in front of the urinals, waiting for customers, so usually she just sat in the bar drinking beer or eating her favourite ice-cream sundae with whipped cream and sprinkles on top, and watched, glassy-eyed, as the grandpas circled the toilets.

I was from Poland, and she from Slovakia. Things always worked out for me, for her almost never. My lectures fell on deaf ears: 'Get to work, Dianka, *arbeiten*! Even if it's just for fifty schillings!'

To which she would reply indignantly, 'Ach lass mich! Ja sem žena leniva!'

Once she did get her arse in gear, all she'd do was sit and drink beer with the guy, coax him into ordering her an ice-cream sundae, and say to me, out loud since he couldn't understand anyway, 'Jużem se sweho byha znalasla . . . Kukaj se, podiwejse, jaki byh!'

All the while the 'stud' she was bragging about would be some run-of-the-mill, moustachioed yokel from the Austrian Alps. But try explaining that to Dianka after he'd bought her ice cream and lit her cigarette (with his BIC lighter).

'I think he gonna shaft me tonight . . .' I wasn't sure what she meant because in Polish the word for 'shaft' meant to cheat, while in Czech it meant to fuck. But I could see they wouldn't be doing it in Czech anyway, but in French, and end up Polish-style with a broke Dianka back turning tricks at the train station the next day . . .

But whatever, it was good having someone like Dianka on the street. She'd be out there eating in front of the döner shop or drinking coffee in front of the Eduscho cafe. While I'd be smoothing out my bank notes, turning those scowling Austrians this way and that so they all faced the same direction, bundling them into wads, wrapping them in rubber bands. It was a lot of work, but I had a natural predisposition for it: my eleven-inch *Schwanz*. And a different story for every trick too. I'd have my Krzysztof croaking a different way each time. I told this one guy he'd got stung by a bee and had an allergy and that was that. Dead as a doornail. Another time I had him going off to use the crapper at the train station, back home in Konin, and never coming back. And when the toilet lady and I broke down the stall door, I continued, it was empty, except for a puddle of blood on the floor . . .

'Dianka, you're not cut out for this line of work. You're not enough of a materialist. I know you're from the East. I know your Bratislava's only an hour's drive away, but still.'

Once there was this customer who'd run her ragged—spitting, kicking, fucking, pissing, beating. Oof, he did everything really. She'd had enough. She rang for a cab. She wasn't too familiar with the stairwell though. The stairs were steep, and through the open entryway she could see the cab waiting for her out in front. So she hurried down, started running down the steps, carefree and happy that she had it all behind her and a decent wad of cash in her pocket—five hundred schillings. Then suddenly, just as she got to the last step, the world disappeared, there was a great thud! Dianka blacked out. Coming from Slovakia, she wasn't used to such clean, clear windows. She wasn't used to many things. And later it pained her no end that the cab driver had seen the accident, watched her careening head slam against the windows at full force, and she was embarrassed about that.

Things went downhill from there. She had less and less money. She'd even started to live on the streets, so she ended up looking like shit. It was a vicious circle: she had no money, so she looked awful, but in order to make any money, she needed to get some rest, have a bath, put on clean clothes . . .

She was on her own now, in the U-Bahn, and her shoes were chafing her feet so badly she couldn't even go roaming around Vienna. She hobbled over to Alfie's Golden Mirror, the hustler bar, sat down in a corner, and without drinking, without smoking, without eating, simply watched the goings-on, quietly humming Slovak rock songs and Dara Rolins, who back then was still called Darinka Rolincová.

It was like a game of roulette: you might make five hundred schillings in a night, but to really earn money you had to invest it first. Because sometimes you'd have to sit there for hours before landing a customer, during which time you'd end up drinking five deliriously overpriced coffees, five Fantas, five beers, five whatever, because the bartenders (Norma and Vincent) made sure that the escorts ordered at least one drink per hour. So what you made in one day you'd spend over the course of five just sitting and waiting. And you'd be chain-smoking those Austrian cigarettes, Milde Sorte, which are extra light but always give you headaches!

Dianka watched the successful boys with envy, sitting there at the bar, stuffing their faces with enormous schnitzels and fries or potato salad or pork chops and fried eggs. And sometimes they didn't even have to pay for it because they were with some fat, bald grandpa with a wallet. And with beautiful, fresh lemon halves to squeeze on the meat, on the fries, on all that wonderful grub! She swallowed her own spit and smoked a cigarette she'd bummed off someone, which tasted like crap on an empty stomach. She wondered how long before they threw her out, since she couldn't invest any money in their business now. Even if she did manage to dig up a few schillings, she knew what would happen next—she'd trick once, then have nothing five nights in a row, she could lose it all. Even the Romanians had been dry for two weeks! And what Romanians they were! My God! Through their oversized, baggy white trousers they showed Dianka what gorgeous, fat cocks they had, stretching the stained fabric around them. In their broken

German mixed with Russian, they asked her if she wanted to see for herself, starved as they were—two weeks, *nichts*. They wanted schillings, cigarettes, they'd even smoke Austria Drei, but what could she give them? They were handsome and masculine, without that antiseptic look in their eyes that the Austrians, Swiss and Germans had. They were straight, eighteen years old, dark features, bushy black eyebrows! But they sort of reminded her a little of the Gypsies, and Dianka was afraid of Gypsies, like the ones in Slovakia. They stood around and made bonfires, their eyes mirroring the flames . . .

An elderly customer, Dieter, a copy of Günter Grass's *The Rat* and a *Wiener Zeitung* under his arm, made the rounds of the bar, looking like the professor from *The Blue Angel*. In a threadbare sports coat, with a little pipe. But he didn't know what he wanted. He once called Dianka over to his table, bought her drinks, then said, 'Heute bin ich müde, lass mich alleine . . .'

Then they made a date for Wednesday, although Dianka really wasn't sure he'd live that long.

Vincent was behind the bar today, a tall, likeable Austrian, who was merciless when it came to ordering drinks. Out of the jukebox came torch songs and *Schlager* from yesteryear, and the years before yesteryear, even Edith Piaf. In the next room young Eastern European escorts were playing the slot machines. One African escort was there, unwashed, unattractive, foul-smelling, and Dianka knew she was homeless, that she'd got sucked into the vicious circle, and that she'd end up there herself too, if a miracle didn't happen tonight. Then that sweetheart Vincent gave a nod to the bouncer to escort the boy discreetly off the premises. Outside, in the cold, you couldn't smell the beer or food. There among the parked cars would walk the hookers who weren't allowed into Alfie's because they were too poxy. The ones who'd refused to give the Czech mafia a cut of their earnings, so their faces got cut with a razor. The ones who didn't want to give the bartenders, Norma and Vincent, their due—a piece of arse now and then and every month a dividend.

Suddenly a jolly band of local playboys burst in—middle-aged, colourful scarves or motorcycle helmets on their heads, chains around their necks, rings on their fingers. Noisy and jolly, straight from a land called Miami, a land of movie stars, cocktails and red convertibles pumping music at full blast. A land of moonscape wallpaper and faded dreams that was only as far away as the imagination of the next playboy. They ordered whiskies, smoked Marlboro Reds—they couldn't care less if smoking kills. Bald and monstrously obese, in the way only the wealthy can be, because wealth always exaggerates a person's distinguishing features— thought Milan, philosopher of the Bratislava housing estates. After all, when someone eats too much but they're poor, they just put on weight, but if they're rich (and for Dianka all Austrians were rich), they end up looking like one of these behemoths. Or let's say you had a really campy queen who happens to be wealthy, she'll probably have on an entire jewellery shop, a coat of gold, furs—enough to trump any opera diva ... In any case, the playboys' bellowing filled the bar, they were completely out of control, but of no use to Dianka as long as they were only entertaining each other. She'd been around long enough to know that only the shamefaced, solitary grandpas stuck in the corner were worth eyeing. The bald men unleashed another volley of rowdy guffaws. All the while the real 'rowdies'—the beautiful young Russians—were sitting quietly in the back, fumbling in the pockets of their grubby jeans for their last coins. There was yet another type of customer who was deformed by wealth: the forty-something queens with their awful faces, their grimaces, each reminiscent of a different species of animal—weasel, parrot, owl—all of them dripping with jewellery. Within seconds those prima donnas would be joined by beautiful, two-metre-tall boys from the land of glittering lights and cheap entertainment, who'd come to bring them their coats or take them away, to move their ashtrays closer and light their cigarettes, boys who'd give up their places next to the door for a chance to be chosen . . . they even pulled out their chairs and seated them.

But even as the boys hurried to serve them, the queens just batted their eyelashes and slapped them clumsily, tenderly, or made indignant faces: 'You look like a turd. I'm taking someone else home tonight! Pooh!' Although they were old and ugly, they didn't show the least sign of balding (transplants) or greying (dye), they had no wrinkles, and they were tall, well fed. It was only their jaded expressions that betrayed their real age. They'd had every-thing replaced. But old age passed off as youth doesn't actually look like youth, it looks like old age trying to pass as youth! They put on airs like those old-time Czechoslovak actresses, those old girls with their shoulder-length perms . . . Old gazelles with their bracelets and rings and cigarette cases and lighters, and all of them smothered in diamonds, rubies, a hoard years in the making. And there right next to them was a table of strapping bears with huge bald pates—a gang of taxi drivers. They were knocking back beers, smoking those little brown cigars, cracking up for the whole bar to hear. Tin rings with skulls on them. And if they weren't bald, then invariably they had their hair cut in a mullet, sometimes down to their arse in back, a crew-cut up front, with highlights.

Now one of them swaggered like a sailor to the jukebox and picked out a whole variety show of bad German disco tracks about love. With backup singers. A woman's warm voice rippled out of the jukebox. Dianka looked over at their beer and schnitzel and chewed her nails.

And then an ageing couple all tricked out in leather would come in, leather police caps on, black rubber boots, moustaches, an MA-1 or a leather jacket, leather trousers, chains. You could see it took years for the whole package to come together, years of savings from their white-collar pension put away in the coffee canister.

Time and again one of those decrepit, doddering old codgers would pick up a fresh-faced youth with cheeks like apples and take him across the street to an hourly room in the Hotel Stockholm. There he'd grope him clumsily with his trembling hands and drool on him a little, but not much more than that. Before he swallowed, he'd need to spit out his false teeth. And when it was over he'd pop a heart pill, to quell his heart's revolt against all the excitement.

In the other room the macho moneymakers were playing billiards. On and on and on, for six hours already. As if they didn't need to work! And they were ordering sandwiches too! The expensive ones ... garnished with a spoonful of caviar, anchovies and a slice of lemon, served right at the billiards table—service on top. And then there were those sandwiches with sausage and pickle and tomato ... or the best one, the beef tartare sandwich with the minced onion ...

Every now and then a skinny, nervous, bald queen would walk in, order a beer and spend the whole evening flicking her lighter on and off. If you asked her for a light, she'd just look at you for a moment with a completely vacant stare. Later a group of Polish grunt would enter. Straights. Eyes brimming with banality, hostility. They were only here to make money, they choked back their disgust. They wore white tracksuits with POLSKA emblazoned in big red letters across the back or red with a white eagle. Or football jerseys, Pogoń Szczecin, Wisła Kraków, Arka Gdynia ... It was their honour they were defiling now. Immediately they were like: 'Fuck, man, I'll annihilate that piece of shit if he doesn't give me that hundred schillings.'

Dianka was deliriously afraid of this group. But there was one really nice Pole with them. She heard him telling someone else how he'd just come back from France, from Cannes, how he hadn't made a penny, and in fact was cleaned out, and how if his friend hadn't cleaned up on a slot machine they'd have had no way to get back, they would've got stuck in the vicious circle there. Then he stopped, there was no need to explain to anyone in that bar what the vicious circle was.

And then there was that other Pole, that sweet-talking Eleven-Inch—famous in all Vienna and even in Salzburg, even in Linz and Graz for his massive ... pole. He was beautiful, with dark eyes, black hair, gracefully tapering cheekbones. He was always around, always up to something, wheeling and dealing, smoking cigarettes, chatting away in German, although he didn't know the language, but he spoke it anyway. He was in his element here, in constant motion, constant transformation ... He'd get dressed for work in the morning and always smelt of Chanel Égoïste. Dianka could only admire him, but as for herself, well, she preferred not to, lazy and lousy girl that she was ...

Now Dianka got up and walked out of the bar, out of its heavy air thick with the smell of cigarettes, schnitzel, beer, sweat, cologne ... She walked to the little park next door, where others were stamping their feet on the ground to keep the cold at bay, others like her—so broke they couldn't even afford to sit in a pub. And others whose faces got cut by the Czech mafia. In the cold their sweaty fingers stank and tasted like cigarettes. Here, on the street, it all looked just like it must have in the past. Everyone standing, old, fat and bald customers walking between the parked cars along the street or sitting inside them, impassive as alligators, only the hands on their zippers still moving mechanically. Sometimes someone beat someone else senseless, or else the filth would come around and everyone vanished into thin air.

And right then, just when she'd lost all hope, Dianka ran into that lawyer, Jürgen, who for the next three months would make her his house slut. In exchange for cleaning and sex, he took care of Dianka's legs, which were chafed to the bone, and all of the illnesses she'd contracted during those five days of being homeless. When she'd had to sleep ... no, in fact she hadn't slept anywhere. Because they shut the U-Bahn station, pulling those grates down from the ceiling, like they did in castles in the olden days. They shut down everything, the drawbridges were raised, it was red lights everywhere for Dianka of Bratislava! The first night on the Vienna street seemed like it would never end. Norma threw him out of Alfie's around ten at night for eating nuts from the dispenser without paying (Slavs do that), and Milan just stood in the freezing cold until daybreak. But nothing happened. Snowflakes fell against a background of lit streetlamps. That was it? That's all there was? Sometimes an elegant Mercedes floated by, but Milan no longer dreamt of fancy cars, he dreamt of his own room, of a flat in a tower block in Bratislava, of his mother making supper (open-faced cheese sandwiches with tomato and onion), of a mug of hot tea, of doing homework.

Around five in the morning Dianka started eating snow. From the cement planters, because she thought it had to be cleaner than the snow in the street. She hobbled down one of the main roads, studied the shop windows, and had a taste of that unique and inimitable flavour that the West acquires when you don't have a single penny to your name. A convertible full of Arab men cruised past blaring music, 'habibi habibi' or something like that, and vanished around the corner. A woman wearing a white fur coat was walking a white greyhound. And Dianka watched them from inside a doorway, pretending it was warmer in the recess because there was no wind. She stood there biting her nails, and the woman with the greyhound strolled by like in a commercial, and Dianka thought about beating her up, or at least pushing her down, for being so clean, like she'd just had a bath, with her white teeth, her white dog, in her white fur coat, at least the white fur would get dirty. She'd pop her good!

The dog took a piss and shat, his mistress collected the poo with a scoop and put it in a little bag, threw the little bag into the trash, then started coming towards the doorway where Dianka was standing, in order to take refuge in the beautiful, warm, expensive flat that she owned. Dianka had never done it with a woman before, but as the lady passed by she did her best to give her a lingering look. But those who've hit rock bottom, or are about to, are no longer attractive, people can sense the loser in them and they turn away.

She tried to get into an underground car park, thinking that even the cars must have it better than she did, but she tripped the alarm and had to get out fast. And so, for five days and five nights she shambled all over that fucking city. When she went down the less-frequented streets, she would take off that awful shoe and expose her festering wound, in the cold, in the snow. It was better to freeze. She'd station herself on bridges and watch the Danube with its enormous, slow-moving ice floes. She inspected the kerbs with a beggar's certainty that she was bound to discover money there at any moment, that it was statistically impossible for her not to find anything. In the U-Bahn station there was a vending machine, and in that machine, behind the glass, chocolate bars, croissants, hot chicken wings—everything. She just needed to find some coins, and she spent every night searching for coins. And every single bottle cap looked like a coin, every pebble embedded in the tarmac!

The last money she'd had . . . where to even start? Three days earlier she'd wanted to call home and ask her parents to drive down and fetch her, but the phone ate her money. She pounded it with her fist, but nothing came out. There was a sign with a toll-free number to call and report such incidents, but of course it didn't work, all she got was an automatic message with some little Hitler rattling off whatever. But Dianka took her revenge on those Austrian bitches by stuffing the payphone with sticks and matches (matches that would've come in handy about now).

She sat down on a busy street and simply started to beg. She had the feeling that the moment she went from standing up to sitting down in front of one of the buildings, she would cross an important threshold and become invisible to others, as if she were living in a different dimension. For an hour or so she observed

Vienna from her ground-floor view, Vienna of the hurrying steps, of the shoes and trouser legs, the briefcases and handbags. Most people were attired in expensive, elegant high boots and dress shoes. And they were all rushing, as if they were being chased. That hurrying footwear was uptight, excited, anxious to make it to some concrete destination, and none of it could be bothered to actually ever stop.

And not a single coin landed on the scrap of cardboard she'd scrounged from a rubbish bin.

She came to despise all the people getting into their cars, driving off to their opera, reading their newspapers in their little Eduscho cafes, carrying their shopping in their pretty department store bags, running through their snow, kissing under their statues, and giving each other gifts of chocolates shaped like the head of their Mozart. Dianka glared at the huge boxes of chocolate like a starving bitch, although she would have preferred a hot dog. Whole window displays of chocolate, each individually wrapped in gold paper, painted with the profile of the Great Composer in an enormous grey wig. Open round boxes of chocolate the size of carriage wheels shimmered in the empty street's nocturnal light. Dianka had crossed a threshold in her hunger and was feeling it less and less now. But she looked at those boxes of chocolate and couldn't tear her eyes away, so highly improbable and fascinating had the luxuries of that world become, as they do for anyone who is suddenly completely destitute. A poor man dreams of work and enough money to get by, a beggar dreams of nothing less than millions! So there Dianka was at five in the morning, gazing at the window displays of Montblanc pens, Rolexes, fur coats, Louis

Vuitton bags . . . A single thread from one of those bags could feed her for a week! That was the weirdest thing of all.

Distant bells were ringing, crimson garlands lit up, then went dark, and Dianka had the feeling that at any moment, out of the fog, here in front of the shop, a carriage drawn by a legion of reindeer would come for her and whisk her off into some fairy tale or other. She wasn't quite sure which one best suited her: the one about the little match girl who froze in the snow? She'd stuffed her last matches into the payphone, and anyway, smoking was awful! It did nothing at all to make the hunger go away. Or maybe the story of Kai and Gerda was better? That must have been one of those Scandinavian fairy tales, because Milan remembered only that it was full of ice, whiteness, blue skies and wealth. Just like Sweden. But the best would be if out of the fog a coach made from a pumpkin would materialize and carry Dianka off to the ball, and even if the prince was eighty years old, wore a toupee or had a comb-over, even if he couldn't get it up, he'd still be able to pay for her, buy her new clothes, help her get back on her feet.

There were these lights set up everywhere, and Dianka noticed to her surprise that they were rigged with photosensors, because whenever she went near them they would start playing 'Jingle Bells'. In the window display a chubby, red-faced Santa Claus held out his hand to Dianka, but there was nothing in it, no bag of gifts . . . And in that empty, bitterly cold night, little bells really were ringing, but instead of reindeer came a combination street cleaner and rubbish lorry, which in Austria all looked completely space-age. Dianka felt very rubbishy herself and couldn't help thinking they were coming on her account.

Dianka eventually stopped walking, because every time she took a step her shoe would cut into her foot, practically to the bone. Those beautiful loafers, detested now, were a reminder of the life of prosperity (Ralf! Alex!) she'd had not long before, when instead of saving her money for times like now, she spent it all on heaps of new clothes. ('Geld sparen, Geld sparen, Dianka! Du musst Geld sparen! Billige Schuhe kaufen, billig essen.') But later, when she lost the flat she was renting from this one Brazilian queen (Sierra Ferreira da Silva), she stashed all those treasures in a locker at the train station, threw in a coin and . . . and they were still there, but in order to get them out she'd have to deposit five hundred schillings or something, because the meter was still ticking! The blinking display had kindly informed her that if she didn't remove her things within the next twenty-four hours, she wouldn't be able to get them out at all. Or something like that—she hadn't entirely understood what those Austrian pigs had written there. At any rate, it had told her to have a nice day, and that always meant bad news.

Dianka was no longer able to walk or stand up, nor could she put up with the sadness emanating from all the Christmas trees and lights and jingling, carolling bells everywhere. She was so done with that whole green-and-red festival of kitsch. That night she'd had her fill of fog and tears, enough to last her a lifetime. The fog was red from the lights. Red smog.

But then: a miracle happened! Dianka, filthy and hungry though she was, found a trick in the Kettenbrückengasse U-Bahn station. It was a small station, where like everywhere else no one bothered to lose their change, but for some reason Dianka liked to sit there.

Oof. A fat, sweaty, unshaven Arab smiled lasciviously at her sixteen years and fawn-coloured hair. Milan thought he might kiss the Arab for joy, right there in the subway. She was already counting how many chops, French fries and sandwiches he'd be good for . . . How much could she get out of a guy like that? Not much. But there was a shower at the Bahnhof; you just tossed in some coins and the doors parted. Only a few inches though, so that two people couldn't make it through at once. You had a half hour entirely to yourself. Washing was wonderful, but being entirely by yourself for a whole half hour—that was pure bliss! To be off the street finally, to be alone finally! She'd go and get washed up, and put on a pair of fresh socks, which she would buy at that discount supermarket, SPAR. It would be a holiday!

The Arab guy couldn't host. That's how people said it: 'Can you host?' 'Hast du Zimmer?' As if to spite her, he didn't even have his own place. But Dianka wanted to get the whole thing over and done with as soon as possible, so she was about to drag him off to the bushes in the park or the toilet in the U-Bahn station, when he, Ahmed, insisted he knew the perfect spot. He took Dianka to an underground car park that had some public toilets. They zigzagged between the variously coloured cars. It was dimly lit, the only bright thing was a red sign with the word *exit*. They shut the door, and Ahmed sat down on the toilet. It was all so gross, he had breasts like a woman's, except they were covered in hair, and he reeked of sour sweat. Every few minutes he would break into idiotic laughter and order Dianka to lick his revolting, sweaty body from head to toe. Or he would fart and laugh as if it were the funniest joke he'd ever heard. Dianka did lick him, but all the while she fantasized about the cigarettes and chops. Suddenly someone started pounding on the door of the stall—it was the attendant! The parking attendant! The guardian of all those underground car parks, leading all the way down into hell! In a fluorescent vest, yellow, maybe orange. He banged on the door and bellowed. Dianka didn't understand a thing because he was yelling in German, and for her to understand he would have had to be yelling in Slovak. Instead he yelled in German, but Dianka had no problem imagining what he meant. In a word, they needed to get the fuck out, because the Polizei was on its way.

'Verdammte Schwule! Verdammte Schwule! Macht auf!'

Well, the guy opened the door and with all his might pushed the attendant away and made a dash for it (without paying!), and Dianka was seized by the even fatter and even more repulsive Austrian guard. If this were a porno, the kind Dianka liked to watch when she could afford to sit in the Kaiserbrundl sauna, the guard would now be pulling out his cock and commanding her to pay in kind. But because this was real life, the guard landed his fist in her face without so much as a hello, and she began to bleed. She fell on the floor, on the tiles. The guard grabbed her by the collar, screamed something about the police, then threw her a bucket, a mop and a rag. Dianka tried to escape, but the fucker grabbed her by the ear and held her with all his might. He kept holding her by the ear, like she was a schoolboy. She was afraid she might never escape, our Dianka, and that she'd end up as cheap labour washing the floors. The guard cried alternately 'Polizei!' and something like 'scrubben!' It was her choice. 'Eizer you gonna scrubben zis whole car park for me right now, or I call ze police! Fucking queer!' Dianka chose to scrub. Bawling to high heaven, hungry and filthy as she was, she had to clean the entire multistorey car park, and then she had to clean the toilet. After two terrible hours she simply walked out into the night, empty-handed, knackered. That's what they called it. She lifted her head and noticed an enormous luxury hotel in front of her. The Sacher Vienna. Snow was falling. White flakes fell majestically and slowly, as if they were uncertain whether to settle on the pavement or on the pretty black Mercedes. Only one room showed a light. She'd seen her share of such hotel rooms with customers—the king-size beds spread with luxury gifts for their wives from Frey Wille, bottles of Chanel perfume in the bathroom, room service bringing up champagne on silver trolleys. The light went out, and Dianka thought to herself, in Slovak, how unjust it was that so many rooms should go to waste, empty all night, while she was freezing and had nowhere to sleep.

How many times had I told her: 'Dianka, calm down. This is a job for people with steel nerves. Who can learn Deutsch, go after the Geld, and fuck the Männer with the Mercedes cars in the underground car parks! But you should go to Munich, to Zurich! Vienna is no good, Dianka, kein Geschäft. Don't be surprised if I tell you how many customers I had today: eleven—the magic number. But I know how it's done! Anyway, if someone calls themselves "Dianka, Princess of Wales", but they're not actually her, then that's fucked up . . . I mean, look at the real Diana— does she walk around looking like shit? Is she out there hunting tricks like you? Ponimaesh? Capito, you little hooker? Dianushka? Milanushka?'

Now, at five in the morning, in front of the shop with the musical chocolates, my words must have been drifting through her head like snowflakes. Mozart. The Vienna Philharmonic. The Vienna Conservatory, to which Mario Ludwig was leaving his entire fortune. The mask and the rose on the poster for the musical *Phantom of the Opera*, which was playing at the Theater an der Wien, where tickets cost twenty large dinners including dessert. The chocolate violins, the chocolate pianos, keys of white chocolate punctuated by keys of bitter dark chocolate. Vienna was all classical music and chocolate, it was just a shame there was no free kebab for hungry Dianka. They would always have vacant rooms in the Hiltons, and they would always be throwing Dianka out of the U-Bahn, out of the garbage bins, out of the doorways of houses. A crash course in capitalism for a communist kid from ex-Czechoslovakia. No money? Here's an arse-kicking, now get the hell out. Money? Here's an arse-licking, welcome, make yourself at home. That night Dianka realized that the West in its entirety was like an electric amusement park wired on high voltage. The little lights kept on blinking whether you were having a wonderful time or dying in the gutter, Milan, you beautiful angel. Milan, you piece of shit. Milan. you syphilitic twink. The lights were perfectly indifferent, and eternally festive. For the rich, that is. Other people didn't exist. Just as long as no one took the plug out of its socket.

And Dianka, even if she didn't realize it, turned into a socialist that night. Except that in her opinion it was socialism that had caused her beloved Slovakia to be yoked together with those horrible Czechs. Slovaks were Gypsies too, and Dianka started to look around for a place where she could pitch her tent. Oh, if she were to run into a Gypsy caravan now, she thought, walking unattractively through the neighbourhood with her nose to the ground, on the lookout for spare change. If suddenly she were to hear the neighing of horses and asked, 'Where are you going, friends?' And heard, 'We're journeying with our caravan, returning to Slovakia. We're done purloining the horses, tain't our world here. Come with us!' 'Yes. I'll join you! I'll be a Gypsy with you!'

'Shit, I'm hallucinating,' thought Dianka.

Dianka limped back to Alfie's. Holiday decorations had been hung on the door: wreaths made of boughs of fir and decked with colourful baubles. She was half-certain they wouldn't let her in. She entered. Thank God Vincent wasn't behind the bar, because he wouldn't have let her sit there without ordering any drinks. Tonight that old queen Norma was the barmaid. Jolly, campy, good-natured, but sometimes cruel, she had a moustache, a big hoop earring in one ear, and she'd spent her whole life at Alfie's. Dianka approached her and said, in English, 'I am hungry.'

She looked at her like a starving animal, but Norma wasn't sympathetic. She threw a couple of schillings into the peanut dispenser, a measly handful tumbled into a little drawer; and beaming at the entire bar, she said something that was meant to destroy Dianka's reputation for ever: 'Madame here is hungry! And look, she's angry too! Ladies, may I present: Madame de Hangry!'

Fucking bitch. Blasen my Arschloch, you cunt!

There was no way Dianka could pummel Norma over the bar. She had to be nice to her and smile, because she had nowhere to sleep, and Norma was famous for always having a lot of homeless boys staying at her place. She asked if she too could spend the night there and was told, 'Ooh, it's really tight . . .' Norma was currently hosting a horde of Gypsies (a caravan, after all!), whose manners were just atrocious. The ones Dianka had met in the toilet, who hadn't got off in three weeks, who'd showed off their extravagant, hard-up cocks to her. She'd have to wait until Norma finished her shift, around five in the morning, and seeing as there was a favour Dianka might do for her, maybe there was, after all, a mattress in the kitchen that Dianka could sleep on . . . Was there a door to the kitchen, Dianka wondered, to keep the Gypsies etc. out? But she never got a clear answer.

In the meantime, she went to the toilet to wash her face and hands. From all corners her new nickname trailed after her: Madame de Hangry! Dianka remembered how it was back in Bratislava, when the boys went off to Vienna one after the other and came back well fed, tanned from the winter sun, wearing chic new clothes, and with stories about the great wide world.

It was midnight. Exactly three days and three nights had passed since Dianka had last slept. And what a sleep that was! The U-Bahn was shut between two and five-thirty, but through the grates came warm air from the vents and Dianka fell asleep to the mechanical whir of the floor scrubbers and escalators. The vagrants all slept in these crevasses, the bantam vagrants at least, because the real ones, the diehards, the elderly junkies, they all knew how to stay inside the U-Bahn. Inside. And how to evade the purge. When at three in the morning the Great Expulsion began, they were safely tucked away inside closed-off underground corridors only they knew. There they had their lice-infested pillows, their plump pet rats, the shopping carts they'd stolen from the super-market, the candles they lit.

But Dianka still hoped her situation was temporary and that she'd never achieve that level of initiation. She still hoped to be reinstated to Austrian society and maybe one day even pay taxes for prostitution. She was a prostitute of the working class. Her customers were always either muttering glumly, 'Morgen arbeiten', or whispering excitedly, 'Morgen keine Arbeit'. For them the world was divided between workdays and the weekend.

THE POLE

'Dianka, have you ever thought about where your problems come from?' I asked her once again after running into her in the U-Bahn at Karlsplatz. Once again, she was limping because her shoes had chafed her ankles, and her wrists were wrapped in bandages. Once again she'd been screwed over by the world and other people. Again she was on the street, again she'd been shafted.

'Look, Dianka, this is no way to live. It's no good, not at all. Look at me and my life. Now you go back on that street and tomorrow return to Bratislava, As for me, I got my Eleven-Inch, the most famous *Schwanz* in Vienna—"Oh ja, mehr, mehr, Eleven-Inch!" My tricks start feeling me up in the cab just to see if it's true what people say. I gotta tell you, my Mama told me it runs in the family, because my Papa's was just as big. And what my grandma had to say about my grandpa, mein Gott! Seems that was how he survived the concentration camp. And he spoke in German too, when he was doing it, just like his grandson. That's how he got into the Party after the war, and how they got their garden allotment and got to jump the queue for their car. Now I understand why Grandma would look at me that way in the bathtub, bringing in the towel, then the bubble bath, then seeing if I didn't inherit his genes after all. Anyway, if Grandpa really did have a chopper like that, no wonder my poor granny had such a high-pitched voice ... Mine's long, but it's also thick. Some people are too scared to take it from behind, afraid they'll split in two. Other queens practically jump on it. I'm like: "You. Will. Die." And they're like: "I. Vant. To. Die!"

'It's just a big chunky meat-balloon with veins. And it gets hard at anything. Even if you stick a hamster in there or a frog, it gets hard just like that. It gets hard if my trousers are too tight, and it gets hard if they're too loose . . . "Mein Gott, was ist das?!" my customers whisper reverently. And when they do, you know you'll be getting a nice tip. I mean, that I'll be getting one.'

'Ich. Und jetzt du? Mein Gott!' I rolled my eyes like I was expecting the heavens to take their revenge. Don't be offended, Dianka, but Slovakia isn't exactly a world leader on the cock market. Hungary is, even if it's right next door. But Slovakia—kleine Schwanz, Dianuschka, ne je to dobří! And with all that beer you drink it's "hello belly!" but "goodbye willy"! But it's not the end of the world—what you lack in one department, you can always make up for in another. And you've got such a glorious, delicious little tush, Dianka. Put that little booty to work!

'Ich gehen nach Zurich now, Dianka, arbeiten mit Million-airen in Schveetzerland. Big Geld, big Schwanz, big Bank, Schokoladen, Rolex, don't get me started! I'm gonna be a porn actor, Dianka, grosses Geld! Shayna shvants in moyl, shayna shvants in arschloch. A reiche Mann from Munich kommen mit mir nach Liechtenstein machen Shopping, schöne Kleider kaufen! I'm getting the fuck out. Was denkst du? Crazy, right? No more Austrian fascist stink-eye for me. Vergiss das, Dianka. They can kissen my Arsch. When you got money, hundred schilling, just for being you, and they give you a promotion, cuz you look like an angel. Ich denke: I'm still young, beautiful boy, I get the fuck outta here and take that Deutsche Bahn to Switzerland! And I'll be eating fricassee with millionaires, just like in the movies. I'll let you know what happens in the next episode. Now for a commercial break. Tschibo frische Bohnen, awaken the senses. Ooooh, Melitta: the flavour of Europe in every cup!'

When I was around, you didn't need radios—I spoke all the languages and even came with advertising!

DIANKA

Her head aching, music pounding in her skull, she sat at the bar. Norma placed a great big glass of beer in front of her, like a gift from heaven that had found its way to hell, and offered her a cigarette. There was even an uncomplicated customer who took her into the toilet where he asked to be kicked in the balls—good clean work and on-site, just very poorly paid. Weird to get paid for this, she thought, kicking him with all her might. She was too short, so she had to stand on the toilet. He asked her to put on a pair of cowboy boots with spikes that he'd brought with him in a shopping bag from Aldi. Later he told Dianka that he liked it when guys were kinda manky, especially down there, that it really turned him on and would she meet him in a week, but make sure not to wash at all until then. (He had no idea what an easy task that would be for a homeless sex worker.) Dianka said she would have to add an indemnity to his fee for all the customers she'd be losing that week on account of being unwashed. Of course that nutcase didn't agree to it, so she immediately went to the sink and began flamboyantly splashing water on herself . . .

That night went on and on. Dianka fell into a stupor from lack of sleep and exhaustion and caught herself, for example, gazing at an escort from Africa and wondering how long she'd have to stay unwashed to get as dark as he was. Wasn't it Napoleon who liked his lovers not to bathe because he wanted to smell their bodies . . . And she thought about how many customers were at Alfie's tonight (she counted: almost fifty), and how each of them must have at least one gold tooth in his mouth, and if you were to kill one of them and pull out that tooth (or teeth) with pliers, you could probably sell it (or them) at the pawnshop.

Suddenly someone started shaking her violently. 'Madame de Hangry! Madame de Hangry!' She woke up with a start. She'd been sleeping with her head on the bar. Norma was standing over her, the last sloshed customers were dragging their feet, so Norma turned on all the lights as a sign that the party was over, the mood soured and suddenly it was bright as day. The music cut off mid-phrase, and Norma announced to the whole bar: 'Meine Herren!' and something else, no doubt she was saying it was time to fuck off.

It was five in the morning. Norma set down a mélange in front of Dianka, a Viennese coffee with milk. But she was so asphyxiated from the cigarette smoke, drunk and tired, that she didn't have the strength to appreciate it. Soon she would at last be able to sleep on a real bed! Well, on a mattress in the kitchen anyway. The last customers had filed out into the cold, completely wasted on white-wine spritzers. Norma was behind the bar eating schnitzel and potatoes paired with an energy drink. Eventually she rang someone up and talked for a long time on the phone in Gypsy, Dianka recognized the sound of the language from Bratislava. It was like Romanian shot through with Russian, something corroded, festering, rotten. The difference between real languages and that mishmash was like the difference between the fragrance from fireplaces where rare woods were being burnt and the stink that came out of a Gypsy slum, where they heated with rags doused in lighter fluid and frozen dog shit, old boots, park benches, plastic bags from Aldi, cosmetics long past their sell-by date, artificial teeth. She had a funny feeling, a bad feeling; and it had to do with Norma's phone call with the Gypsies. Who were they? Why was she calling them? From here, at this hour? To all her questions, Norma just answered, 'Geemmma', which in Austrian dialect meant *gehen wir*—'let's go'.

The cold, fresh air was like a slap in the face. They walked over to Linke Wienzeile, where Norma's station wagon was parked. Sitting inside were three ugly Gypsies with big noses. Of course, Dianka knew there were attractive Gypsies too, but these three were clearly congenitally deformed, their mothers must have smoked when they were pregnant, lapped up water from puddles opalescent with petrol and torn radioactive pigeons from limb to limb with their bare teeth.

One of them, a beak-nosed guy decked out in gold, was behind the wheel. They drove through the dark city without stopping, down streets lined with ancient townhouses on either side, as if they were cruising along the beds of dried-up rivers. Some of the windows were already filled with dirty yellow light, with the smell of early-morning coffee consumed with a makeshift breakfast, no time to sit, workers getting ready for their shift in the factory.

Despite Dianka's prayers they stopped in front of the Dead Dog, where the wreckage of the night would finally run aground. Open until seven, the pub was a repository for whores and harlots, thieves and vagrants, where anyone was welcome to come and quaff the watered-down vodka and smoke to her heart's content those shop-floor cigarettes, Milde Sorte or Austria 3. Why did they need to go to another bar at this hour? She didn't know that when you've been in a bar all night, you're unfit to do anything else but drink and smoke to the end of time. She looked at the faces on those criminals, those out-of-work proles, and realized she couldn't care less. Norma was chitchatting with the bartender about some shady deal or other. Dianka took in her surroundings. Housed inside a railway viaduct, the Dead Dog was the trashiest bar in Vienna and probably the only one open after five. There was always another drink to be had there, and the dregs from all the other bars were drinking it: Arab escorts in vests with 'Dolce & Gabbana' plastered across the backs, grandpas in chaps, a teenage transvestite in a blonde wig and four-day stubble applied with grey pancake make-up, fat bitches with lust in their eyes. They knocked back vodkas and bought packs of Austria 3 from the vending machine. When Dianka heard Norma's 'geemmma' again coming from somewhere overhead, she no longer wanted to leave. She wanted to stay there, slumped against the table, watching the trans-grandpa smoke his filterless cigarette all the way to the end and the old witch behind the bar smack her lips in slow motion like a beached fish gulping for water . . .

They stopped in front of the ornate facade of a nineteenth-century apartment building. The Gypsies piled out and told Dianka to wait in the car, but after a bit Norma came back for her. Exodus from the warm car, into the cold! They stood at the front door and one of them opened it with a bunch of keys, obviously not his since it took him a while to find the one that fit. Eventually Norma opened the door and, shushing one another, they all headed upstairs. Fourth floor. The smell. The creaking steps. Behind the sturdy doors on every landing old people were drinking coffee or still asleep. Five o'clock. Norma opened the door to the flat on the fourth floor and it occurred to Dianka that the plot was taking a new turn, that a new story was about to begin, when all she wanted to do was sleep.

It was soon clear to her that this was not Norma's flat, the one she'd been expecting to sleep in, on a mattress in the kitchen as Norma had promised, but that it belonged to someone else . . . someone who seemed to have diligently collected everything for a hundred years and then died—at least fifty years ago, given all the dust. One of the Gypsies immediately grabbed a grandfather clock as big as a wardrobe and started hauling it down to the car. Norma handed Dianka two candlesticks. She was poor. Her ankle was already scarred over from the chafing. She hadn't slept for four nights straight; even worse, it looked like she wouldn't be sleeping tonight either. And then there was the new nickname, Madame de Hangry, which made her want to have a go at some pensioner, pull out his gold teeth and sell them in the underpass, then move to Zurich with the money. And now, instead of sleeping, she was confronted with a completely new, spacious, sprawling narrative, some late-night larceny in a stranger's flat. She didn't know what she was doing, hanging around with Norma. She didn't realize that Norma always immediately fell into some convoluted plot, a Gypsy story, a thief's story, a story about dusty flats soon to be emptied of their grandfather clocks and dust-covered fans.

She kept having to shift around in the back seat, half-buried in the pile of junk, and the station wagon seemed to be endlessly capacious. That flat was crammed full! A million bottles, hundreds of glass animals and other grubby knick-knacks, lamps, tins of hair pomade, a radio from the fifties, ashtrays made of conch shells or glass bricks, nude German ladies with fans and fluttering birds on the wall, their rosy, fat cheeks protruding from their arrogant, innocent faces, decades-old dishes in the kitchen . . . Ah yes! In the kitchen, atop a refrigerator which Dianka wouldn't have opened even with a gas mask on, was a large glass jar that someone had no doubt used for saving small change—five-mark coins, five-franc coins, schillings, dollars. And the kitchen was empty except for Dianka, and now the jar was empty too . . . It would be hard to expect Dianka to feel bound by some sense of morality. One can be human only under human conditions! And now at last her inner thief had been awakened. Now her eyes began scanning the glass-brick ashtrays for gold rings among the buttons and paper clips. Now she understood why fate had brought her to this place!

With the car packed to the roof with junk from the flat, they drove out of town (instead of to Norma's, as Dianka hoped). Ugly Vienna melted away, the people guzzling their last-call beers in front of bars disappeared. They crossed the bridge over the Danube, the ancient tenements receding behind them, and kept going until they arrived at a field situated between what looked like hangars, former factory buildings, rain falling on everything, rain and sleet, and on the horizon, slowly, the sun was coming up. Inside the car, the Gypsies' cigarette smoke made Dianka want to puke, but whenever she tried to open the window, they said it was too cold: *kalt, kalt, kalt.* Out in the field, in the darkness, some people were standing around in the rain and sleet. They were laying things out on newspapers, like in a surreal flea market. In the dingy head-lights of Norma's car they looked like bags of potatoes. On news-papers with headlines printed in Gothic script stood clocks, silver tea services, the contents of mouldy flats in ancient, ornate

Viennese tenements whose ancient former inhabitants had died slowly, of cancer, in agony, over the course of years. Norma went out and spoke with the dealers, and then the Gypsies started taking out the antiques, but Dianka had already fallen asleep, despite all the commotion around her, all the chowchescu, the macarescu, the makuna hothotta. When she woke up, they were at Norma's and it was already horribly light outside, that greasy winter light. She tried to stand up, but found herself already being tyrannized by the Gypsies, with the consent and at the instigation of Norma. The 'joke' consisted in their having put a sausage on her belly and binding her hands together so she wouldn't be able to reach it— a clear allusion to her new nickname.

In Norma's flat the walls were entirely covered, from floor to ceiling, with shelves full of cassette tapes and compact discs— thousands of compact discs, which at the time were still a luxury—and between them stood an enormous stereo tower, large as a wardrobe, with glass doors. And here the long-awaited scene finally played out: Dianka fell asleep on that infamous mattress in the kitchen, which she had been dreaming about all night. Of course, someone else was already sleeping on it, another boy, but he kindly moved over to make space for her. The Gypsies and Norma wandered back and forth over her head, smoking, chuckling, making coffee, playing Depeche Mode and U2 when really they should all have just gone to bed, because they hadn't slept the whole night either! Eventually, however, the flat fell into blissful silence, interrupted only by the refrigerator suddenly jolting to life and the sirens of ambulances passing by outside the window, which served as a constant background music for the city, until gradually, eventually, it all faded away and died. But the flat, filled with veils of cigarette smoke, smelt like a nightmare. The sweaters and other clothes that Norma, the Gypsies and Dianka had been wearing now gave off the stench of the night's pub crawl—cologne, grease, cigarettes, vodka, sperm. And without a shred of curtain or shade covering them, the windows were no help against the malevolent daylight.

Dianka was flying into an abyss and couldn't care less. She was dreaming of her Mama and of Bratislava: since her dreams still hadn't made the switch to the new Viennese operating system, their reality was running late by about a year. There she was at school; to be precise, she was smoking by the boilerhouse next to the playground, where she would go smoke with her friends during recess—that was how they sinned back then! She really wanted to smoke, but the rain was coming down in buckets and kept putting out her cigarette. Then suddenly the rain got very warm, hot . . .

It was a brutal way to wake up. The Gypsies were kneeling in a half-circle around her head, jerking off and peeing on her. What startled her into consciousness was the urine of one of them as he 'wrote' something on her face. They were all cracking up. She tried to break free, to escape, but they held her down, laughed, spat in her face, peed, and one of them even flushed. Dianka suddenly understood how something that in normal life is quite naturally a source of joy can, under duress, become the most ghastly of abominations. She escaped the flat, ran away from that idiot, Norma, who was standing in the kitchen doorway, smoking and cackling. Dianka was on the street again, and once again the street was inside her.

Still, she had the *treasure* she'd stolen from the jar in the old flat. She found a toilet, shut herself in a stall, and scooped out everything from the vast pockets of her filthy denim jacket. A good thing she'd slept in it, because if she'd hung it up in Norma's hallway, the Gypsies would have looked after it . . . Crumbs of tobacco, bits of tablets, old U-Bahn tickets, a button and the loose change from the flat—the insides of her pockets told the story of her life in Vienna. The bus ticket from Bratislava. A handkerchief crusty with red snot. A condom. But none of that was important—what was important was the money she was spreading out on the toilet-seat cover. She'd seen a sign advertising an exchange counter near the train station that accepted small change. At a low rate, but now she saw she'd been fucked: Deutschmarks, Dutch guilders, Swiss francs, French francs, Swedish and Norwegian and Danish crowns, British pounds! Evidently the guy just chucked into the jar whatever money was left from whichever trip he'd just returned from. There must have been at least twenty dollars in there! For that amount Dianka could easily spend a night in a hotel, take a bath, wash her clothes, eat, and still have something left for drinks and ciggies in the bar—as long as Norma wasn't working!

But she had escaped from Norma. Like a tourist, she exchanged the small change for schillings and hobbled over to the gay-friendly Hotel Urania at Obere Weissgerberstrasse 7. She knew it because it also rented rooms by the hour, and she'd been there often with customers. She knew the bathrooms all had extra-large and comfy bathtubs in them. 'Gay-friendly' was putting it mildly for the Urania. I don't know if the place had ever seen a straight person, aside from the Thai cleaning staff.

For the first time Dianka tasted the sweet fruits of thievery, of opulence and luxury with someone's else money. She liked it very much and solemnly swore that from that moment on she would steal as much as she could. She would take revenge on the rich for those empty rooms in the Hilton, for those Mozart bonbons, for those greyhounds on Louis Vuitton leashes. Lying in that gay-friendly bathtub, in that gay-friendly Hotel Urania, Dianka decided never to return to Alfie's, so she wouldn't run into Norma and the Gypsies again or hear that awful 'Madame de Hangry' whispered behind her back. She'd start going to the Alte Lampe, on Heumühlgasse, where she could still always pick up some rich old guy, not even necessarily as a trick. Even if it was for free, guys like that tended to fall into 'relationship mode', and that meant financial security. She went there, all freshened up, and immediately knew she'd have to pick up the old guy sitting at the bar, drinking a mélange, smoking Milde Sorte and reading the *Wiener Zeitung*.

He turned out to be a lawyer and a psychopath. He locked Dianka in at home for the whole day and went to work. And she had to do the kitchen, all the chores, the computer . . . and be bored, run the vacuum, dig through wardrobes stuffed with boring suits on hangers wrapped in plastic slipcases. The Western middle class needed objects to fill their flats! Slipcases and slipcovers for everything! Shoetrees, umbrella stands, napkin rings, knife sharpeners and knife holders, coat racks and coat hangers, ironing boards, food processors, blenders, air fresheners, humidifiers, vacuum cleaners both upright and prone, toasters, espresso makers and coffee grinders, and outside the kitchen windows the mizzle and drizzle of dirty rain and sleet . . . As if under a spell Dianka wandered around this kingdom of things like Alice in Bourgeois Wonderland. But when fate brought her face to face with a completely inscrutable appliance, she froze. The lawyer explained it was a device for punching eyelets in shoes, so the shoelaces would pass through more easily . . .

In the cupboards she found neatly stacked boxes of fragrant laundry detergent, washed-out polos from Lacoste and other designers, mounds of balled-up socks, row upon row of hangers with white and blue button-down shirts . . .

Eventually she started to regret that she'd ever run away from home and come to Vienna, where she ought to have been quaffing champagne every night and the streets were supposed to be full of hot guys and fast cars. Instead, she had Jürgen, an old, balding lawyer who freaked out over the slightest infraction, hitting and shouting and carrying on. Someone who wiped his arse with chamomile-scented cotton pads could only be a freak! Dianka looked suspiciously at all the unfamiliar contraptions. What, for instance, was that enormous electric brush for? It looked like it was for cleaning bottles, but it had some kind of setup on the handle, buttons, 'ich das nicht verstehen'. What a laugh the 'brush' caused when she turned it on. It was a giant vibrator!

One time she washed her hair with shampoo she'd found in the bathroom, and Jürgen threw a shit fit because it was the very special shampoo for the silver hair—his—and it was very, very expensive, and she must to stay far away from it. And once he beat her to a pulp, for no reason at all! That too. He'd told her countless times not to use ze metal spatula when scrambling eggs in ze

Teflon pan, she must to use ze vooden spoon! So what, big deal . . . Because vherever ze coating is scratched, ze pan vill burn! Dianka really got it in the neck for that scratched pan. That's when she realized what the first commandment of the urban professional middle class was: 'Thou shalt not use metal utensils on Teflon, only ze vood!' And these commandments had been revealed to the urban professional middle class by their yuppie god, scratched into the surface of two Teflon skillets . . .

In the end, Dianka rebelled. She began doing things wrong on purpose just to provoke him. She made a show of using the above-mentioned shampoo until her hair started turning silver from it. She wiped her arse and feet with his Towel Only For Ze Face. She stuffed down so many Geriavit Multivitamin Vitality capsules from his supply that she began to glow. She guzzled the liquor from his liquor cabinet using the time-tested Slavic method of replenishing the decreasing volumes of alcohol with water from the tap. And—although Jürgen had expressly forbidden it—she called up Edwin, her friend from the good old days, her American . . .

(Edwin was a playboy, a rich kid. He drove around Vienna in his white convertible, dressed all in white. Cowboy boots with heels. Leather pants or white jeans. A Walkman. Leather jacket with fringe. Long, wavy, blond hair with highlights. Tattoos. American manners. Chewing gum. Marlboro Reds in the soft pack. A flat decorated entirely in white, mirrors on the ceiling.)

She told him she'd slip out and visit him that evening, asked him to wait. And Edwin once again gave her directions on the U-Bahn, because Dianka didn't really understand public transport.

She waited until evening. That's when she had her daily walk, when she was allowed to go out for an hour on her own. But if she didn't come back at the agreed time, there'd be hell to pay. Edwin loved poppers, which were already illegal by then and could only be found in porn shops as 'CD-washing fluid'. He waited for her near Hammergasse and took her back to his place, his white-and-pink, electrically heated bed. Edwin didn't care about time; he banged Dianka on his big white bed, while she kept trying for half an hour to screw the cap back on the poppers, but whenever she had it nearly screwed on, another wave of Edwin would send it flying, and the poppers would spill on the sheets . . . In short, she didn't have a chance to look at her watch. Terrified, Dianka said goodbye in a hurry. She ran down the stairs to the vestibule, and the glass door to the stairwell snapped shut behind her. In front of her was the exterior door, which turned out to be locked— she would need the key to get out. She tried to open the glass doors, but needed to use the intercom to do that. But what was Edwin's last name, what floor was he on? She hadn't paid attention when he'd brought her upstairs, how could she have known she would need that information later? So there she was, trapped in a space just a few square feet, time ticking by. Jürgen was probably already cursing her name. And probably no one would come through the lobby before morning, because those Austrian yuppies had all gone to bed hours ago. She rang one of the buzzers for the first floor; a woman answered, but Dianka's German wasn't the best. She tried to explain her situation in the same language she spoke with me, a mix of Slovak, German, Russian and Papiamento, but the voice started shouting something about the Polizei, so Dianka hung up. She made herself at home on the stone floor and thought about how everyone in Vienna, really everyone in that rotten city, lived in pre-war buildings . . .

When she arrived home at three in the morning, Jürgen refused to let her in. He'd thrown all her clothes out of the front door. At last, though, Dianka whined and cried so much that he gave in and let her sleep there that night, he was afraid of what the neighbours might think, and Milan kept sobbing louder and louder. But he wouldn't let her sleep in his bed, she had to sleep on the floor. And that night Dianka slipped into the bathroom, took the blade out of his safety razor, and ... well, that's how she got those cuts on her wrists.

She had wanted to appeal to the lawyer's emotions, and it worked. Once again Dianka ascended to the role of mistress of a modern kitchen and bathroom. A life of wretched stability set in. Jürgen sometimes took her to a deathly boring name-day or birthday party for this or that 'gay' he knew, a lawyer or a doctor ... Every one of those gays had a boyfriend and a kitschy flat that smelt of all-purpose cleaner. The partygoers would entertain themselves with little games, like who could eat a whole piri-piri pepper. Dianka dreamt about Alfie's. It seemed to her that while being a whore on the street was dangerous, it was full of adventure, like being a sailor on the high seas. Here, it was warm and dry, but full of boring, empty small talk, banal jokes, having to go out to the balcony to smoke, having to take off your shoes when you came in to keep from scuffing the parquet. These people were cut from a different cloth than she was. With their pedigreed cats (bad-tempered, completely hairless, with devil ears!) and their designer demitasse sets ... They actually were capable—just like in the television commercials—of having long debates about the superiority of one brand of dishwasher tablets over another. They aspired to nothing more in life than their salary and health insurance.

Dianka felt like she was suffocating in hell, in a pink-upholstered prison cell that smelt of air freshener and potpourri sachets from IKEA ... Those flats, those gays ... Everything was gay this or gay that. When they wiped down the counters or had their floors mopped, they always laughed and said they were using 'Mr Queen'.

Dianka decided to take advantage of the fact that Jürgen no longer locked her in the flat when he went to work, so she could go to the dry cleaner, to the baker, to Aldi, to get dishwasher tablets when they ran out, to get meat for dinner—although she had to buy that at the *Fleischerei* because ze regular shops zey are nicht gut ... Dianka walked around with her shopping list of scribbled Slovak words for different dishwashing liquids and kinds of meat (and in parentheses how each was to be pronounced in German), and looked longingly even at the drug addicts keeping warm in the U-Bahn. They were free. Then, timidly at first but eventually more brazenly, she started turning tricks again. Not at Alfie's, where someone might see her, but in the U-Bahn, in the Karlsplatz station, 'Umsteigung zu den Linien U-Eins, U-Zwei und U-Vier' ... During the day practically nothing happened, but at least it was a way to escape doing laundry. She was standing there eyeing the compact discs, to be precise, she was looking at a bald Sinead O'Connor on the cover of *Nothing Compares 2 You*, when suddenly someone said 'Hallo, wie geht's?' to her. She froze! It was one of those stupid lawyer queens from the piri-piri party! She would have to be careful!

She ended up going to Alfie's after all ('why not?' and 'I'm screwed anyway!' and 'just think what Norma will say when she sees me, posh lady of the house that I am now, like on the cover of one of those TV magazines'). She took a seat at the bar, ordered a beer (even though there'd be a 'breath-test' later), lit a cigarette, and started thinking it all over. Break up with the lawyer. Rob him and get out of Vienna. But where did he keep the expensive stuff? He certainly had enough jewellery, cufflinks and tie-pins, all of it from Frey Wille, so definitely valuable. She'd take it all. And then she'd have to beat it. Boys go missing all the time, and then you hear how they're in Germany now, or Switzerland, wherever there's business, but the johns, the customers, are so naive, and they're so hot for Eastern Europeans ...

And that's when Dianka met Trashmaster. A cardinal scene in the blockbuster of her life—a silent movie, as it turned out, since he never really talked, and when he did it was only in German, and even that was some kind of Bavarian mumbo jumbo, while she spoke Slonglish. A diamond on the trash heap! For now all she saw was a young stud bristling with heterosexual allure, totally out of place in the care home for old queens that was Alfie's. With his tattoos, cropped black hair, biceps and tight jeans, everything rock hard like he was made out of metal, a vein running across his forehead, he was like a character in a gay comic book. Later it turned out that the concept of 'sexual orientation' was irrelevant for the Trashmaster: here was a human (although he looked more like an animal) who fucked anything that moved, plus a lot of things that didn't. Dianka claimed she even once found bestiality porn in his flat, a videotape titled *Miss Piggy*. She said he had a crusty sock there filled up with dried sperm. And a hole in the upholstery of the sofa bed, which was lined with a load of toilet paper larded with Nivea cream.

But that was later. Now, they were having a hard time keeping it together, now they were sloshed at one in the afternoon, they were already three sheets to the wind, plastered with beer, wine spritzers and vodka, all the drinks you weren't supposed to mix, already heading to the Hotel Stockholm for an hourly room, and although it was right across the street, to Dianka it was taking ages to get there. When the queen at the reception saw her come in with a gangster like that, she asked for the money up front.

'What happened, Dianka? You got a new target market? What happened to your doctors? Your fat senior citizens with their pension cheques just cashed? Your lawyers still unasphyxiated by their Frey Wille neckties? Your accountants with their three pillars of a financially secure future?'

'Why yes, I've changed! Just so you know: I've changed! In case you were wondering: I've changed! I'll be getting my arse pounded at one in the afternoon now, I'm a thief now, I'm wicked to the core, I'm a Gypsy! Now it's just gangsters with six-packs for me, and they don't even have to pay, we'll go off into the world together (since ideas like this crop up when people get drunk) and con old people out of every last cent of their pension cheques, especially the lawyers! But now I really need to go up to our room, I can't hold it any more, I feel like a bag of pudding, come on, hurry up! Give me a towel, you whore, if I'd come in here with a lawyer like Hermann or Günther, you'd give me one! No, don't bother now, I'll wipe my hands on my trousers, but I really need to go. Give me the key or I'll break down the door!'

Now Dianka was nursing her hangover with a can of Gösser beer, gliding noiselessly to Munich in a spotlessly clean night train together with her stud. Vienna was over. *Alles verloren.* She lay with her head nestled on his belly and, lulled by the gentle sloshing of beer, was transported to new destinations, one Oktoberfest after the another, because that was how she imagined Munich. She was clutching that fucking lawyer's electric shaver in her hand. Her eyes were shut, and under her eyelids her last twelve hours in Vienna flickered feverishly, to put it mildly, past. How like a heifer she had been brought together with her bull in an hourly room at the Hotel Stockholm. How his nipples each had a cat's head tattooed around it, and the rest of his fleshy body was entirely inked, you could read it like a rippling illuminated book. His cock was a truncheon, always erect, even after coming. Their chemistry had them eating each other raw, right down to the kidneys and entrails (which, unappealing as those bits inside us were, Dianka was glad were invisible). When they'd fucked for the third time, that bitch from the reception started pounding on the door, demanding they pay for a double and their hour was up. To which Trashmaster, instead of paying the bill like an uptight lawyer would do, killed her with a burst of laughter that sounded awfully like a horse's neigh. And after they'd outsmarted her, they left, laughing their heads off, to go have another beer, with a vodka chaser. Then Dianka needed a minute to go back home, as little inclined as she was to call that hostile place a home. And there, waiting for her, was an entire council, or conclave (Dianka didn't know the word), an entire courthouse, let's say, of lawyers, including the queen she'd run into in the U-Bahn, the one she'd recognized from the piri-piri party, who'd immediately gone to Jürgen to communicate the important information that that boy of his was out whoring around while he, Jürgen, was at home. Dianka's meagre belongings were already packed in a shopping bag from Billa, she stole a couple of CDs (*The Phantom of the Opera!*), went to the bathroom under the pretence of urinating and helped herself to a bottle of the shampoo for silver and blonde hair, the electric shaver and some perfumes. She jammed it all into her pockets, and without any further ado, she left. Outside, on the street, like a lion in a cage, that beast, the Trashmaster of Munich, was skulking and smoking. Once they turned the corner Dianka pulled the loot from her pockets, and they outwitted their pursuers once again, arriving at Westbahnhof. It's hard to say how they communicated because Trashmaster didn't even have a solid command of German, speaking instead a misshapen Bavarian, and again, with Germans and Austrians Dianka usually spoke a variant of broken English. But they understood each other perfectly, chattering in pheromone. Dianka was already putting away her third hot dog, and he was drinking one beer after another, telling her—inexplicably—how amazing business would be for her in Munich, how there was a bar for escorts there on—*nomen ist omen*—Frauenstrasse, how Dianka could stay at his place as his sister had gone out of town, how in Munich he would have to leave her for a bit at the train station because he had some things to sort out . . . Now Dianka was travelling by train cradled in his warm crotch with its undiminished boner, trying to make out the hazy contours of her own future, playing with the electric shaver, turning it on and off, staring at the distant lights outside the windows. My hair is blond, so it's fine to wash it with shampoo for silver and blond hair . . . such were the desultory thoughts drifting through Dianka's noggin . . .

Sometimes she even unzipped his zipper, pulled out that fat monster and wrapped her mouth around it, as he watched the corridor, keeping a lookout for anyone coming.

THE POLE

Mein Gott! Teufel! Hilfe! Kill me already! How can you let yourself go like that, Dianka? You're a mess! You really can't do anything in moderation, can you? It's because you're from the East! When you kick up your heels, the champagne starts to flow, and you drop Rolexes into wine flutes as tips. But when you let yourself go, you go all the way . . .

This was all just more of your Eastern Bloc ridiculousness, Dianka, more baggage from that post-communist country of yours where the Gypsies are in power now and every puddle shimmers with petrol. More communist-era postcards from your collection, and empty cigarette boxes and Coca Cola cans, and comic books and dreary school days. But it's all over now. And now *meine Damen und Herren* . . . I raise the tablecloth with my hands, the orchestra strikes up . . . and whoosh! I tear away the tablecloth! And what do we have here? A beautiful, delicate piri-piri pepper, gleaming red, fastidiously washed . . . And who will eat it? Will it be you, Milan? Few skills are as highly valued in the West, so if you don't know how, you'll have to learn, you'll have to take a course in how to eat exotic hot peppers, how to drink lemon juice, how to consume things you don't like and still keep smiling!

You're knackered, Dianka, you're frothing at the bit, you're shagged out and on your last legs, your feet are chafed again and you don't even have comfortable shoes to change into! And business in Munich is *scheisse*! Shit weather, and everything expensive like pig! Ah, West Germany at last! Well you'd better wash up and comb your hair, or else you'll just make the rest of us Eastern boys look bad!

And there you were thinking you'd got yourself Prince Charming, but that wise old bitch from the Hotel Stockholm already had his number: 'He won't pay.' And if only you'd listened to her instead of making a run for it, you'd have heard the rest of what she said: 'Nothing but trouble, that one. Mister Trouble.'

O mein Gott! Wo sind deine winter shoes, Dianka!? Having a tiny willy doesn't mean you have to live your life this way, Dianka. Look at the Thais. Who cares what they have down there, they all drive around in convertibles like kings!

I got myself a pager, Dianka, but I won't let you touch it as you've got grubby hands and that grime under your nails! And look at your fingers, they're covered in warts from never washing, from poking around in other people's arses, from being homeless for over a week—one day out on the street and up come the warts. They're caused by a viral infection, you know, from poor hygiene (like dysentery). There's ointment for them, but you wouldn't even know how to ask for it at the *Apotheke*, would you? So you've got warts. And those cold sores on your lips from only you know where. And herpes too. All those spots on your face and no money for a facial. You probably have lice, syphilis, gonorrhoea, who knows. In any case, I sure wouldn't risk it with you. You've really let yourself go, Dianka, and you think you're going to make it out on Frauenstrasse? Even your Trashmaster won't have you any more. Remember how mad he was about you when you first came here? But back then you were a flubsy Austrian housewife, a lawyer's wife, with air freshener spritzing out of your arse, wiping your arse with chamomile-scented wet wipes, peeing air freshener into your own mouth, your hair glistening from that silver and blond shampoo you washed it with . . . Look how quickly taking up with Trashmaster has turned you into trash yourself, like a junkie!

Even if they let you into Tabasco, I'm sure no one will want to come near you. I wish I didn't have to tell you this, but you stink. Really, I can no longer keep silent about it. We're in Germany now, Dianka, where people smell like laundry detergent and Fa deodorant and shower gel. Why can't you turn on the TV sometime and watch the commercials? What's on people's minds? Laundry detergent.

So there are these two housewives, like you used to be, they run into each other on the street, both with mohair sweaters on, one green, one pink, and the one in the green starts gushing: 'Ach, ist er neu?' and points at the other one's sweater.

And the other one goes: 'Ja, ja, neu, neu . . .' and winks at us: *mit Perwoll gewaschen.*

You need to learn how to take things, Dianka. If you steal a guy's watch when he takes it off before sex, he'll be looking for it again right after . . . Or let's say you find yourself a regular john who pays well, if you go and pocket his shaving cream while you're in his bathroom, you've just lost a customer!

Listen, I'm a klepto too, but stealing is an art like everything else. I do it exceptionally well—I guess you could say I've a call. But you? You must remember to take things he rarely wears, so he doesn't make the connection between your visit and their disappearance. Don't steal anything that's just lying around in the open. And don't clear out the minute you have it under your coat like you're running away from a fire. Stick around, chat for a bit. He's human too, after all.

Respect your customers. Be good to them. They've been sitting all day in their banks, in front of their computers, they've only just taken out their contact lenses (fortunately for you), and all they want is someone there who understands them. But you! When you go off with someone, you mope and make faces like you're going to your own beheading. Like during communism. Little Princess Dianka deigning to fraternize with a commoner . . .

Certain behaviours that may be acceptable where you come from, with the Gypsies in that Slovakia of yours, are simply unacceptable here. That's why I'm giving you this. It's a loan. Wait, get your paws off it! First, listen to me! Here, I'm giving you two thousand schillings. You're homeless, and a homeless hooker can't earn money. Go get yourself to the Bahnhof, take a shower in the pay toilets there, and invest in some soap. Otherwise, Dianka, I just don't know what to tell you. And don't spend it all on crap, on your Kinder Schokolade and Kinder Surprises! Here, take this packet of tissues and wipe your nose, you're dripping snot, I can hardly stand to look at you. Now put that money in a safe place and get yourself a hot meal, something solid, and not an ice-cream sundae with whipped cream and syrup, drizzles and sprinkles, crumbly bits and pirouettes, dried fruit and coconut flakes!

GOLD RUSH

You keep spending your money on luxuries and then you run out. Do you remember the 'gold rush' that took all the escorts by storm back in Vienna? Suddenly everyone was wearing gold all the time. It was a fad. Nothing but gold and more gold. It's not like you're getting back any of that money you spend on clothes and, as every hustler knows, there's no telling when you'll next hit rock bottom (like, no offence, you, Dianka Spencer of the Seven Sorrows, current residence: Central Station, next to the toilets). Everyone was turning tricks like mad, sucking dick under the bridges while looking out at the murky blue Danube, but they had their thousand schillings, they'd save them in a jar, and off they'd go to Kaufhalle to get the next bracelet. They wore them like Gypsies. The more senior they were, the more tricked out in gold they'd be. On every finger a signet ring, and it was a crying shame when everyone got busy and you couldn't buy any more, or even trade in for something larger. Luckily it was easy to sell the earlier, more modest versions for scrap. Even here, in the underpass at Karlsplatz. So you could wear all the necklaces you wanted. Five big gold chains at once and earrings in your ears. You'd be staggering under the weight of it all, so you'd just stand there and have a smoke, pull out your Dunhills and your gold S.T. Dupont cigarette lighter. And if you already had a gold lighter, why shouldn't you have a gold pen and keychain and a Louis Vuitton portemonnaie? You needed them—giving head is hard work! You didn't leave home in the arsehole of the world not to have them! So the boys began festooning themselves in gold, like protective armour against the spectre of indigence and ruination, until the most gold-bedecked hooker of all, an African queen named Maputu, was mugged and killed in a dark alley on her way home. She too had buckled under for that pawnshop. More than just the gold lighter, she had a gold cigarette case too, and, for all I know, she even wore gold condoms when she fucked . . .

Well, behind all that prosperity and gold lurked old Mario Ludwig. Do you remember, Dianka, how when Mario died under suspicious circumstances (leaving everything to the Vienna Municipal Conservatory, although we were the ones who had been conserving him), the putas suddenly weren't so clever any more, but instead queued up to sell their gold for scrap, at rock-bottom prices, like it was copper? My God, did the price of gold ever drop in Austria then!

All I have left of him is my Dupont lighter, which ran out of fluid long ago, and I haven't a clue how to refill it. That's all that remains of the Romanov fortune! But I'm not throwing it out or having it fixed or refilled, maybe I'll get a new flint for it. Even broken, it always looks so fancy on the bar next to my cigarettes, let them see I didn't get off the boat yesterday.

Mario Ludwig was my first customer, back when I first got here. In gambling, you have the law of the first win, right? How you always win the first time, but after that it's lose, lose, lose. When it comes to turning tricks, there's the law of the first customer: the first one is always the best, and after that it's the luck of the draw. It's true. Once some friends and me went to Monte Carlo to play the tables (yes, with Mario Ludwig I really lived the life!), and right off we swept the board. The other people though, they just nodded their heads at this sign of encouragement from fate before wiping us out for good. And of course we ended up losing our gold to the city's various twenty-four-hour pawn shops and had to hitchhike back.

So there I am, going into Alfie's, scared out of my wits like it's my first time. I go up to the bar, Norma rolls her eyes up to heaven like Christ on the cross, like who's this little parvenu and has he even paid her to let him work there? Well, there may be the law of the first customer, but at Alfie's it's just the law of the first night. The first night with Norma that is, that vile queen of a bartender, that moustachioed slag with the pockmarked face. In other words: *weg, hau ab, raus, Wien kein Osteuropa!* So I order a beer at an ungodly price, to which Norma always adds her date of birth. She twirls a coaster with the face of Mozart on it, rolls her eyes and crosses them like Jesus. Other boys next to me nudge one another and exchange knowing looks, they laugh: 'The new one doesn't know she needs to pay Norma first, ha ha. Ooh Norma, look at that hot new thing, but has she paid? Has she even fucking paid? Fresh meat delivery, direkt aus Polen!'

Shhh, I could hear them speaking Polish and didn't want other Poles to recognize me. They started horsing around, slapping each other on the back . . . Generally, if a customer knows how to say *powoli, powoli, langsam, langsam,* it means he's hooked up with Poles before, because most of them are straight and in no hurry to have sex. Other than that, he'll typically know a few other words too, like *koorvah* (fuck), *yehbahne* (fuck!) and *keelbahsah* (fuck?). Powoli, powoli, but surely!

But Norma just chuckles. She wipes off an enormous mug shaped like a log and devours me with her eyes. She paws at her zipper, tongue flailing between her lips, her moustache wet with foam. Now she's eyeing the darkroom, she wants to take me back there to exact her toll, when all of a sudden an elderly man walks in, clutching a cane with an amber head. Everyone begins bustling around him. One of the Poles holds the door open for him, but he walks on his cane directly towards me and takes the seat beside me at the bar. Norma right away starts fawning over him. When he orders an herbal tea—nothing special—she brings it to him on a silver platter!

Well, the king may have the right of the first night, but the emperor's prerogative trumps his!

Nothing like grandpas, the shrivelled old grandpas! They're the only good customers, the only reason for places like Alfie's to exist!

So there's Mario Ludwig sitting next to me, and the boys all stop smiling and start glaring at me with envy, already calculating their losses as it's obvious they won't be making a schilling off him tonight. He's already been with all of them a dozen times already, and whenever a new product hits the Vienna market, Mario takes him for a test drive, showers gold all over him, and pays by the minute. Never again will he pay as well as he does that first night. Mario has the face of a cod—I don't know why I thought that, but that's how it was. The head of a cod or a carp sticking out of an elegant suit jacket with a Gucci pocket square. It feels like I'm sitting next to a big fish, and I'm smiling the insincere smile of a ballerina who, despite having had eight abortions, still keeps dancing *Swan Lake*, baring her discoloured, sixteen-year-old teeth.

Anyway, conversation with Mario may not have been very stimulating, to be sure, he was a little hard of hearing and slightly dim, but at least I didn't need to bust my balls trying to speak German like a *kinner* . . . *kindergartener* with him (like with Günter). He was chatting with another customer at the bar, and the whole time he kept turning to me to tell me that the guy reminded him of a bee, *eine Biene*, and every time I had to roar with laughter. Just in case I didn't understand, he made a buzzing sound and waved his hands around his head like wings until I was embarrassed for him because the other guy was right there and fuck if he didn't look like a bee!

Meanwhile, I was making the most of my good fortune, hitting him up for packs of Kim cigarettes and schnitzel and fries in the full-monty version, for coffee, vodka, beer and those delicious toasts that Norma made so well.

He kept ordering me beer, but after that herbal tea he stuck to red wine, some kind of heavy vintage Burgundy. He smoked his Murattis, which he lit with a gold Dupont, and mumbled to himself, to which all I had to do was smile and nod politely, *ja, ja, ganz genial, wirklich, ja, ja, aber natürlich!* Or else he would suddenly turn and leer at me with those vacant cod-eyes of his, his tongue lolling out, completely pervy. I always welcomed the chance to have an intelligent chat with grandpas about politics, and I was happy to agree with his opinions as I had none of my own, so *kein Problem*. If that's not what he was after, I was happy to play the moron all night too, and roar with laughter at every belch or fart, as long as he paid.

Suddenly he turned out to be completely wasted, breaking glasses, puffing into the ashtray until the ashes floated up and into Norma's face like the cremated remains of all the Viennese hustlers who'd ever died of AIDS. If any of us had pulled a stunt like that we'd have been thrown out on our arses long ago. But here we had a situation where the more Mario acted out, the more everyone sucked up to him. Maybe when he was fucked up he gave bigger tips or something, or maybe they were just conning him. So when he sent his glass of Burgundy flying and it shattered to bits, they all clapped and shouted 'bravo!' Norma immediately gave him a new one, came out from behind the bar with a rag and right there, on her hands and knees and between his legs, started mopping the floor! With such graphic displays of capitalism, it's no wonder the other hustlers were so wet for money.

I wondered what was going on in his head, psychology being my forte after all. I had a feeling he wanted someone to hit him. So I tried a little experiment: 'I think you were very naughty just now.'

And what do you know, he flinched.

'Ja, ja, aber schlag mich nicht!'

Don't hit me, meaning: hit me. There you have it.

He suddenly fell into a funk. He opened his Louis Vuitton card case and out of a whole row of credit cards selected one, always the same one, Diners Club. He paid, signing the slip with his black Montblanc fountain pen, and shuffled out. And you, silly boy, didn't know whether to follow him or not, whether he would take you with him or not, because he didn't even look back over his shoulder. But the other escorts looked at you like, what are you, stupid? Go out after him, what are you waiting for? The most he'll do is tell you to go away, and there's no harm in that, so go!

They laughed and made humping motions with their hips in my direction. I stubbed out my cigarette, checked to see if he'd paid for everything I'd got, the schnitzel I ate at four o'clock, the cola vodka I ordered after that quickie at six . . . It was all paid, *er hat alles bezahlt.*

Outside the bar I was attacked by the fresh, sharp, freezing cold air, and he was standing like an orphan in the middle of the street, leaning forward, then backward, as if he were sleeping while standing. Ten metres away he was getting chatted up by this one African hooker who wasn't allowed in the bar because he stole, had AIDS and stank. It all started when he tried underselling the other hustlers and the Czech mafia cut a swastika in his face in the toilet. He just went downhill after that. I stomped my feet and the chode ran off.

So there was Mario Ludwig, trying to hail a cab with that Louis Vuitton man-purse of his, his cod- or carp-like head sticking out of his ascot like the bowl of a lowercase *g* (for Gucci). Under normal conditions no one would have stopped for a drunk like that, but this was Mario Ludwig—none other than the infamous Maria Louisa—who evoked the same response in everyone: 'Pull over, there's money in this.' He plonked himself down in the back seat, gave me a look like he'd never seen me before, gestured for me to get in, lewdly stuck out his tongue, winked and gurned and grabbed my thigh, and in a completely incomprehensible German announced his address to the driver, who became immediately obsequious.

The other boys had already advised me to get out of the cab as soon as we arrived and go around to open his door for him— as sloshed as he was, I'd get points for it later when he was adding up. Had I let him walk ahead at the entrance? Had I made sure to walk behind him (always a few steps, as if he were the Queen of England)? Had I lit his cigarette with sufficient deference? Had I helped him off with his coat?

We drove up to his mansion block, and I was actually surprised that with his lucre, he didn't live in a mansion of his own but in a single (large) flat. He explained later that he'd have been lonely on his own in a house, and that the building belonged to him, so he saved the best unit for himself. Anyway it was beautifully renovated and lighted, heads of lions or jellyfish maybe, can't remember now.

Mindful of my instructions, I opened the door for him, kept my distance a few paces behind him, and picked up his fanny pack when it fell on the pavement. It was funny, having to be on my toes like that, going around with a drunk. He was really pretty hammered, and we'd hardly made it into the crimson-upholstered box of Mozart balls that was his flat, when he started swigging away like a madman again. Of course I practically had to rip his coat off him first, to avoid any complaints later on. My God! There's no way I could drink like that while working; either I'd end up getting sick all over a Persian rug or a bed or something, or I wouldn't be able to get my eleven inches up at all. Or else I'd have no problems getting a stiffy, but because I'd be trying so hard not to vomit I wouldn't be able to control it. Meanwhile, this one here's swilling Johnny Walker Gold Label. He gets undressed down to his jeans and stands at the mirror, clutching his bottle of the most expensive whisky in the world, making faces like, 'You still got it, you handsome devil you . . .' He lights a Marlboro from a pack from before the health warnings, and immediately starts playing at 'Come to Marlboro Country'. I very politely assure him

that yes, totally, he's a supercowboy, even if—although I don't say
this—his body is as white as the belly of a carp, he has sagging
breasts and on his paunch there's a scar where his appendix was
taken out. But he just keeps playing at being the cowboy, putting
on a leather Stetson he got as a souvenir at the Grand Canyon,
and I honestly can't drink another ounce of alcohol, otherwise I'll
vomit, I'm ready to collapse. I mentally added up the day, all I'd
had to drink and how much. I'd got up at two in the afternoon,
made my way to Alfie's at four, it was three in the morning now,
so I'd been knocking back for eleven hours! And he'd been forcing
drinks on me at the bar the whole night, as if he didn't realize he
was compromising the quality of the services to be rendered.

Suddenly two little doors opened up in the clock, and a cuckoo
appeared, cuckooing the new hour, and all the air went out of him.
As if he were a balloon and the cuckoo had nicked him with its
beak. He wasn't a cowboy at all any more, just an old, inebriated
banker. He sat in the kitchen, lost in thought, and forgot all about
me. It occurred to me to take advantage of his state and have a
look around the enormous flat, decamp to the bathroom to have
a wash. I walked down the hallway looking at the portraits of dour,
medieval, Protestant housewives, all framed alike, until I made it
to the bathroom. That was the most beautiful bathroom I'd seen
in my life. Everything in grey and black granite, even the cosmetics were in black containers like from Chanel or something . . . So
fresh and fragrant, and the water so clean you could drink it right
from the tap without letting it run first. Next to the sink was a
TAG Heuer watch worth a fortune . . . The black floor was pleas-
antly warm under my bare feet. I took a bath, sprayed myself with
colognes, styled my hair with gel and struck poses in front of the

mirror titled 'Alexis at Her Bath', then went back to see what Cod was up to. He was lying naked on an enormous bed, wincing like a prima ballerina who has to give herself to the manager of the cinema in exchange for a role in *Swan Lake*, and his decrepit body was a stark contrast to the perfect home interior around him. He was the one piece of dreck among all those perfect things. He lay there, withered and yellowing, in the starched rose-print sheets, took a whiff from a bottle of poppers, killing off his remaining grey cells, and held out his hand to me. I went to him. The fragrance of freshly washed laundry that pervaded the entire flat was spoilt by the solventy, lacquery, nail-polishy pong of the poppers. In the mirror I saw how beautiful I was, especially next to him. I saw my high, narrow cheekbones and the low-cut bangs of my black hair . . . Of course I didn't appreciate those things back then . . .

Then we started to have 'sex'—*mein Gott!*—it was more like psychotherapy in bed. He bought and consumed boys with his eyes and judged his own virility with them too. But while the beauty of a young man may make a thousand promises, it does not always deliver, especially not if the deliveree is an impotent lush with varicose veins and haemorrhoids. We snogged a bit, and he spilt all the whisky and told me to lick it up, while he lay there writhing and making weird noises, gurgling noises, like he was gargling liquor. It was clear this wasn't it, the whole scene, it wasn't what he was after. He'd lifted it from a movie, but had no idea what he really wanted, why he'd dragged this skinny boy home with him. But as long as he was paying for it he felt obliged to 'perform', and it wasn't clear which of us was forcing himself more, who was faking it more, who was actually working here. Each of us was waiting to get 'laid' by the other. But either there's chemistry or there isn't, and when there isn't, that's when the theatre begins, the pretend moaning, the whimpering and rolling eyes, because two people who've landed in bed together almost never have the courage to say outright that the sex isn't working. For me it was still good because at least I'd be getting paid. But he couldn't even get it up, even for one second. I beat him a few times, and he pretended not to want it and begged me to stop. But you couldn't really call that 'beating'—I mean, as I was expecting a nice honorarium in the morning, I was afraid to give him a proper thrashing. He kept going on with his 'I know I was bad, I was so bad, but I won't do it any more! Don't hit me!' (Hit me.) Thwack! and he'd lick my feet. I felt like I had it under control, so I started operating on autopilot, while my thoughts turned to my own problems, especially the financial ones.

Eventually, he spoke: 'Excuse me, but I want to stop. Get out of here.'

I kept beating him half-heartedly a bit longer, then leaned down to lick his nipples, he was paying for it after all, but he raised his voice: 'Nein! Raus!' as if any more fondling would only make him vomit. I pulled back: the last thing I wanted was a quarrel with Cod. Luckily he passed out and immediately began snoring in a peculiar way. I was thinking that if I really did leave now, I'd have to wake him up to get paid, and it would be only too easy to get on his bad side. So I thought I'd just have a nap at the foot of his enormous bed and wait until morning, when Gramps might be more favourably disposed, despite the massive hangover he was sure to have. I looked at him: death warmed over. He was naked and completely wet (from the whisky and pee—he'd ordered me to pee on him), stripped of all his posh clothing, which at least blocked out the pitiful image of his wrecked body. He was lying on his belly, with his white skin turning yellow and wrinkled arse, repulsive; and all around that chode were gold and silver salvers and marble toilets in the bathroom, all of it worth a fortune.

Oh well, at least I'd kept my part of the bargain. I picked up the bottle of Johnny Walker Gold from the fluffy pink carpet; even the dregs were massively expensive. I extracted the pack of Marlboro Lights from the shambles of his clothing on the carpet and went to the kitchen. I made coffee in the complicated espresso machine (which I was well acquainted with, other rich customers all having the same one) and smoked. Well. Thank God it's Friday. Time to clock out! In the enormous silver fridge I found sausage, cheese and olives, all top-shelf, Italian, or Mediterranean rather, and made myself a little late-night snack with Cod snoring in the background. Why do rich people have to be so unhappy? We Eastern Bloc boys, we'd be over the moon to have the equivalent of that fridge (OK, the equivalent of all the kitchen appliances together)—I really haven't thought about this for ages. That's just how it was. After a certain point, lucre stops putting out. Past a certain threshold it starts exploiting its owner, even if they're firmly convinced that they're the one exploiting it.

And then began the tedious wait for daybreak. Cod yelped and moaned in his sleep. When he was quiet, the whole flat filled up with the ticking of the cuckoo clock. I was hoping it would finally get light out and Cod would wake up, lavish me with the gold and jewels, or not (I still had no idea), and send me home.

Home. Well . . .

THE MANY-HEADED DRAGON

Back then I was living with a group of Thai hookers in Liesing, which is insanely far from everything, but it was free and came with victuals. Because they worked in the laundry of a hospice somewhere, they would feed me with spicy chicken and shrimp and in exchange got to suck me off as much as they pleased. They really lost it over my Eleven-Inch, whenever they saw it they'd swoon and roll their eyes and wring their hands . . . Their own willies were like children's crayons . . .

I didn't know how old they were because they all looked like little guppies, grub for paedophiles, but one of them was evidently nearing forty. Their little noses, their little ears, their little mouths, everything miniaturized.

I really loved them though. What a scene that was, how we met! I was walking down the street when suddenly this convertible pulled up next to me, the door opened, and inside was an entire preschool of Asian queens, smelling like reused frying oil and incense, in place of the speedometer an altar to some guru or other fatty, and oriental music blaring at full volume. On the floor of the car was a basket with ginger, roots and strange herbs sticking out. I got in, I mean, what did I have to fear from those Lilliputians, it's not like they could do anything to me. (Although later, when one of them was giving me a massage, it turned out the fucker was strong enough to crush me like a bug!) They started groping me with their little paws, and I looked to see if the police were anywhere about, because this would definitely fall under paedophilia. I was Dianka-level broke at the moment—well, it happens to the best of us, *einmal ist keinmal*—and they were inviting me to their place for dinner. In that faraway district of theirs, Liesing, where they had a four-room flat in a tower block. They opened the door for me, set out on the carpet an array of spicy Eastern delicacies, boiled up some rice, distributed chopsticks. It was a miracle. Everything was super spicy and smelt weird, and there was chicken, but the sauce was hard to stomach. I cant't say if I really care for this kind of food. You have to really watch out with other cultures and peoples, they're all so strange and unfamiliar. And in their hilarious Thai English they came on to me, explaining that they'd seen me before at Alfie's, that in addition to working in a laundry (because of the insurance and their residency permits), they worked there too, servicing those old paedophiles who went to Thailand every winter (although if those Austrian grandpas knew how old the Thai Queens really were . . .). Despite their size, my queens were ancient, there were customers they'd been servicing since the seventies, they'd been here forever. And to think all those kiddie fiddlers who'd been going off to Southeast Asia for endless chicken were getting spoon-fed other old men, Asian-style, immutable and wise . . .

You could say the Thai Queens never did anything except as a group. They were like an octopus or a many-headed dragon, they always appeared out of nowhere and always together, suddenly, silently, they wandered barefoot through the flat, leaving their tiny footprints on the bathroom tiles, never less than three of them together . . .

They were already 'set': while East European boys had at most six years, from fourteen to twenty, to make money (after that they'd need to have saved up for some other kind of business, a tanning salon—anything), these queens never changed at all. Customers died of old age, new customers were born and grew old, but their youthful meat, provender of paedophiles, never spoilt . . . But Europeans were incapable of telling them apart, so even if one of them died of old age, they probably just sent a cable back to Thailand—we have an opening—and an identical one would be on her way, with her nylon red-white-blue bags, her plastic shopping bags, her cache of chili peppers and hot sauce, incense and cassette tapes with praying gurus on the covers . . . And if a customer asked, Where's my favourite boy today? the boy would reappear!

Those trolls they say haunt the Swiss Alps? They were them, a tribe of trolls that never left the cave.

It was all them.

So I'd head back to my Thai Queens, sleep on a mat enveloped in the smell of curry, and later take the U-Bahn to Kaufhalle to look for some new sexy duds. I had my eye on a pair of Diesel jeans and cowboy boots. A leather jacket with fringe would be great too, a real Western one. But Grandpa would have to pay for that directly—they were expensive, right? Why should I spend my own money on it? I was lying next to Cod on his enormous heated bed. I looked at him. He was lying naked, whistling every time he exhaled. I gently covered him with a light blanket—after all, he was paying—and imagined what I'd buy if he left me a million . . . Or two million . . . The list was long:

1. A CD Walkman that plays on repeat, and a lifetime supply of CDs.

2. Jeans and a jeans jacket from Levi's, or some even better brand.

3. A Diesel leather jacket . . .

4. Black Calvin Klein undies with the string that goes in the arse.

5. Wella Sanara shampoo and conditioner.

6. Chanel Égoïste perfume . . .

And as I fantasized about these various luxuries, I fell into slumber. Once again without brushing my teeth first, once again without my pyjamas on, once again in a stranger's bed. I imagined walking in to Alfie's Golden Mirror tomorrow night, where all the whores had been starving for weeks. The doors open, and I walk in, dressed all in white, everything new (and white Davidoff cigarettes), I put my Walkman down on the bar and listen to my own music because theirs is crap . . .

In the morning it was like this: Carp (I suddenly realized he looked more like a carp than a cod) wasn't upset, he just silently opened and shut his mouth over and over, just like a carp—clearly it wasn't his first day in the bathtub—and seemed bewildered, wobbled a little, turned on his side.

We drank coffee together in silence and ate toast from his Dualit toaster in his enormous kitchen adorned with Laura Ashley bouquets. Coffee in cups decorated with little roses, little roses on the window curtains. I wanted to say something. But what? I certainly wasn't going to bring up yesterday. But he kept talking on his phone, completely ignoring me, going off to get a fax, his pager buzzing, and all of a sudden he was steering me towards the door and saying goodbye, thrusting money in my hand I wouldn't have time to count, and then I was gone. Not until I got to the U-Bahn was I able to pull the wad out of my pocket. It was a lot. Much, much more than I ever would have guessed. I'd be able to leave my Thai Queens and move into a five-star hotel for months. No more curry odour! I'd be able to buy all new everything and walk in anywhere 'all in white'. And there'd be much, much more left over for hard times.

Oh Dianka, you really should have seen those faces at Mario's funeral! I looked at that coffin garlanded in crimson and coats of arms, and I was happy to think of that drunken pervert's dumb dick being finished off and shit out by the worms.

It was a strange ceremony. The trees over Vienna's Zentralfriedhof were filled with the twitter of birds, and it was clear that even after death the wealthy aristocracy doesn't fraternize with plebes. Clustered around the headstone inscribed with 'Mario Ludwig von Whatever zu Who Cares' was the family, little grey-haired countesses and doddering grandpas for the most part, fatigued from squabbling in court with the Vienna Conservatory, accompanied, at a distance, by representatives of the Conservatory, while much further away stood those who were the true conservators of the Dearly Departed—nearly a hundred sixteen- and seventeen-year-olds all festooned in gold and dressed not in black but in all the colours of the rainbow, wearing Nike and Adidas, smoking cigarettes, blowing bubbles with their chewing gum, even though they were in a cemetery. A few Thais in hoodies playing handheld video games. I was the only one in black. I always thought black was sexy and made you look thinner, so I had a lot of black clothes, some even with sequins. Black shoes, black stockings, black trousers, black belts, black watches, black shirts, black glasses . . . Well, maybe I went a bit too far with the black fedora, but if I hadn't gone too far, then I'd have had to take it all seriously, and really, I wanted to make a scene. And all this without showing off an ounce of gold, although God and Mario Ludwig knew I could've scrounged up a little something. In any case, I was the only one of us who in any way resembled an aristocrat, and the family eyed me suspiciously: was this some illegitimate grandchild who'd been hiding out in a Swiss boarding school all this time?

So where are *his* attorneys? One Conservatory representative gave me the side eye too. The other boys would obviously start picking their noses as soon as the funeral was over. No one had any idea that all Mario had left me was a gold S.T. Dupont cigarette lighter, a broken one at that ...

In any case, that was the moment when I understood that I needed to conduct myself in manner completely different from the other boys.

I stood there inching incrementally closer to the family, and the blackness of their attire gradually sucked in the blackness of mine until it absorbed me. Eventually I found myself in their midst, like a grandson. Concealed between the other headstones, musicians of the Vienna Philharmonic were playing ... One old countess, moved by the sight of tears flowing down my young cheeks, reached out and grasped my shoulder with her bony hand as if she were adopting me with the gesture.

Once the funeral was over and after conferring with the other grandparents, the same grey-haired countess invited me to the repast—and that, Dianka, was the famous Party of the Princesses, a story I'll be telling for the rest of my days ... I've even charged extra for telling that story before ...

The banquet for Mario Ludwig took place the next day in a baroque water palace on the banks of the Mauerbach in a large park on the western edge of Vienna, a neighbourhood called Penzing. It was a place that would have been suitable for the Vienna Philharmonic to perform in, were it not for their excessive proximity to the Vienna Conservatory. There was, however, the *Wassermusik*, strains of which were coming from the garden.

I was dressed like a good boy from a Swiss boarding school, in a Ralph Lauren polo shirt, hair slicked to the side, totally farting higher than my arse was tall, but I still didn't know how to conceal my defects *auf Deutsch*, and because of that, even as I was entering the palace, I still hadn't ompletely worked out my story. I only knew I needed to make a lot of contacts in that most elegant of worlds, maybe enquire whether someone might not need a chimney sweep, for instance, and if that didn't work then at least steal something. In the meantime, paparazzi were standing at the entrance, eyeing me as if I might even be the young Prince William.

The fête took place in a garden directly on the water, among cream-coloured arbours housing tables bedecked with Laura Ashley rose-decorated tablecloths crowned by silver platters of hydroponically grown and genetically warped strawberries the size of fists. It wasn't your typical banquet but, rather, a breezy, bubbly garden party of the 'strawberries and champagne' variety. The cream-coloured trellises of the arbours were overgrown with tea roses, no doubt genetically modified as well. The surface of the lake surrounding the palace reflected the setting sun.

I put a lot of effort into learning by heart that Mario's family name was von Sinzendorf und Kaunitz-Kinsky (I wrote it in a beautiful Gothic script on my palm), so I had up to three names to choose from for myself. Each would require a perfect high German, and not my low Polish German, but my looks were enough for all three names. 'An acquaintance from Oxford'... Different lines from the series *The Career of Nicodemus Dyzma* kept running through my head: 'A good friend from the English racecourses ...' If only that elderly pervert had been a bit younger, my seventeen years clearly rhymed with that rabble of seventeen-year-olds from the funeral. What could I say to them? What could my connection be to that drunken senex, Carp? And how would I explain living with my Thai Queens? Perhaps it was better to maintain an aristocratic reserve, and if someone asked about the rabble I could simply, charitably suggest that Mario, bless his soul, had always been one to succour orphans . . . In short, I was in a bit of a bind.

When offered alcohol, I politely demurred, conscious of being underage, and sipped instead a glass of orange juice that tasted so intensely of orange that the oranges it was made of must have been genetically tweaked and vitaminized. Suddenly I had an image of myself as the boyfriend of some elderly wreck, sipping my juice while sunning on a lounger in the garden, decked out in white Lacoste, wearing a cap with a visor, or maybe just the visor on its own—just like in the Rafaello commercial . . . That was my dream!

We were seated at tables inside the large gazebo and set to work on the genetically puffed-up strawberries with whipped cream. The man beside me was a dead ringer for Gombrowicz, and I understood that fate had sent Gombrowicz to me, as my cicerone, since Gombrowicz too had been of an . . . aristocratic . . . persuasion. Anyway, if it weren't for him, I still wouldn't know what to make of that party today.

This Gombrowicz was a cynic, a real piece of work, he had a permanent smirk on his lips and bitter knowledge of the world emblazoned on his face, the kind of face one sees only on old waiters and hotel porters, and he hadn't the foggiest as to how I had come to be there. Why, if it isn't the little Countess von Slutshausen de Moorcock! He winked knowingly at me, as if to say, 'So of all those twinks at the funeral only this little trickster managed to worm his way in, huh! You'll go far, kid!' Of course, our conversation was happening entirely in facial gestures; the spoken part of our dialogue, for the first half hour at least, was given to enthusing over the weather and the strawberries. Later, however, he gently steered me away from talk of low-growing fruits. It turned out that the lady seated to my left, who was dressed modestly in black and had blond hair with gold highlights, was one of those genuine princesses whose pedigrees date back to the fifteenth century. She had studied art history in order to marry well, and that she had done. She wasn't particularly clever, but she was genteel and had all that was needed for getting by in this world, languages and such. In fact, it was the more modestly attired women here, whether silver-haired or blond with high-lights, who were the princesses, and the ones tarted up with Chanel jewellery . . . were something else. For instance, the one across from us raving about the tea roses, with her Marlies Möller coif, dressed in all white and all Chanel, with her white Chanel watch, Chanel rings that glowed against her bronzed and liver-spotted fingers—she had been a cleaning lady who worked for a senile aristocrat, tidying up after him, wiping his arse. She'd seduced him on his death bed, ran off to get the priest to make it all legal, and was set for life . . .

Anyway, that one, with the liver spots and bronzed skin, with the helmet of grey hair turning to violet, to rose (roses were her métier), was named Charlotte. My Gombrowicz hinted with his eyes that she'd be liable to pay me a fair wage to clean out her chimneys. As I approached the boxy cream-coloured cocktail dress, the tiny Chanel watch, the long, orange-lacquered finger-nails, I was overcome with the sweet scent of old lady. It was the two charred pork scratchings of her boobs in front of my nose that gave off that strange, treacly odour, and her cleavage was all freck-les and liver spots, as if she were made of liver, of liverwurst, to be prized out of the sandwiches in my lunchbox and chucked into front yards on the way to school.

I took my leave of Lady Liverwurst, although I might well have lost a good client, and turned instead to the demure one in black, with the balayage and barely any make-up. And so it began. My Gombrowicz translated into an exquisite German when she, the medieval one, asked where I was from.

Nothing could have caused me greater distress than to be asked such questions as these, to which I had yet to confect an answer. I considered saying, and almost did say, that I hailed from Montevideo, born and raised in its beautiful capital, Pernambuco. But then, I thought, Poland had and in fact still has an aristocracy, albeit without as many liver spots, and it must be knocking about somewhere still, so I told her I was from Poland, from Łańcut, Potocki my name, Georges Potocki, and in case she asked, I explained I was a direct descendent of Barbara Radziwiłłówna. Georges Potocki Ponimirsky de Łańcut (although my real name's Teresa von Orlowski ...), so very delighted to meet you. And fol-lowing the true ancient Polish tradition, I kissed the hand of my Medieval Lady, which prompted her to panic.

'I beg your pardon, madame. In Poland, we value the customs of chivalry above all else ...'

'Ah, la Pologne ...,' she drawled, and it was clear she had nothing else to say on that lovely topic.

'Yes, Poland, Poland,' I repeated, and I was unable to pronounce the word any differently than I would, say, 'more, more', or 'slow down, slow down . . .'

'I see, I see . . . yes, Poland . . . ,' she said, driving her fork into the heap of meringue, whipped cream and raspberries that comprised her Pavlova.

We could have gone on conversing like this until the end of days. Was it time to bring up my pedigree, my big feature?

'Ach, Polen, natürlich! Why, recently I read in *Bild der Frau* a true story about a German lady from Frankfurt am Main and a Polish man and how they fell in love . . . Love really does conquer all!'

But she suddenly fell silent, remembering that the story continued with him robbing her blind and driving away in her car . . .

So I began telling her my own story, that is, the story of my well-known family, the Potockis, of the Silver Pilawa line. My father, having travelled to Africa, was stricken with malaria from a tsetse fly and died. I was in my boarding school in Switzerland at the time and was playing in my Ralph Lauren polo when I received the terrible news . . .

Witold G. informed me that Mario Ludwig had probably died 'in the arms of a whore' who had left without reporting his death to anyone and that many things had evidently simply vanished from his opulent home. Everything pointed to his having died of alcohol poisoning—the levels in his blue blood were off the charts. He was found in the bathtub, his head submerged, a rose floating on the surface, and neither his wallet nor a single watch was to be found in the entire flat, although every trollop in this town knew he had a special vitrine for his timepieces. There, mounted on their velvet cushions, Mario's Rolexes and Pateks, his Graff Diamonds, Breguets, Chopards and Hublots ticked away the time between wind-ups . . .

What surprised me most was that everyone except Witold G. was convinced that the whore had been a woman. The police had ruled out foul play, and since Mario only ever socialized with prostitutes and never had anyone over, and what losses there were would be difficult to determine precisely, a forensic investigation was never even initiated. It was anyone's guess how much had gone missing, but it was the Vienna Conservatory's loss now, and they were sure to get over it.

The only person who knew the precise inventory of that loss was me . . . For I was the whore Mario had been with when he croaked. And he croaked like a fly on rat poison! It was I who gave him shot after shot of Absolut vodka, and although I was terrified when it happened and wanted to run away, an innate opportunism and the fact that I had yet to be paid for my services that night made me stick around a bit . . . So yes, I was lying when I said that all I'd inherited was a broken S.T. Dupont lighter. In fact, what really happened was this:

I was lucky Carp hadn't picked me up at Alfie's or in the sauna or on Karlsplatz or anywhere else where someone might have seen us together. We just met on the street that night, an especially elegant street—the Ring. Mario wasn't likely to make the rounds on Karlsplatz anyway, not unless they'd installed a marble commemorative plaque for him there. So the pigs could do all the investigating they wanted at Alfie's, no one there had seen me with him that day. Anyway, there I was: 'Oh, hallo, Mario! Gayen veer? Vee gayt's? Nach Cafe gayen?' I was thinking: It's always better to gayen with him than not to gayen, and maybe he would take me home again. But our love had just gone through its eighth crisis, and any minute he wouldn't be taking me anywhere any more. I'd have to play my cards right this time.

The cafe we went to was so glamorous and cosmopolitan: Black men dressed immaculately in white were smoking cigars, while a woman in a fur coat despite the heatwave walked by with two greyhounds to which she bore a remarkable resemblance. Everyone was so sophisticated, as if an exhaustive cleansing had taken place there and elements of the worst sort had all been expunged. The coffee came in a thimble-sized demitasse, all of two millilitres there at the bottom, for only two million. I was given a miniature sandwich made of egg, garnish and beluga caviar. I scarfed it down. A tart for dessert. And Dumont cigarettes, the kind Alexis smoked on *Dynasty*. Someone in the background was quietly improvising a little something on a grand piano, lid propped open. I thought to myself: 'What do I have to do to get rich? Jesus, they all look like greyhounds here . . .' And then it occurred to me, I should take advantage of Mario Ludwig's greatest weakness and 'slip something' into his drink. But there wasn't time to prepare anything, I wouldn't be able to skip off to the pharmacy at that hour to pick up some drug that might interact violently with the alcohol. I'd have to wing it.

So I turned up the charm, fluttered my long eyelashes, licked my lips like a kitten lapping milk, and stood up to go to the conveniences, my bubble butt in full view. I winked and smiled enticingly. To what effect, you already know. But first, I said, 'I'd like a cognac. You have one too—you look like you need one! What's that, darling? Nothing happening on the stock market?' Oh, if only you knew, old man! 'What horrible problems you have,' I said out loud, and under my breath: 'They'll be a lot worse before long.'

Regardless of how much Gold Label whisky he'd drunk in his life, how many luxury cigarettes he'd smoked, and however much expensive caviar he'd polished off; regardless of what lavish clothes and accoutrements he wore, to what elegant resorts in Cannes and Monaco he jetted off on holiday, how many millions he had stashed away in his bank accounts; regardless of how many cars he owned, even if all of them looked the same; regardless of all the cosmetics he smeared on his ghastly face, all the young and beautiful bodies that warmed his hideous body through the winter, and all the Mozart balls he'd ever consumed—regardless of all these extravagant circumstances, I can tell you: Mario Ludwig died the death of a vagrant under a bridge.

He drank himself to death.

It was easy, even too easy, to persuade him to swill at home along with some sexual servicing. He had never worked, so when he wasn't dealing with his stock portfolio, he had plenty of free time. So there we were, at his. Gramps immediately began pouring out generous shots of frozen Absolut, then went off somewhere and came back tricked out in an unfashionable tartan skirt and a mismatched teddy fastened at the crotch, his octogenarian dugs safely tucked away in their lacy sheath. He handed me an old frayed whip, bent over the armchair and tore off his plaid skirt. A white bottom appeared. He buried his head in his arms, and from somewhere behind that protruding withered white arse, Mario whimpered, 'Ach, nein! Nein . . . ! Don't hit me . . . !'

I told him I wasn't lifting a finger until he had a drink with me for my birthday. It was my birthday! (By the way, if you ever need to squeeze more dough out of a generous trick, just tell him, 'It's my birthday today and nobody remembered. I'm so lonely ...' Just take care you don't have your birthday too often, no more than once every few months. In a pinch you can alternate it with your name day, although name days never really work in the West ...)

Anyway, it was my birthday, and I wasn't touching that whip until he'd had a drink with me. So I approached him with a treacherously full glass. 'Bottoms up! I'll be offended if you don't! You know how Poles are! A horse, a sabre, a bottle ... Pole and German brothers be ...!'

'Ach so! Johnny ...! Wann hast du Geburtstag? Heute?!' No one was going to give me a present, but that's OK, I would get my own ...

'Drink up, Gramps. Na zdrowie!' I spoke Polish to him, and he laughed and slurred after me 'na zdlovia'!

Debil. Moron.

'Now then, now that you've been anaesthetized by the alcohol, I'll give you a whipping you'll never forget!' Usually I had to lay off at some point because there would always be a 'day after'. But this time there would be no day after!

Mario usually took me to the ATM to give me my honorarium. Now, I'd be taking it myself. I thrashed him until he was nothing but moaning and flailing. 'Take that! Take it! For having had your whole life ahead of you, for all of your luxuries, your schillings and Deutschmarks and your New York Stock Exchange! For looking like the Carp you are! Take that! For your trains always being on time! For your fucking Mozart balls!'

I was exhausted, so I stopped beating him. I fell on the armchair, out of breath, and he was lying on top of his torn skirt, his superannuated arse smeared all over with blood, whimpering. I went to the bathroom and washed up, sprayed myself with Paco Rabanne (the cosmetics would be coming with me as the Vienna Conservatory certainly didn't need them), made myself coffee in the Nespresso machine and went back to Carp. He had, as it were, come to, although he was trying not to sit down. I poured him another glass of Absolut. Drunk as he was, he would keep on drinking. He'd lost all capacity to reason. I didn't even want to be nice to him any more, since there wasn't going to be a next time, so I just shouted orders at him: 'My birthday!'

'Jawohl!' he saluted me, the skirt back around his waist, and now he had a jaunty woollen beret with a big pompom set at an angle on his head.

'Now,' I said, 'Let's get the treasure! Show me the safe where you keep your treasure!'

'Jawohl!'

Could it really be this simple? I wondered as I walked with him down the hallway. Could it really be this beautifully simple, with him just opening up the safe for me and . . .

But no. When we got to the safe he got muddle-headed and stalled. He couldn't remember the combination. Had his last healthy brain cell awakened in a tidal wave of vodka and bolted in a panic for the interior? He sat down on the sofa in the room with the safe and began puking on the beautiful cream-coloured shag carpet, his body diminishing incrementally.

'Oh, I'm going to have to take care of you, you're clearly sick. Du bist krank! Arzt, Arzt, Apotheke, where's your Apotheke? Where? You got any medizinische Drogen?' He pointed. I put him to bed and threw myself at his bathroom cabinet.

Have I ever mentioned how much I love pharmaceuticals and colourfully packaged vitamins and diet supplements? I kept an eye out for what I would take for myself, but first I needed to find some pills that would interact negatively with the alcohol, with each other, and ideally with Carp's life. I threw a bunch of benzo-diazepines, antibiotics and who knows what else into a small bowl, most of the names meant nothing to me, but the idea was to take a little of everything. Aspirin—why not? Anti-diarrhoea meds? Awesome. Suppositories? Sure—and he can take them all orally: it's not like he'll explode or anything. Here's something for his heart. And here's . . . sleeping pills! Ten of those, please! I took them to him with another glass of vodka, but he was sound asleep and snoring away in the room with the safe. No darling, not so quick.

I put the pills and the vodka down on the night table and shook the little bugger. I threw the first CD in the tower into his stereo and turned the volume up as high as possible. It happened to be the Viennese recording of the musical *Cats*, I remember it so well from those days in Vienna. Oh the memories! It almost worked too, but Gramps was slipping through my fingers. Eventually I got him to chug the whole pharma-vodka cocktail, but he still wouldn't open the safe (to be fair, in his state he wouldn't have been able to open a suitcase, even one without a lock). Well, we'd have to figure out another way. I forced him to drink another glass of vodka, fisted a bunch of sleeping pills up his flabby arsehole (the body can absorb them there too), and put him to bed. Meanwhile, I went off to peruse and slowly gather in one place all the things I wanted. The cosmetics and perfumes in the bathroom. There was so much! I looked in the mirror. What a fucking god! I repeated my Ten Commandments: You're your own creator. You're all that matters. You're only in it for yourself.

I pulled out the largest (wardrobe-sized) Louis Vuitton rolling suitcase I could find and started packing it for my new, beautiful life. From the bathroom, where not even the Fahrenheit shower gel eluded my grasp, to the closets full of clothes Gramps had procured at all the Harrodses and Galeries Lafayettes the world over, shoes with shoe trees inside them, often made to measure, but we wore the same size, so . . . Then came the Montblanc fountain pens, the Cartier and Chopard ballpoints, to die for . . . When I saw them I went back to push another handful of pills up his arse, all I wanted was to ditch this place as soon as possible and take off for Zurich with my loot. So, fifteen Patek Philippe watches, ten Rolexes, all the Hublots and Cartiers! Luxury-brand wallets and handbags, bottles of liquor from the bar (only the very topshelf bottles though), and then there was his office. All the pens in his desk went right into the sack. I pulled the drawers open, but my hands were shaking—good Lord, a thief wears a burning cap, but the murderer a whole electric helmet (cf. Nałkowska's *Diaries*: 'My hair was broiled in an electrical helmet.')—Suddenly, I felt like I was having a heart attack. What was that? Oh, the cuckoo, that idiot cuckoo from the clock. It had been here the whole time, no good Austrian home would be without a cuckoo clock. But my heart was pounding its way up to my neck, and I had to sit down on the velvet-upholstered armchair behind his desk. Like Lady Macbeth I stared at my hands, covered as they were in imaginary blood, but every surface I'd touched had my fingerprints on it! I began wiping the desk with my sleeve, but as soon as I started, I realized it wouldn't even matter. My fingerprints were all over this house anyway, there wasn't anything I could do . . .

All of a sudden I heard a horrible bang, followed by a crack! I froze in terror, but then everything went silent. My heart was beating somewhere behind my eyes. I tiptoed to the room where I'd left Mario. Empty. I began searching all the rooms and finally found him lying on the floor in one of them. What had happened? He must have come in for something, then lost consciousness, and at the last minute tried to grab the table, but got the tablecloth instead, and fell on the floor, pulling the tablecloth and all the porcelain knickknacks on it down with him, and knocking over the chair as well. What was he looking for? Why had he used his last reserves of strength to come in here, to this room that, compared with the rest of his flat, was inconspicuous?

I looked around. There was an antique grandfather clock with a pendulum and porcelain face—I certainly wouldn't be taking that with me—and framed pictures on the wall: those were probably worth something, but they weren't really my style (unless of course they were Louis Vuitton). There was a tiny desk in the style of Louis XIV or some other basic fuck, I really hadn't a clue—for all I knew it could've been in the style of Queen Bona. But maybe there was something inside the desk, something Gramps was just dying to keep me from finding, trying with his own body to block me from finding, something that might very well be the code for the safe!

More importantly, I realized that as long as Gramps had fallen and not cracked open his skull, he could easily fall again. I lifted him and threw him against the edge of the table, and it worked: he fell with a thud on the floor (not so easy to get the thud here since the carpet was so soft). He started muttering something under his breath, although he should have kicked it long ago, and I began to feel like I was in a horror movie. The desk could wait, I needed to finish this business once and for all. I hauled Grandpa under my arm to the bathroom, where there were lots of sharp edges made of finest granite, and started throwing him at the bathtub and against the floor until finally I managed to get a deep gash in his head.

I dumped him in the bathtub, plugged the drain with its beautiful silver stopper, and ran the water. Now, people have different views on this, but I knew I'd need his head to be submerged. Once enough water had flowed out of the Philippe Starck faucet, I pushed it in, like the carp in the bathtub for Christmas. A Carp waiting to be slaughtered, waiting for the Christmas Eve dinner slaughter. I grabbed hold of his face and pushed it down into the water. Glug. Glug glug. He started moving. Just like the carp when it's pulled out of the bathtub and hammered dead. My God, how many more lives did Gramps have left? There I was, holding this sloshed nonagenarian's head in the water, and he was thrashing and splashing all over the place. But a hundred years' difference in age is still a hundred years and not to be underestimated. Eventually Grandpa stopped moving. I kept holding him down in that crystal-clear spring water direct from the Styrian Alps, as if I were doing my hand-washables there, until my lower back started to hurt (I couldn't kneel because my trousers would've got wet). A last little bubble of air wandered slowly, leisurely to the surface.

'The devil didn't save you, so you weren't a witch after all,' I said, a reference to the practice of swimming a witch.

Eventually I left him. I looked myself over in the mirror, checking whether my face had changed from the experience of becoming a murderer, but it wasn't much in any case, and nothing visible to the naked eye. As I'd suddenly become very rich, however, I did begin to look a little like a greyhound.

I returned to the room with the ancient escritoire to see about those other valuables he'd been so determined to safeguard. I pulled open the drawer. It looked like albums for collecting stamps. And there, inside them ... Oh God, what is wrong with these people?

It was a collection of coffee creamer sachets, the little packets that you tear at one serrated end and squirt the milk out. This is what he was protecting, knowing with his last ember of consciousness that he would die with a thief in his home. In Poland the foil always tears every which way when you open them, but not here. In any case, these all had pictures on them: here a castle, there Mozart, the Alps, cows, white crosses on red ... Evidently the hardcore collectors have a special device for extracting the milk and when they find one with a picture they don't already have they take it home and open it delicately. I suspected Dianka of collecting Kinder Surprise gadgets the same way, but that was nothing compared with what these perverts did. I was sure that, as with stamp collections, these albums must have contained some rarities, defects or super-valuable specimens, but it's not like I was going to sell them. Let the Conservatory deal with them, the creamers could stay.

Having spurned the creamers, I continued my inspection of the flat, pulling my suitcase after me, until I could hardly get it closed. This had become a full-on heist. The cuckoo cuckooed five in the morning. The 'new me' sat down on the shag carpeting, poured herself a glass of Johnny Walker Gold Label, and smoked a cigarette, flicking the ash directly on the carpet. Inebriated as I was, I began chatting with myself in the mirror in different personae: 'Fuck everything, I'm my own creator now! Fuuuuuckkkkk eeeeevvverryyyythiiiiiing! I'll go shopping in Monaco, ja ja, einkaufen gehen!, the world's biggest whore, and when I'm done with my shopping I'll move to Zurich, and Austria can go fuck off . . . Fuck these bitches with their scowls and jowls. . . I'm so sure he's got something else squirrelled away here that I haven't found yet, I'll have to do another walk-through . . . Oh, what's this? A little jewellery box made of gold? Awesome. Here you go, little jewellery box, hop-hop into the Louis Vuitton, which now I'll have to sit on to zip shut . . . There we go. Just what's left of the whisky and then I'll be going. Fuck.'

At last I pulled the door shut, grabbed the handle of my wardrobe-sized suitcase, and slouched off towards the life to come. Everything was different now. Visibly so: I staggered with my suitcase through that affluent neighbourhood where no one ever smiled, swerving this way and that, trying to get as far away as possible as quickly as possible. The farther I got, the easier it would get. Muttering under my breath, 'Oh fuck, oh fuck . . .'

And there I was, with unparalleled impudence sitting at table at Mario Ludwig's funeral banquet, although it looked no different from a garden-variety garden party or a baby shower. No one wept for Mario, least of all I. In the meantime, here was Charlotte coming up to me with an enormous rose in her hand, which she had plucked. And up she started in English, expounding and expatiating over me, as if I were a rose she might just pluck as well!

'What a wonderful young man, how cultured, and what beautiful eyes you have, so dark, very Italian, you must be from Italy! Oh, those Italians! *Animali*, as they say . . . It was so heart-warming at the funeral to see you shed a tear for our dear, wonderful, inimitable Mario . . . (I'd learnt how to do that in drama group in high school, by the way.) Come with me, boy. Your dinner companions will forgive you for abandoning them, and here, I have a rose for you, a very large rose, and an even larger strawberry, I spit out for you instead of eating it!' (Oh you would have, you whore, but being at a wake you wouldn't dare, said the scandalized looks of the genuine princesses.) The blackened scratchings of her dugs were right in front of me, the smell of perfume mixing with the scent of old woman and jewellery baked in the sun. I thought to myself, no sweat, I'll just have to retool as hetero, if only for a night; but I cringed, and my Gombrowicz winked at me: 'Go for it, slutso.'

Back then I was the proud owner of a cell phone, one of the first, a Motorola, the size of a man's shoe (and when the lid was open, the size of two shoes). The Czech mafia had introduced a new fad: everywhere there were adverts and tart cards for phone sex. 0-8-0-0-C-U-M-M-I-N-G. Call me at the Club! Wet-n-Horny Here! *Je to Roskas!* Or: Willst Du Nur Wichsen? Call me: nool hoondert noyntsish aynts aynts aynts aynts aynts aynts! Ach, das ist zo hayse noomer nool hoondert noyntsish aynts aynts

aynts—aynts aynts aynts! Escorts who provided live services also advertised for phone sex: on TV after ten, in the gay papers, all over. All you needed was a cell phone.

You needed to charge those 'shoes' all night if their batteries were going to last throughout the day. Their phone books had only men's names in them. The boys would coolly slip them into the back pockets of their Levi's, where you couldn't not notice them due to their antennas, which stuck out even when retracted. So I had my own phone, but I couldn't give Charlotte my card because it was quite obviously and unmistakably the tart card of a hustler. Along with my number it included a photo of washboard abs and, in German, CALL ME! in red letters. So she had to write my number in her notebook.

Her cream-coloured visiting card was inscribed with the name *Charlotte* (a name that made me think of big fluffy cakes and was well suited to the meringuey atmosphere of the banquet) *von Liechtenstein* (a country in the middle of nowhere populated by me and two dudes in a room in the Hotel Sonnenhof in Vaduz, which cost three times as much as it would anywhere else). Below her name was a single word: *Prinzessin*. What a vocation. She lived in a villa in Zürichberg, the Louis Vuitton of neighbourhoods, where Zurich's wealthiest, scowliest residents lived. There was no way to meet anyone there, the average age of inhabitants was seventy. Like steamer ships crossing the Acheron, streamlined black limousines emerged from their underground garages and coasted down desolate streets, their blackened or mirrored windows thwarting any view of possible passengers inside. They may as well have been radio-controlled and completely empty, floating empty to pick up the shopping, returning empty home, no need for   anyone to open the gates, they was automatic too . . . Zürichberg didn't need inhabitants to be the perfect neighbour-hood.

So there I stood at the door of Charlotte's palatial villa. I was dressed as she had requested: in a snow-white-and-navy-blue sailor uniform with an enormous collar, a belt, and a cap with an anchor on it. She had sent everything to me the day before by courier.

I rang the bell and she opened and immediately began to coo and warble over me as if I were a bouquet of roses. As before, her hair was a large, messy spool of candyfloss balanced on her head, courtesy of the most expensive stylist in Zürichberg. Violets and pinks in her hair, orange on her lips and talons, in one hand a cocktail glass with a pretentious drink the colour of fluorescent toothpaste. She looked at me as if I were Kurt Cobain standing on her doorstep. I had no idea what was in store . . .

Dressed all in ecru, she spread out on the white sofa, and it was clear I would have to sit next to her, at a distance that infringed upon my moral rights.

From the speakers wafted a medley of distinctly nautical melodies.

She lit a cigar, poured two glasses of Jack Daniels, neat, then pulled out of a case a large false moustache, which she then put on! Thus began her transformation into an old, sun-weathered sailor. She snatched from her head her candyfloss do, which turned out to be a wig, and from her eyes the false eyelashes . . . She left the room and a moment later returned in an authentic United States Navy uniform, saturated with sweat and enhanced at point zero with the vestigial bulge of a genuine sailor's erection . . .

As she hadn't yet taken off her baubles, her rings, earrings and dainty watch, I helped her remove them, thinking they would make a good tip for my extraordinary services, all the while making threatening, even maritime grimaces at her. I knew one thing: I must never laugh. Then she unbuttoned the grubby fly of her sailor trousers and pulled out a massive strap-on dildo . . .

Lord, you may have created us in your image, but here I think Your hand was a little shaky . . .

With the rolling gait of a true seafarer, Charlotte led me to the bathroom, where it soon became clear, after her wig landed on my head, that she was going to dress me up too—as her. Soon, I was standing there in her furs, three strings of pearls around my neck, my nails painted tangerine, my lips scarlet, false eyelashes carefully pasted on my lids—all confected with unmistakably feminine expertise by this bald, moustachioed sailor! I asked her if there was anything in her biography that might explain our little game. She reeked of old lady, she stank of matron. A long-haired white cat, which had been slinking between our legs the whole time, looked up at his mistress mistrustfully. Charlotte poured me another drink, but like a true sailor, she herself guzzled the whisky straight from the bottle. I, on the other hand, left on my glass a smudge of orange lipstick looking like a big question mark. Her wig smelt like all the perfumes in the world combined with a hint of dowager. She lit up a Kim Slimsize. I found it hard to imagine a sailor smoking Kims—too chic for a man's hands—much less actually witness it. She took a long, deep drag, then exhaled.

She walked over to the gleaming white baby grand piano and brought back a photograph in a white wicker frame. A sombre, elderly gentleman peered out, his mouth looking like the slot of a piggy bank, his eyes like a demand for payment.

'Prince Michael von Liechtenstein, my husband. You know, I'm not actually an aristocrat. My maiden name is Gurke, which means pickle. I was his cleaning lady, and I had to clean for ... excuse me one moment ...' She goes and gets a second photograph, one that hardly deserved to be framed.

She put on a strap-on, buckled up, and ordered me to bend over; and as if she were taking out on me all the wrongs that sailor in the photograph had done to her, she began pounding me, all the while telling me her story and gently biting my ear.

'I was born in Graz, in 1933. So I'm exactly sixty years old, and for fifty-five of those years I wasn't an aristocrat at all. But I always wanted to be. Graz has always literally been in the back of beyond. And the Thirties, well, you know—crisis after crisis, Austria under the spell of Hitler, skyrocketing inflation, paper money used to kindle the kitchen stoves, the Weimar Republic's chaotic end. Then all of a sudden—parades, parades and flowers in the windows, bosomy lasses serving steins of beer, and everywhere marches struck up by orchestras in the background. My parents were avid supporters of the Anschluss of Austria to Nazi Germany. Father worked for the railways, and his whiskers curled around three times, like a train-conductor walrus! He was a great fan of law and order. Mother would make lard sandwiches for his lunch and always remind him, "Whatever you do, don't throw out the waxed paper!" But he wouldn't have thrown it out anyway—he always folded it into a perfect square and brought it back to be used again. And there I was with my dream of becoming a singer ...'

I left her, and hobbled down the street as if I'd just been ridden by five sailors. She'd paid handsomely and I decided to leave for

Switzerland that same night. With all my treasures, my money and my souvenirs of Mario Ludwig in his fat Louis Vuitton suitcase.

I went back to my Thai sisters in Liesing, but no one was home; two were in the laundry, two in the brothel and one in the massage parlour. I packed my things and left them a note in English: 'I go. I sorry, dont remember me bed'—like a farewell letter to a lover. I thanked them for taking me in and for the massages (they massaged me non-stop, slathering exotic oils all over my skin, after a good drubbing from those little mitts of theirs, I felt like spitting up my liver!), for the spicy chicken and all the orgasms while kneeling down . . . 'I've met a millionaire and am off to Zurich with him. Love, your big mascot Michał'. I could already see them reading it, crying, rolling their eyes, nattering to one another in their language: 'He go Zurich! In Zurich, many, many men! Big cock! Eleven-Inch! Oh la la! This so expensive!'

But I still didn't know, then, that once Thai sisters in the West adopt you, they won't be letting you go that easily . . .

I took the U-Bahn to Wien Westbahnhof, not far at all from the Dead Dog, and set my sights on new horizons.

DIANKA

Dianka Spencer, Princess of Wales, sitting on a park bench, pulls from her bag a Kinder Surprise and with her filthy fingernails delicately unpeels the foil. She sniffs the egg, which smells of chocolate, vanilla and coconut. Now's the moment: she'll bite the egg and once again discover to her delight that the chocolate inside is white! As the egg cracks it releases a subtle fragrance. Carefully, she extracts the plastic capsule, one half of it clear enough to be able to see that the surprise is in there, like a nut in a shell, but it's hard to tell what it is. And voilà . . . it's a ball! Chequered black and white—because somewhere in the world, something important having to do with football is happening, to which Dianka has been sweetly oblivious. And there's something else: a piri-piri pepper! And a tiny Teflon pan. A device for debobbling the jumpers of grandfathers. A tiny shampoo for blond and silver hair—just enough for a gnat. And here, faster and faster, more gadgets come tumbling out: keys to a flat which no longer exists, an ice-cream sundae made of plastic, a miniature piggy bank with a slot for an arsehole and an innocent look on its face . . .

Dianka eats the rest of the Kinder Surprise egg and licks her filthy fingers. Gypsy Girl all over.

Munich was just like Austria, only different; it was all a bit more: more clean, more austere, more alien and more rich. Trashmaster woke Dianka up at dawn. The train intercom kept shouting 'Moonchen!' every five minutes, informing the passengers which connecting trains would be departing when and from which platforms, which side of the carriage to alight from, not to forget their belongings, etc., like it was dealing with imbeciles. The train moved slowly, and so perfectly smoothly it seemed to Dianka they weren't moving at all, except for the lights and what looked like factory buildings sliding past outside the window. On the platform she immediately noticed the air smelt different there. The escalators had a different odour, a different kind of grease in the gears. And the U-Bahn too. A different voice announced the stations. People in suits holding briefcases were standing on the platform at six in the morning, scrubbed clean from head to toe, redolent with shoe polish and toothpaste, with perfectly blow-dried hair and white teeth, they looked like cyborgs. They glanced at their expensive watches. It was clear they could hardly wait to get to work and to work until close of day, zealously contributing to the erection of German *Ordnung*. Dianka stood there, mouth agape. In Vienna everything was so cosmopolitan and colourful. But here? Not a chance.

Trashmaster left Dianka in a corner of the train station and told her to meet him in one hour in something called the DB Halle (DB meant Deutsche Bahn, she knew that at least), in a place called Cafe Mephisto.

'Where is that?'

'It's right here, around the corner.'

Mephisto was such an apt name for the Trashmaster that Dianka, charmed by the coincidence, didn't ask anything else. He left. Dianka was so utterly exhausted, her nerves so frayed by the last few days, but at the same time she was so relieved that she would never, ever have to return to that revolting city, Vienna, never again have to see the Gypsies or Norma's ugly face or that awful lawyer, that she sat down on a bench and fell into a blissful stupor. Now and again her ears picked up the elegant strains of the loudspeaker's announcements: 'Meine Damen und Herren, auf Gleis zwei . . . Ich wiederhole . . .' With her last bit of change Dianka bought an espresso (in a porcelain cup!) and a delicious sandwich of steak tartare and minced onion in a fresh, crispy baguette. But he wasn't there. It was already seven-thirty. Where on earth was Cafe Mephisto? There was the cafe she was sitting in, but that was a Tschibo, nothing at all like a Diabolo. And there was no reason to go down that hallway; there was just a wall there behind that corner. Once again Dianka was broke and on the street, or rather in the train station, and in Munich, which for all its wealth and elegance had little use for penniless boys . . . At last, around ten or so, she decided to walk to the end of that hallway after all, where what she had thought was a wall turned out to be a security blind and behind it the entire DB Halle opened out, ticket counters, shops, cafes and of course the infernal Cafe Mephisto too. But it was so late that even if Trashmaster had waited for her there, he surely must have left by now.

Thus did Dianka slouch into Munich, hardly knowing whether she was in Germany or Switzerland. She'd given every-thing, even the safety razor lifted from the lawyer, to her Trash-master, who was supposed to take it all home and then come get her. She was so overcome with yearning for Trashmaster that she circled back to the DB Halle and once again past Cafe Mephisto—coffee for five marks!?—and there he was! He too had almost given up, he too had come back one last time. They fell into each other's arms, the tattooed muscle bear with the unibrow and heaps of black fur everywhere else, and Princess Dianka Spencer, queen of the people's hearts. Have you need of a safety razor? Some shaving cream perhaps? Princess'll be happy to do you for, she'll sort you right out. Chop chop!

So began Dianka's magical week, her week of fabulous fucking! Trashmaster's girlfriend had gone off to Klagenfurt for a kindergarten teacher training; and the Beast himself had taken the week off from the landfill, which he spent splitting open Lady Dianka, downing enormous beers with Lady Dianka, as if it were already Oktoberfest, visiting the Olympia Shopping Centre with Lady Dianka, doing it outdoors, even in the empty, last car in the U-Bahn, when they returned one night completely hammered to Trashmaster's one-room flat on the outskirts of Munich.

'I really have discovered a pearl in the trash!' Dianka thought to herself proudly.

Trashmaster lived far out of town, forty minutes with the S-Bahn. Tower blocks in the suburbs, a tiny flat—smelling of air-freshener of course, which barely masked the stronger stench of his two cats and the litter tray . . . A lot of videotapes of porn, in the bathroom one little sample of Chanel Égoïste, from the window a view of perfectly trimmed lawns and an Aldi. Dianka couldn't remember much of that crazy week, having been habitually and brutally raped without any right to appeal—which irritated her but excited her even more. He, naked, muscle-bound, cat tattoos around his nipples, a cock of steel that never drooped, washboard abs (also of steel), scratching his stubble. The cats on top of the wardrobe, watching everything, and the cats on his chest. The bestiality porn (pigs, goats, etc.), the weed, the amphetamines, beer, vodka, poppers. Eating wonton soup from plastic containers while sitting on the carpet—Dianka had never had it before and fell in love with it! She loved the duck bouillon, the spices . . . Then Trashmaster started disappearing for hours at a time, and Dianka got bored watching zoophilia porn in the flat by herself, but maybe she wasn't the target audience, and she would brood, thinking how every guy is aces at the beginning, but by the end he's locking her up in his flat. By the time he got back, she'd be seeing him in a different light. She'd have got to know the nooks and crannies of his shack only too well, the secrets only a flat knew how to tell. But it was worse when they didn't reveal anything, like now, with Trashmaster. Empty shelves, empty cupboards, an empty kitchen . . . If a female had ever lived here, she would have infused it with a touch of her flowery-powery, blossomy-possumy, squirrelly-girly womanliness: Hello Kitty, a plant on the windowsill. But none of that here. Dianka, who was increasingly hungover or coming down from a high, started to get paranoid. Maybe he's some kind of serial killer? Maybe he doesn't really work at the rubbish tip? After all, given the linguistic barrier, their conversations were limited to moaning and groaning and the occasional 'gut, gut', when Dianka had serviced him well, or 'nein', when her teeth got in the way. It was only in the corner of the room, next to the mattress where their romance had bloomed, if that is the word, that some of Trashmaster's personal belongings lay scattered— harnesses, dildos, buckles and other instruments of torture that he never actually used.

Trashmaster suddenly got bored with Dianka, practically from one minute to the next, during a third orgasm in a row. He fell onto the mattress and lit a cigarette.

'Let me to show you something.'

He took her to Frauenstrasse, to the infamous Tabasco Bar.

'Du musst arbeiten, Dianka!'

She already knew that song—from me. 'Morgen arbeiten, heute arbeiten, du musst arbeiten, ich hab keine Arbeit!'

'Fifty-fifty, halbe Kasse für mich, halbe für dich, du musst Wohnung zahlen, ganze Woche mit mir wohnen, nischt zahlen? Oh la la, Probleme!'

In Munich the market for prostitutes was entirely in the hands of Arabs and Turks, to whom Dianka really did have an allergy—to their smelly kebabs, their filthy, tombak-ringed fingers, which they used to count their Deutschmarks. Tombak looks like gold, but like everything with those Turks and Arabs, it's a scam, a knockoff, counterfeit, and tarnishes after a few months. The Arab women walked around so completely veiled only a slit for their eyes was left. No wonder, Dianka thought, their men run after everything that moves, because how can you find the hole under all those curtains?

It occurred to Dianka that Trashmaster might not be German at all, but something even worse, some kind of Germanic variety of Arab, or who knows, even an Albanian pimp; in any case, he was something a whole lot cheaper, more tin than gold, or worse: painted plastic! Besides, he had a gold tooth and started milking her for money like a real pimp. She'd left Alfie's in Vienna, but here was another bar for boys from Eastern Europe, Tabasco. Make the sign of the cross and let's go in!

The first person Dianka ran into in a Munich bar was Norma— Norma of the Gypsies, Norma who looted antiques from the flats of dead grandpas, Norma whom Dianka had been chuffed to bits about never seeing again. She was perched at the bar together with another Vienna queen Dianka knew only from sight and a Czech hustler. She was drinking wine, smoking Milde Sorte cigarettes, happy not to be behind the bar for once, and already well lubricated. Dianka felt a surge of pride: 'That slag will wonder how I got to be so worldly. I mean, how did *she* get to *Munich!*' But Norma at once started shouting to the whole bar at the top of her screechy, hoarse voice:

'Ohhhh! If it isn't Madame de Hangry! Why is Madame so, so hangry? Herzlich Willkommen, Madame!'

And so Dianka's hopes that by changing her country of operations she could lose that distressing nickname were dashed to dust. And that awful Norma, with her hoop earring and bald pate and moustache, just stared at her from across the bar, her eyes bloodshot and swollen, like 'What? What are you going to do to me? Once Madame de Hangry, always Madame de Hangry, wherever you go, all over Europe, I'll find you, I'll come after you and in every new bar I'll be there to welcome you! Ja ja, willkommen! In case you ladies don't already know her, may I introduce: Madame de Hangry! She's the one who used to turn tricks for hamburgers in Vienna! My Gypsies would come to blows over her! Too broke for a boy? No problem. Maybe you have a crust of bread on you? Here, I have someone for you, and I won't even take a bite for my commission . . .'

And the guys in Tabasco all took up her new (old) nickname, and it stuck in Munich too.

But here the patrons were more pedestrian than in Vienna and had something even malevolent about them, thuggish. Mostly they were Poles in tracksuits, something evil lurking in the air.

Meanwhile, that brute, the Trashmaster, told Dianka she had to move out, since his girlfriend, clean and pure as a new Kleenex, was on her way back from the kindergarten teacher training in Klagenfurt, in fact she was just then getting off the S-Bahn, just then turning her key in the door, just then hanging over them the sign with *Das Ende* written on it, *Fine, Koniec, That's All Folks!* She was just then scooping the used condoms from the floor around the bed, irrigating the houseplants, shovelling out the litter tray ... *The End*—of Dianka's fatal attraction! Well, the girlfriend wouldn't be staying clean and pure for long, as long as she was anywhere near that pigsty, the squalor of the mattress of the Trashmaster ...

Now, suddenly, that animal (*das Tier*) turned into a brutal, beastly Albanian pimp, and with his fur-covered, tattoo-covered, animal paws began cruelly seizing the lion's share of Dianka's meagre earnings, and sex hardly paid better in Munich than it had in Vienna, although everywhere else in the area the prices were much higher. Dianka tried to put one over on him, hiding a hundred marks in her underwear, but his pimpish intuition told him something was up and Dianka got it right in the snout, blood everywhere! Well, she hardly looked very princess-like then, our Dianka. And it happened in the very same Olympia Park where they had gone on those romantic walks at the beginning!

And where on earth was she going to sleep tonight? Could anything be more exasperating than the fact that night came every night, that it never even got tired of it after all these billions of years?

If all there was was just a single day, released once and for all, like a movie, and you didn't have to worry about always having to spend the night somewhere, Dianka could have sorted something out. But always, just when she'd come up with something, just when she was sure she'd hit on a plan for changing her lousy fate, for breaking free from Trashmaster, from Munich, for finally ditching the new nickname and the old, or for dodging another night spent in an all-night bar, came the night. The audacity, the fuckery of the universe. Unannounced, the city was suddenly saturated with colour, the light of day transformed into vivid neon, pulsing rhythmically to the words 'Live Sex', and Dianka was at home in the sordid, seedy red-light districts, unlike her namesake, who was probably in Buckingham Palace. Suddenly the passers-by passed by more quickly, dressed more sharply, cigarettes dangling from their lips, hunger radiating in their faces. The dope fiends were on the prowl for dope, the queers for a cock to suck, the whores for money, Arabs for anything that moved, traffic backed up in the streets, the U-Bahn ran more sporadically, more and more people were out, all done up for a night on the town, with bouquets of flowers, bottles of wine ...

And there was our Dianka without any flowers or bottles of wine, but for that with a face gleaming blue, then red, then yellow, reflecting the neon signs of the adult cinema. She felt stressed out by the neon signs, harassed by the Arabs, provoked by the smells of meat from the Turkish döner shops. She wished she could enter one of those cabins, throw in five marks, and sleep for an hour. If it wasn't for all the carrying-on on the TV screen. Because who wanted to watch TV after work and end up watching more work? So she walked past the adult cinema, and the next one too, since in this neighbourhood it appeared they only rented retail space to adult cinemas, dirty bookshops, or bars with darkrooms.

The way it works with these cinemas: There's no attendant or anything, you have to 'insert coin' for everything. You walk in and wander down the little hallway, and on either side are booths, most with their doors ajar and no one inside. But fairly often there'll be an Arab standing in the door rubbing his crotch, and it's unclear what he's after, because he's straight and doesn't respond at all when Dianka winks at him. 'They're all perverts, no getting around it,' Dianka yawns sleepily. Eventually she shuts herself in a booth and inserts coin. This is so much better than the reality outside. She wants to be alone, momentarily alone. No matter how much it costs, she doesn't want an Arab to even look at her. And if only she could tune out those Germans all around her. She throws her denim jacket over the monitor so she won't have to see the porn, turns down the volume, and sits. And there she is, alone. It's only when she's alone, when she's started picking her nose and chewing her nails, that her fucked-up life starts to scare her. Because she's all alone with her thoughts, and she doesn't want to think—not about what will happen next, not about the decisions she'll have to make—being the lazy and lousy lady that she is . . .

It's 1993. Dianka is sixteen years old now. She walks through the little park, where it's still possible to find a trick now and then. She's stashed away the electric shaver she stole from the lawyer along with the rest of her shit, panties, etc., in one of the train-station lockers, which you have to keep feeding five-mark coins, just like the booths in the adult cinema. The only difference being they don't have porn on in there for the shaver to watch, or not watch. Dianka sometimes feels like she's her own baggage, her own rucksack. Her body bothers her—it's an obstacle, a problem to be solved. If only there was some way to stash herself away in a train-station locker like her own extra bag . . . But how would she insert coin from outside then?

Dianka has no choice but to keep being, although God knows she couldn't be less interested in being. She has to be at five in the morning, when she's her own worst enemy. She still hasn't disappeared by six, when she's at her weakest. And she keeps persisting at seven, eight and nine. Who invented the hours? It must have been someone with a nice, cosy bed, someone who wasn't homeless!

She bought a kebab and sat on a bench in the little park, content, dreaming of castles in Spain. She spilt some of the sauce on herself, but who cares—she lit up a crumpled Marlboro, because now she was where the flavour was, in West Germany, where everything was so shiny and expensive, even a poor person, here, in this park, would be impressive to folks back in Bratislava: 'Where'd you get those jeans, Milan, are those original Levi's? And those cigarettes you're smoking now, and those shoes.'

In the meantime, the following situation was happening in the park: there was one old Black queen, who wouldn't be getting anything today, and there was a bleary-eyed white who must've been in his forties, the word 'customer' written all over his face (*Kunde* in German, which Dianka always pronounced 'Kundel'). So Dianka uncrossed her legs, because crossed legs is a decidedly unsexy way for a young harlot to sit, and spread her thighs invitingly, her hand with its grubby fingernails and cigarette between two fingers cupping her crotch. She cast a glance at him without really looking at him, the codes of cruising being hardwired. But the white guy was jumpy, her gesture was driving him mad, he went off into the bushes, started doing something in there, then came back, moving nearer, then further away, then suddenly ran off, totally weird, right past Dianka, without even looking at her. The little drama was starting to get on Dianka's nerves, when the man sat down. The merciless light of the streetlamp left no doubt as to the degree of hygiene of Dianka's fingernails and jeans, her greasy hair, the zits on her nose. But who cared—Dianka's grottiness was no match for a German daddy's libido.

The guys here were all the same. They were all made of lies, price tags, S-Bahn and U-Bahn lines, and on payday the taxi too, more-or-less filthy bachelor pads, more-or-less withered plants on the windowsill, and generic, easy-to-forget names like Klaus or Otto (anything was fine, as long as it wasn't Jürgen). This particular specimen also featured oval, wire-rimmed glasses, a briefcase, and something of the bureaucrat in his face. After their boring, bureaucratic sex on the inevitable mattress was over, he lay there and said to Dianka, who was standing in the window smoking a cigarette and, having already tuned him out, wasn't even listening: 'It no good here, you know. You should go to Zurich. You'll be swimming in it there. Geh nach Zürich!' Somehow this sentence made its way through the cloud of smoke enveloping Dianka's head; she'd already heard it somewhere else, in Vienna, from that charmer Eleven-Inch. Could his wiener really be that big? All those millionaire customers!'

If she'd been able to speak any language well, Dianka would have said then, 'Could you please repeat that? Wiederholen bitte?

I was lost in thought . . .' But instead she asked him where she might find this mythical Zurich, in what country, on what continent. If this had been her geography class, she would have had a coughing fit and left the room by now. It turned out, however, that Zurich was only a few hours away on the express train, and this guy actually worked as a conductor, inspecting tickets between Munich and the Swiss border. And then what, I walk to Zurich from there? It's close enough from the border that I can buy you your ticket.

'Come again? Entschuldigung?' Dianka asked, not being used to strange men helping her with her biography.

'You won't need to buy the ticket from Munich to the border because I'll be checking the tickets, and I can cover your ticket from the border to Zurich. But let's go, I have to leave for the train station now!'

It later turned out that he wanted a very considerable reduction in price for her services, but for Dianka it was worth it, because what would happen next, looming ahead of her like an iceberg, was the fabled city of Zurich! She soon learnt that this modest metropolis was located in the wealthy and picturesque neighbouring country of Switzerland; that it was associated with chocolate, watches, diamonds, gold bars, Swiss francs and the world's best cappuccino; and that the mountains there were home to trolls, Wilhelm Tell, lakes and prudent, Protestant penny-pinchers (although they didn't pinch too hard). She learnt about the Nestlé Company, how it was the holding company of Milka and Rolex and all the others. She learnt all this on the train from the train guard while he wasn't checking her (non-existent) ticket. Outside the window the landscape became more and more undulating and hilly, full of lakes and vineyards. Once the train even entered an endless tunnel, industrially bored into the mountains of gneiss and granite by those prudent, Protestant people.

The train station they were leaving from wasn't the one where Dianka had stored her dingy backpack, so she had to rush over there first to get her belongings (which were mostly other people's belongings, like the electric shaver she stole from Jürgen, etc.). She had nothing now to keep her in Munich or Vienna, and was getting excited about her new life, when suddenly she found the key to Trashmaster's flat, which she had forgotten to return. It was a modern key, of a type completely unknown in Bratislava, a flat shaft with little holes in it that opened both the building door and the flat. At first she tried to throw it away in the toilet, but toilets here were completely different, there wasn't a hole to squat over, and the key wouldn't flush. Then she went to toss it out of the window, but none of the windows would open. Suddenly Dianka realized that this beautiful silver key, which now that it had no use value was beautiful in and for itself, was literally the only thing in the entire world that actually belonged to her. As well as, maybe, her grimy Levi's jacket and her disposable lighter. The key was hers. So she decided to keep it as a token of remembrance; after all, there had been so many wonderful moments with Trashmaster before he turned into a sadistic pimp ... Dieses Tier! And it would be fun to imagine him flipping out when he realized she hadn't given it back, oh if only he could get his furry paws on her now, he'd rip her to shreds like a bulldozer sorting out a plastic bag on the dump! Like everything else, keys were expensive here. She also hoped Zurich was too far out of not only Trashmaster's league but

Norma's too, for her nickname, sign of her miserable life in Vienna, ever to follow her there.

Three hours later the train stopped for a long time at a station. Dianka's friend the train guard wished her well and gave her fifty marks along with the ticket from the border to Zurich—which cost so much that Dianka panicked, wondering where on earth she was headed. How would she manage to survive there? A half-hour train journey for that price? But now she had only her reflection in the toilet mirror to pose these questions to. Once again she was all alone in the world—along with the key to the flat of some chump in Munich, a disposable lighter and a Levi's jacket on her back. The train entered the tunnel. The loudspeaker emitted a woman's voice speaking something that sounded a little like German but was actually some kind of Yiddish, or Dutch, or Gypsy. Gypsy German. Dianka immediately felt at ease when she realized she'd be living with the Gypsies, with her people, the mountain people!

THE POLE

And who's the first person I should run into at Carrousel Bar in Zurich? Who else but that muttonhead Dianka, that is, you! You were sitting in the corner there like a mouse in a mouse trap, devouring an ice-cream sundae, freezing cold ice cream, not a care in the world about gaining weight, not even working the bar, not even following the hungry stares coming at you from every corner, you the fresh meat. You might've been thinking—but normal thoughts, not those super-dodgy typical East European thoughts, of course, like how to get hitched with a local and get a residency permit, how to come and go without your passport getting stamped, how to ring up Poland or Slovakia using tokens instead of coins—but it was enough to look at you to know that you weren't thinking at all. You weren't interested in any of this: how we were young, beautiful, skinny and poor; how we came from the new Eastern Europe, freshly liberated from the bonds of communism; how we never put on weight, although we ate hamburgers all the time, while our customers were old and bored and rich, and still got fat on their organic greens. How their country had a negative birth rate, but even when those old queens popped out a kid after forty, the English exams for getting into kindergarten were so hard the child would end up a drug addict or later in life develop a fetish for baby bonnets. Do you have any idea how much lucre they have? The czar kept his money here and it's still here, in a safe under Paradeplatz. Ceaușescu kept his money here too, and was never able to withdraw it. All the African dictators too—Bokassa, Mobutu, Abacha. Germans during the war. It's all still here. It pays to be a neutral country. But now it was time for them to return a little of that money to us, the victims of history. The sexual victims of history wearing skin-tight jeans, their crotches stuffed with socks, a trick every hustler knows ... No, you weren't thinking about any of that, Dianka. Bon appetit. Nice to see you again! That guy over there is totally staring at you. Oh, hiiiiieeee!

She immediately asked me if I would go with her to the toilet because she was afraid of the mafia, and since I was afraid of them too, we went together, making sure that everyone could see that there were two of us going in. Sometimes a newcomer wasn't allowed into the local market, and when that happened the mafia would jump him in the gents and mutilate him, cutting a swastika in his face with a high-quality Swiss Army knife (definitely not one made of chocolate). Newcomers had to make twice as much as anyone else and weren't allowed to undersell.

Luckily I was a new too, and had nothing against raking it in. I quickly sussed out the situation in Carrousel. Basically, there were hardly any escorts, but quite a few old and very rich *Kunden*. It was immediately clear the boys here were very tight knit and there were several different mafias which wouldn't want anyone new sitting at their sumptuously laid table. The Czech mafia (which was the largest), the Russian mafia, the drunken Polish mafia and the coked-up African mafia. Of course there were also Thais there, but they were too gentle to establish a mafia and they had such delicate ears. Everyone at the bar would have had a good laugh: a Thai mafia! (Without a doubt it would have been the deadliest.)

The Czech mafia were a jolly bunch, standing all together drinking beer from litre-sized tankards. Their boss, an unattractive, thick-set dude named Pepe, told me it was paradise here, that the prices started at five hundred francs for a blowjob and went up to a thousand for anal, although there really wasn't an upper limit. He said they wouldn't bother me, unless they heard from one of their informants that I was underselling. For now, though, I'd have to give him twenty per cent of every trick.

'Ten per cent, plus I show you my Eleven.'

SOMETHING ELSE ABOUT CARROUSEL

Carrousel was in Niederdorf, on Zähringer Strasse, one of a tangle of little streets lined with little houses made of gingerbread, flowerboxes, little hearts everywhere and Swiss flags. Inside, the bar's decor was pure kitsch: heart-shaped mirrors, plastic figurines of Apollo with lightbulbs glowing inside, Greek columns, fake marble and American music from the 1960s, every day the same thing, every day for half a century the same music, a sign of how tradition-loving and unchanging this country was: 'I Will Survive', 'Spanish Eyes', 'Those Were the Days', etc. And if someone didn't like it, there was an ancient jukebox in the corner, next to the toilet and the equally ancient cigarette machine, where you could insert coin and purchase this or that hit song, and then everyone would have to listen to *your* music. The escorts played Michael Jackson's 'Bad'. And one old queen, clearly a very nostalgic sort, once must have funnelled a whole bank of change into that jukebox, so all night long the bar got to hear either Hildegard Knef's 'Eins und eins das macht Zwei' or pre-war German *Schlager* like Zarah Leander's 'Kann denn Liebe Sünde sein?' or 'Eine Frau wird erst schön durch die Liebe', or my favourite, which I sometimes played on the jukebox myself, 'Ich weiß, es wird einmal ein Wunder gescheh'n'. (Maybe because most of the johns were elderly queens, the youngest singer on the bar's playlist was Elvis Presley; but the jukebox had a handful of songs for the grandpas and a handful for the twinks.) Then everything would get so romantic, moody in a good way, in this bar, in this country, where the pre-war never ended, because there was never any war. Had anything in Switzerland ever been different? Bars like Carrousel are only possible in countries like this, where thanks to the Swiss people's remarkable conservativism, not only had it never closed, but the panes in the windows and the cigarette machine had never been replaced either, which was why the cigarette ads, like those for beer, were somewhat out-of-date. Of course the bar's telephone number had changed, from two digits to six, but goodness if the air indoors wasn't the same, after all the bar hadn't shut its doors since they first opened! Mario the bartender was the embodiment of this dedication to conservativism: when he started working it was clear he'd be serving beer and playing Gloria Gaynor until the day he died, and there he was today, 'I Will Survive' blaring from the speakers just as loud as it would be fifty years from now. But maybe Mario was reborn again and again, like a phoenix, because the way he juggled those mugs of beer, balancing them on a tray over everyone's heads as he navigated the crowd, and served them with his voice booming throughout the bar 'Zum Wohl mitenand!'—it would take more than one lifetime to learn how to do that . . .

But the Czech mafia loved the jukebox most of all, and probably it was for them that the owners added an entire album of Karel Gott, including his rendition of 'Die Biene Maja', which he sang for the German version of the *Maya the Bee* cartoon. The Russians, for example, weren't interested at all in Alla Pugacheva and her 'A Million Scarlet Roses', although it was on the jukebox too; even I'd played it a few times, since what queen doesn't love Alla?

But as soon as the American music came on, it was as if all of Switzerland, but most definitely Carrousel Bar, turned into an enclave of the USA, somewhere off in the Wild West, in that part of America where they drink whisky on the rocks, smoke Marlboros, wear cowboy shirts and cowboy boots and blue jeans, and listen to American pop hits . . . A shambolic wallpaper mural slapped together from ads showing sunsets over the Grand Canyon and memories of *Midnight Cowboy*, with a bit of David Lynch for good measure . . . All these Swiss nudniks who moments ago, on the street, were accountants or financial managers or ageing real-estate agents, who wouldn't let you even walk past them without charging you two rappens and would quibble over them to the bitter end—once they crossed the threshold of Carrousel Bar they turned into characters out of the movies: stepping up to the bar with the bowlegged, rolling swagger of sailors, ordering their whiskys on the rocks, playing some washed-out hit songs on the jukebox, they settled into two large booths with white plastic Apollos planted in the centre of the tables. And even the Apollos were a little too beefed up, Apollos on steroids . . . The whole bar was glowing with cheap Christmas-tree lights, as if it were a casino, somewhere in Las Vegas, and everyone was singing to the jukebox. The boys were drumming up business, because if the grandpas were going to hire them, they first had to order insanely expensive drinks, the profit from which went mainly to Renzo Morelli, mafioso and bar owner, who probably ran the rest of the sex trade in Zurich—and in Witikon, Dietikon, Opfikon, Russikon, Winterthur, Uster, Kloten and Zug as well. The Czech boys (to whom Dianka did not belong because she was new and was Slovak) would say the name Morelli in hushed tones of respect and fear, because all that was needed was one word from

Renzo for an escort to be banned forever from Carrousel, cut off from the vein of gold. 'Renzo said this . . . Renzo told us that . . . Renzo won't like it . . . Watch out: Renzo might come in and you'll be turfed out.'

Behind the bar, surrounded by bottles in a little grotto, like a tabernacle, stood another lit-up Apollo. From time to time the decor was changed, like when they wrapped the entire bar in tin foil. The door was always open, and when the boys had nothing to do they could sit and admire the view, slightly occluded by late-afternoon shadows, of Bellezza, the shop across the street, where latex clothing and fetishwear were sold by a bored Goth domina with long purple-and-black hair, solarium-tanned skin and platform heels. Further down the street were other gay bars as well as professional female prostitutes of the worst sort, old, cross-eyed, misshapen, their faces botoxed out into permanent grimaces. There was something off about every one of them. One was too tall and skinny, especially considering her extreme age; another was too short and fat; a third seemed relatively normal, but in her own indescribable way she too was 'poor and beshat by pigeons' and, besides, there was always a fly buzzing around her—a zoological mystery, given that it never pestered the others. The better prostitutes were to be found on Langstrasse. But even there, Michelle was the only true lady.

Carrousel Bar opened at four, when Mario reverently raised the ancient blinds, but the first guests never arrived before seven. I would always go right at the start, however, and try to catch a tourist who didn't know he'd got there too early—if *Spartacus* said they opened at four, then they opened at four. In *Spartacus*, the international gay travel guide, Carrousel had a *p* printed next to it, for 'prostitution', and that's how tourists knew what to look for there and weren't put off by the lukewarm description ('pleasant atmosphere, nice music, mainly older clientele . . .').

Escorts in Zurich worked either in Carrousel (upscale and expensive) or around the train station, where the drug addicts were. Zurich was a city of drug addicts, and statistically the whole country was ahead of the game. Sociologists wracked their brains wondering why there were so many junkies here, of all places. Was it the repressive nature of bourgeois society? Were the demands on young people too great? Always having to be better than the neighbour's children, always taking entrance exams, for nursery, secondary school, university . . . just to spend the rest of your days counting money in a bank. As far as I could see, the whole Swiss system was sick, and it was no surprise that young people rejected the idea of leading a normal life and decided to go live in Needle Park.

Zurich is a tiny city with a huge drug problem. As a junkie you get wise to it pretty quick. So of course I had to go right away and have a look for myself. In every city, the train station is where you find the junkies. And Platzspitz in Zurich isn't far from the station. So Zurich really isn't as boring as it looks . . . I'd never seen anything like it before. In Platzspitz, everything happened right out in the open. There was a pavilion in the middle of the park where people camped out all year round. They set up tables, laid out their spoons, then ran around and peddled their wares: 'I've got brown stuff, who's got some white to cut it with?' All in Swiss German, of course . . . You could use right there in public, no different than being at a hot dog stand. Whoever wanted to could shoot up right on the spot, there were hundreds of people just lying there, some with open wounds all over their bodies, others looking like corpses. A million syringes were sticking out of the ground. It looked like a scrapyard . . . With almost two thousand junkies hanging out, a lot of fuzz was making the rounds too . . . From rotting planks and luggage carts stolen from nearby Central Station [the junkies] assembled market stands, laid out spoons on them for heating up the cocktails . . . Hundreds of 'Drögeler', as people in Zurich called the addicts, would crowd into the park, on some days more than three thousand. They would sit on a carpet of syringes, in flowerbeds, in the bushes, jabbing needles into their arms and legs in full view of the gawkers. Some would tear their clothes off in search of an intact vein between the festering wounds that studded their scrawny bodies. Even in winter. They stabbed desperately at their groins or their necks since all the other veins were already infected. Half-naked bodies lay there under the open sky—turning blue from the cold, some were already dead. (Christiane V. Felscherinow and Sonja Vukovic, *Christiane F.: Mein Zweites Leben* [Berlin: Deutscher Levante Verlag, 2014])

Thousands of homeless drug addicts still congregated around the Kornhausbrücke; they camped out in the rubbish, and at night the area was lit up with the tiny fires of disposable lighters, which gave it the impression of a cemetery on All Saints' Day, or a concert or football match in a huge stadium. Practically everyone made their money for heroin through prostitution, so there was abundant supply, poor quality (all those junk-ravaged bodies) and very minimal demand, because everyone, even the unemployed, got so much cash from the state they could afford the drinks at Carrousel. And this whole sordid nightmare was literally a few hundred metres away from Bahnhofstrasse, from Rolex and Patek Philippe, from the diamond jewellers and the subterranean bank deposit boxes holding tons of gold, including Jewish gold, from Chanel and Dior. Maybe one was a by-product of the other.

The strangest thing for me was that while all of those marvels on Bahnhofstrasse were things that we, the escorts of Carrousel, desperately wanted, and therefore got—the Louis Vuitton bric-a-brac, the Montblanc pens, the Rado watches, the shoes, the perfumes, the skin-care products—when Swiss people our age saw them, they just grimaced and spit and huffed, 'Jaaaa, it's so *ugly*...' After a while I had a mind-boggling realization: they were actually ashamed of Bahnhofstrasse! Essentially they were already postconsumer, they were hipsters ahead of their time. All the young Swiss were so niche, so left-wing, so rebellious—Switzerland-hating offspring of the upper middle class with portraits of Mao hung over their beds. They wouldn't be caught dead wearing name-brand clothes; I even felt sorry for them sometimes, how they never took vitamins (despite not having to buy them with dollars at Pewex), refused to own Nikes and used organic cosmetics that could just as well have been manure wrapped up in Soviet-style packaging. Here they were in paradise, in the eye of the hurricane, but they lived like they were in the Eastern Bloc. And words like 'commune', 'communism', 'socialism', etc., peppered their conversations with alarming frequency . . .

Around midnight Carrousel was suddenly packed to the gills. Mario was like an acrobat, serving beers through the air over everyone's heads, scooters and convertibles lined up on the street outside, and men kept joining the commotion, having just left Cafe Odeon, Barfüsser or Petra's Tip Top. Two or three Black men in immaculately white suits with black shirts and yellow ties appeared, they were smoking cigars and pipes, the sweet fragrance mingling with strains of Chanel Égoïste and Dior Fahrenheit, and they had greyhounds on leashes and black poodles!

The escorts didn't give a shit about any of it. They just kept making their rounds, returning from the Hotel Central Plaza with wads of money coming out of their ears, stuffed in their socks, crammed into the tiny pockets of their jeans, banknotes wrapped with black rubber bands and quickly counted out in hermetically sealed toilet stalls, too many banknotes to ever spend all of them, and so they got away with it . . . They landed back in Carrousel and ordered more beers, and again started fielding glances, and again headed over to the hotel with their next tricks. Swiss francs, as brightly coloured as comic books, were indestructible, they could probably even survive a washing machine. And they endured so much—exiled from the elegance of a Montblanc portmonnaie into the pocket of some savage from Eastern Europe, from where they were sure to end up rolled into tubes for snorting cocaine . . .

It went on like this until six in the morning, when Mario announced last call by blasting Queen's 'We Are the Champions' at full volume. Every day it was the same, except Mondays

(*Ruhetag*). Morning came, the magic dissipated. In the harsh light you could see the shattered beer glasses, puddles of beer on the floor. The escorts and their customers were dawdling, as if they still had some business left to sort out, some debauchery to bargain out of the night, and were unable to stop that fast-spinning wheel of cash transactions. If a customer had been giving me the eye half the night, I'd be cornering him now: 'You want me or not? Who do you want, who? I don't got all night, thirty per cent off, everything must go!' By now the Queen song was over and it was insanely bright outside, and quiet, except for the nattering of drunks at the bar, and there was Mario, still serving someone or other a schnitzel or beer. Now the after-hours would start. While most of the patrons were stumbling home, a select few carried on with the party behind closed doors. That's when Renzo Morelli himself would descend into the bar from upstairs, where his flat was. Renzo: stocky, with black leather trousers on and a floral-patterned shirt, a shock of naturally curly, grey hair, a moustache, gold chains around his neck—the very image of a mafioso straight out of an Italian operetta. He sat at the bar, and Mario set down before him a large goblet of Burgundy (there were adverts for this Burgundy on every table; two sips cost as much as anal). He lit a Muratti, laid his lighter and wallet on the bar, and made googly eyes at the privileged boys who had been permitted to attend the after-hours.

But at this hour and in this harsh light the boys didn't look so very appetizing, which is to say, they were knackered, they were infected, they were burnt out, and they were blind drunk. They had pimples. Cracked lips. Filthy hands. Despite the perfume, their armpits were sweat-stained, and by now their perfumes were a mixture of scents of all the customers they'd had that day. They smoked cigarettes, although they weren't old enough. If their mums had walked in now, they'd have all had heart attacks. Look at my son three sheets to the wind at the bar, and chubbers there grabbing his arse with that big butcher's mitt of his, stroking it and pinching it. If my mumsie walked in right now she'd scream: 'Get your arse home! Right this minute! Your father will be having a word with you tomorrow!'

If I were suddenly back in my room in Poland now, the whole flat would reek to high heaven from my clothes—every brand of cigarette, all the then-fashionable perfumes, especially Fahrenheit, the smell of vomit and deep-fried foods. 'Get your arse home! I let you out of my sight for one minute, and boom! you're a prostitute, boom! you smell like shit, boom! what is this insanity? Look at the state you're in! Into the bathtub with you! You'll be getting tested tomorrow, otherwise you'll infect the whole house! They'll have to call the health department to the school. Have you eaten anything? Oh for crying out loud, you've been living on junk food—junk food isn't food, Michał!'

Although we were young, our eyes were old and debauched. Especially at this hour we looked like miniature customers, as if by having them we were gradually acquiring their age as well. Did we have anything to eat? Everyone ate whatever they liked: Dianka liked ice cream doused in condensed milk and sprinkles and M&M's, and I didn't really eat anything at all, just drank and smoked instead. We didn't give a shit, we were happy to eat only dessert for breakfast, lunch and dinner, if only because it meant we'd escaped our mothers' strict supervision. It would have been some ordeal if they were suddenly to turn up here, but Carrousel was inconceivable for them, even if they somehow found out we were living in Switzerland. The mothers only knew that their sons were 'somewhere in Germany', which meant the entire German-speaking region. If you got in once and they never stamped your passport, you could move between Germany, Austria, Switzerland and even Liechtenstein until your tits dropped off. You had something like three months and you had to leave for at least one day, but who could say when we'd entered, it was always 'yesterday'.

Sometimes in the early hours the cops would walk into Carrousel, in full uniform, with their funny green berets cocked to the side, and their dogs. When that happened, the newbies shit their pants out of fear, while the old hands just laughed: those cops never gave anyone the so-called 'teddy bear' (the passport stamp that signified deportation due to illegal prostitution); they were gentle as lambs, and one of them was actually a pretty decent customer. The cops would order beers while we were still in the corners counting our untaxed Hundertfrankenscheins (or Hundred-Frankensteins, as I called them), stretching and straightening them, some of us weren't even hiding it. Instead—like that Greek queen all done up in gold—they'd spread the banknotes out on the table like a hand of solitaire ... The more Frankensteins an escort had spread out in front of him, the worse he looked, as if that monster cash were sucking all the sex appeal out of him. The Czech mafia in particular would be giving everyone the side-eye, because they were normal heteros who were sometimes seized with pangs of conscience. Their girlfriends thought they were here working in a restaurant, or a petrol station, diligently saving up for the wedding and flat. That's what they told them on the phone anyway, thanking them for the laundry they always sent back neatly ironed and folded. I have no idea what kind of idiots those girlfriends were—harlotry has its own stink after all, and they should have been able to smell it. In general the Czechs were like animals, no God in their hearts, going after women, boys, trees, cars or corpses was all the same to them ... And to think they brought us Christianity ...

So once all the uninvited had left, Renzo told Mario to turn the lights off again, then went to the jukebox and dropped in five francs (it was his jukebox, so he'd be getting it back), put on some obnoxious German disco with backup vocals, ate sandwiches garnished with greens at the bar, and raised his glass to the rent boys, eventually choosing one of them—for free, of course, since otherwise the boy would be thrown out of the Carrousel gold mine for good. Although outside the day had already begun and it was light and daytime people in daytime garb were walking around with the *Neue Zürcher Zeitung* in their briefcases, and it was long past closing time for both the bar and the party after the party, it just kept dragging on and on like a slowly advancing train from which a passenger would occasionally decide to jump off. Once the party kept going until three in the afternoon. People looked at the accumulating wreckage of one another's faces, the sallow skin, bags under their bloodshot eyes, chapped lips, tobacco-stained-and-scented fingers and ... on and on, the Carrousel couldn't stop, the music never stopped on the *Titanic* either, what else can you do after finishing your next gin-and-tonic but order another one, what else can you do when your Marlboro Light has gone out but light up the next one!

This, then, was how I landed in Zurich: I spent the night in Carrousel, raked in a tidy pile of Frankensteins, and made friends with another hustler, a muscly Black man, a bit older than me, who everyone called Pavo. Pavo was addicted to shaving his whole body every day, everywhere except the eyebrows. His head was shaven bald, just like the rest of him. He even persuaded me to buy one of those Philips electric shavers with the three rotating heads, but somehow I didn't take to it. The other thing Pavo was addicted to was working out at the gym, and the third—oiling up that buff, shaven bod of his with baby oil. Probably it was only thanks to these procedures that he was able to keep working in the trade, because he was definitely older than nineteen, if not more than twenty, and the market should have spat him out by now. But he figured that buff and ripped as he was, he'd appeal to those queens who were into men, not boys, and who wanted a piece of his knee-length *Schwanz* (his was even bigger than mine, we compared them immediately) which never went entirely flaccid. There were two other guys at Carrousel who served the same market segment—one an old cowboy of about twenty-five, the other a leatherman who was practically thirty. They rarely turned up, and when they did they would drink over by the machines and the jukebox, and it was impossible to tell if they were even turning tricks. They already had car keys and were basically on a whole other level, probably they made extra money outside the profession. Except for this one guy, a really handsome one, but already knackered to death, with the glutted beauty of an ageing stripper from Monte Carlo, an ageing Chippendales dancer, everything synthetic now, highlights, solarium tan—he had a steady income and probably never charged under a thousand. But he dedicated all his time and money to beefcake upkeep. He spent hours every day in the gym, had hair transplants done and transformed himself into his own wax figure. But it paid off because queens all love plastic dolls and dessert liqueurs. And of course he wore a Rolex. But there he missed the mark because Rolexes were looked down on in Switzerland.

But the most successful hustlers were still the illegal, underage twinks, the sixteen-to-eighteen years old did slightly less well, and then the curve took a nosedive. I was still making out all right, thanks to my cock. I was riding the reviews, and sometimes I even gave a customer a whole course of psychotherapy as an added benefit . . .

Pavo's head was full of ideas, he couldn't keep his mouth shut, there was just too much of him. He went around in denim overalls and nothing else, just a bib and braces framing his naked, plastic, brown body. He made friends easily, like someone who's never been betrayed. He reminded me of Huckleberry Finn from *Tom Sawyer*. On his bald head he wore a red knit cap. I confided in him that I had just come from Vienna and still didn't have a place to stay. He knew all the cheap hotels in the city, of course, and had actually just had a fight with the guy he was living with, Hans, who had pinched him and stabbed him with a toothpick, so we decided to get something cheap together.

That 'something cheap' was a little Arab-run hotel that usually rented rooms by the hour, providing lovers with the minimum of space needed for sex (based evidently on an average of three square metres). The biggest and only attraction of this hotel (which didn't even have a name) was that it was located directly across from Carrousel on Zähringerstrasse, just over Bellezza, with its black rubber fetishwear and boots with kilometre-high platforms. We were excited to have a place to bring customers to. You just walked in and rang room three on the entryphone, and the clerk could see you on the monitor. But that was it for the advantages. Otherwise the place was pure scuzz: a filthy dark corridor, shared toilet on the first floor, squeaky narrow beds, windows bolted shut, rusty taps and the clerk listening to 'Lambada' over and over. The 'Lambada' was just too much for us—what the fuck was he on! And if it wasn't 'Lambada', he was playing 'Macarena'. In general both the customers and the staff of this 'hotel' were Arabs. Arabic letters corkscrewed like worms across a computer-printed sheet of paper in the bathroom; same thing in the lift, which was just large enough for one person to cram himself into. But so what. We were young and that was the room we had. Pavo was already looking out of the window: 'Oh wow, you can't even see Carrousel from here, and I was hoping we'd be able to watch people going in and out, like, we could see if it was worth going downstairs.' It was true, the window looked out onto a narrow estuary between two walls, where kitchen vapours floated up and the sun had never shone. Well, what of it, at seventy Frankensteins a night it was practically free.

The first thing Pavo did was take out his shaver, towel and baby oil, and march down the hall to commandeer the shared bath; apparently his hair had grown by a millimetre since yesterday. Later it became clear that commandeering the bathroom, occupying the lavatory and taking up residence in the loo was Pavo's thing. 'Where's Pavo?' 'Have you checked the toilet?'

I jumped on the bed. The mattress was as hard as a rock, but it didn't matter—I weighed about as much as a feather back then. I lit a cigarette and studied the water stains spread across the ceiling. So, I'd finally made it to the promised land of Zurich. It was hilly here, you were always walking either uphill or downhill. The windows all had shutters and there were flowerpots on the sills, the streets were narrow and there were violinists busking in them. On the corner stood a cross-eyed, balding prostitute long past her prime and suddenly there was a delicious smell in the air—she was a street vendor selling roasted chestnuts, handing them to the customers in little paper bags. Everywhere water, a lake, a canal; and everything old, but never ruined, never bombed, spared the wounds of war—this city never even came close. As a result, Zurich was opulent, abundant. The air was clean, you could drink the water from the tap . . . Everywhere were Black men wearing all black and diamond earrings . . . Everywhere it was a bit like France, a bit like Italy, a bit like Germany, but lest you forgot you were in Switzerland, everywhere were throngs of red flags with white crosses in their centres were flapping and fluttering. As if we were in a giant health clinic, the sanatorium of Europe. Zurich smelt nice, it smelt of coffee and cigarettes, perfume and flowers, or maybe it was paint and turpentine, roasted chestnuts, the freshwater fragrance of the lake, the smell of money, of the interiors of expensive cars (vanilla, leather seats) . . . The whole city looked like it was under excavation, I once asked a Swiss if all the pipes in the city had burst in unison, as if on cue; but he said in Zurich they don't wait for pipes to break before replacing them, they calculate when they're due to wear out and replace them prophylactically a few years beforehand, it's less expensive that way, and that's why the city was all dug up.

My Thai ladies in Vienna had no doubt come to terms with the fact that their big white Polish doll with his big Eleven-Inch had driven off into the sunset. If they were here now, they'd be getting not one but two enormous schlongs, no telling which one was better.

Pavo came back with the shaver and asked me to do his back and arse as he couldn't reach them. His arse was naturally hairy, and I remembered my mother telling me how the more you cut it, the faster and bushier the hair grows back. I even wanted to tell him this, but I couldn't remember how to form the construction 'the more . . . the whatever . . .' Well, it may as well grow, he'll shave it either way.

DIANKA

Everything seemed smaller here and more prosperous, yet at the same time more modest than in Germany. It was *Protestant*. Dianka wasn't quite sure what that word meant, but it made her think of grey-haired women who never wore make-up, of not having fresh bread (just crisps or white bread in plastic), of not being able to take a bath (just a shower, to save water) and of a world generally gone to pot. The streets were narrower here, the buildings lower, the cars older, and there was less Dolce & Gabbana and other bling-bling, broadly understood, on the streets. The other boys once took the piss out of Dianka, telling her how when you drove from Germany to Switzerland there was a big sign at the border that said 'Last chance to wash off your make-up'. And Dianka fell for it.

So Dianka's train pulled into a station that was immaculate but modest, and she alighted and, like an orphan girl, walked slack-jawed with wonder. New and different smells, new and different faces. Everywhere red penknives with white crosses on them were being sold, Swiss Army knives. Instinctively, in an underground walkway in the station, she found the toilets, and the entire area around them was a cruising ground! But it looked like this was where the drug addicts went, the boys were dazed, messed up, and the grandpas weren't particularly fine specimens either. Aha, so this was their Karlsplatz of hustling, now she needed to find the Zurich version of Alfie's.

She exchanged the fifty Deutschmarks the train guard had given her for francs, bought herself a Swiss Army knife made of chocolate, immediately unwrapped the red foil with the white cross on it and ate the whole thing. It was hollow, but delicious. She thought of how she would be living here with chocolate Victorinox penknives, chocolate Milka cows and chocolate watches!

She pictured Trashmaster on his way to take her day's earnings from her like the vile Albanian pimp he was. (Why Albanian? She actually had no clue, but how could he not have been Albanian?) 'And now Dianka *nyet*, she is rebel, she make escape, cash gone, key to Trashmaster flat gone!' Dianka relished the thought of it . . .

Eventually she was approached by a punter. A nondescript guy around forty in a jumper and white Adidas, dark circles under his eyes and the faint smell of a Catholic church coming out of his mouth. He took Dianka somewhere in the station for ice cream, since Dianka loved ice cream and basically lived off it, so she asked for an ice-cream sundae. She ordered a cappuccino too, pouring into it all the sugar from the elegant sachets that came with it, not only her own but the guy's as well, and all the milk from the little creamer pot with the lion on the lid. 'The lion is the symbol of Zurich,' the man said and asked her if he could open the creamer himself. He did it in a special way to avoid damaging the foil lid as he peeled it off. Because he collected them and that was one he didn't have yet. There's nothing the Swiss don't or wouldn't collect. While other nations kill each other in wars, conflagrations, the Swiss are busy tending to their knick-knacks, topping up their collections.

The guy sat and watched her smugly as she ate. 'Good coffee in Switzerland, good . . . Poor thing, you must to drink in Germany that garbage . . . In Switzerland, all is better, better money, indestructible money, different coffee, different creamer for coffee, even you take same train from Austria through Germany to Switzerland, when Deutsche Bahn staff come, coffee better, but only when Swiss Federal Railways staff take over train at Swiss border, you see what dishwater German garbage coffee is. Coffee come in better cup, with better saucer, silver urn, with cane sugar unbleached and whole milk or lactose-free . . .'

When Dianka's turn to talk came, she didn't know why, but she was sure the man understood everything she was saying in her hustler-Esperanto. How she had just arrived from Munich without a cent, how she didn't know the city at all, like which places were good for turning tricks, etc., how she was hoping to set herself up in business. Well, maybe she wasn't expressing herself that directly and clearly, but it was enough to look at her to know she wasn't a writer who'd been invited by the Kunsthaus to come give a reading. He just responded in his Swiss dialect, 'Nnnaaaa jaaaa . . . Nnnjaaa ja, zo!', sounds she would later hear many other Swiss men utter, usually when it was time for her to get going.

'I think I know a place you might like . . .'

They walked out of the station and turned left, past the Coop supermarket, and stood on the bridge looking out over the Limmat. It was dark, the air smelt incredibly fresh and clean, and the water shimmered with reflected incandescence from the row of gingerbread facades extending down the bank. After those Molochs, Vienna and Munich, suddenly fresh air, suddenly a small town without a subway! The punter bought Dianka a paper bag of roasted chestnuts in response to her astonishment: how possible? Chestnuts weren't something you ate, chestnuts fell from trees when you were supposed to be going to school . . . They walked and she ate the chestnuts out of the triangle-shaped bag (they weren't any good, but she ate them anyway because they were probably expensive!) and watched the people passing by. There were more people of different races here, Asians, Black people, Arabs, lots of 'Italians'. And there were many people who combined the best of German, French and Italian features (a particularly felicitous genetic combination when it came to the men). And the fellow was just telling her that those three languages were the official languages of Switzerland, so Dianka understand that there was something going on between these three countries. Everywhere the streets were being dug up, concealed behind reflective fences with blinking red lights.

'Where on earth have I ended up? And what will sex be like with these people?' Dianka thought as she walked and chewed the chestnuts, which were too dry, they filled up her mouth and got stuck in her throat. As for the sex, the guy told her not to be surprised, Zurich was a very vanilla city . . . At the sight of Dianka's gaping mouth, he explained: 'Well, it's sex, but you leave your socks on, things like that . . . Know what I mean?'

Dianka felt butterflies in her stomach, as if she were about to take a test in a subject she knew nothing about. She was too embarrassed to ask what he meant, but if she asked other escorts then soon enough word would get out that she didn't know how to have sex with socks on!

'Ye . . . ye . . . yes!' she lied. 'Socks. Of course.'

'And people here are really into swaddling, diapers . . . Things like that.'

'Oh, cool.'

As they walked Dianka looked at the shop windows filled with all sorts of products. 'Swaddling,' she thought. Oh my God, I've never swaddled anyone before!

They walked past a whole row of dusty Arab shops selling spices and veils and stopped at the bottom of a steep slope. The guy showed Dianka how Zurich spread up the side of the mountain, how the city had upper and lower neighbourhoods, and how you could get to the summit by way of stairs cut into the rock or by riding a ridiculously old and rickety funicular train that, with all its folksy decorations, looked like it belonged in a museum. It wasn't so much a slope as an escarpment of rock and brick festooned with greenery. And just like Hollywood with its 'Hollywood' sign, there was an enormous billboard here on the mountainside with curlicue letters spelling out 'Lindt'.

They delved further into a neighbourhood of very narrow cobblestone streets, where every other building had a gay bar in it, and in front of them Black men drank beer and smoked cigarettes, shouted and conversed in Swiss . . .

The guy started telling her about Switzerland, how underneath the streets they were walking on were tunnels full of safes filled with gold. They lost the czar, but his gold and diamonds were still here. An African dictator was assassinated, but his fortune remained, untouchable. Ceaușescu was kaput, but his money was still awaited an heir who would never come. During the war, Hitler had left Switzerland alone, a little sanctuary—and a clandestine storehouse for the artworks and money he pilfered from all over Europe; when he fell, they stayed put . . . Switzerland was a society of modest, frugal, Protestant hill people who manufactured luxury goods for the whole world that they themselves would never buy or use. They saved money and never spent it, separated the recycling, rolled the toothpaste tube to the end and, more than anything—as mentioned earlier—they collected everything and carefully organized it . . .

'Who would've thought?' thought Dianka.

'And you can't be too careful, for AIDS grosses Problem in Zürich, ze viele junkies, ze viele Drögeler, ze many drugs . . .' the punter continued his lecture. 'And you must to watch out for Satanists, because they also grosses Problem, I'm not kidding. Especially for a boy from Eastern European, because who will look for him, who will claim him if he dies, who even knows where he is?'

Dianka shuddered with fear—it was true, no one had any idea she was here! Except for one German train guard . . . but who would ask him?

'Do they . . . do they kill boys?'

'I'm not kidding! Don't hang out with them. And watch out for the Arabs too. Don't go off with an Arab if you can help it, as they'll try to cheat you and not pay. Swiss will always pay. . .'

But this Dianka knew: never trust an Arab . . .

'Well, good luck then. I'll be on my way now.'

He left Dianka abruptly in front of one of the bars, slipped her fifty francs for her first two drinks and was gone. How lucky she'd been to run into him first thing! Clearly this guy wasn't someone who would pay for sex, but he knew what was what and he pitied the poor rent boy without a cent to his name. Dianka's ability to evoke this lofty feeling in others was something she valued very highly. So she stood there at the entrance to the country-western-style bar with the green bench out front, the boys sitting on it mercilessly sizing her up, and she was reminded of when her family moved to a different part of Bratislava and she had to change her kindergarten, and the lady brought her into a room full of other kids who were all friends with one another already . . . The boys were sitting there like they owned the bench and she instinctively knew they were from Eastern Europe. They looked at her and spoke to each other in Russian. They were smoking. They were much better dressed than in Vienna or Munich. Leather, bomber and biker jackets, huge Dolce & Gabbana logos on the backs, leather motorcycle trousers, knee-high boots, cowboy boots, gold chains around their necks, enormous watches, rings, cigars, pomaded hair, a few of them were really beautiful, even kitschy. For Dianka, kitsch wasn't the negation of beauty but rather its highest form. Some of the boys looked like they'd just come off the runway at a Gaultier show, in white-and-navy-blue sailor uniforms and white caps with anchors on them . . .

Dianka stood there hesitating. She was wearing a dirty Levi's denim jacket and blue jeans to match, an all-denim fashion blunder from top to bottom, along with Adidas trainers, dark moons on her fingernails, pimples on her nose, greasy hair, bangs hanging in her eyes, she was worn out from travelling, but she knew her face was prettier than theirs.

A terrible racket came from inside along with old-school American country music. Mungo Jerry's 'In the Summertime', Mary Hopkin's 'Those Were the Days' . . . She took a step towards the door and . . . suddenly landed on the ground! The boys burst into laughter. The one closest to her, in the pink Gucci tracksuit, must have stuck his leg out to trip her. She got up. She knew that if she didn't stand up for herself, if she didn't show them that she too could use vulgar language and stick out her leg to trip people, that is, that she too came from Eastern Europe and drank water straight from the tap without it affecting her, that she hadn't just come directly from home with a lunchbox of stuffed cabbage rolls and a bottle of vodka in her rucksack, but that she'd done her time on the street in Vienna and Munich already, if she didn't show them that, then she'd be their chump forever. She threw a bouquet of Slovak obscenities at them, totally camping it up, then smirked and walked into the bar, hoping she wouldn't see Norma there or once again have to hear that spiteful moniker 'Madame de Hangry' . . .

Although no one appeared to take any notice of her, you could see in that tiny bar the stream of new information coursing through the crowd: 'Fresh meat! Fresh meat!' She'd come riding in from the back of beyond on a cold hot frozen scooter, like Pandora from the box, she'd eat anything, nibble on dried grasshoppers, even the pickle she'd landed herself in, but goodness if she wasn't cute as a button!

Behind the bar Everlasting Mario with the moustache was cleaning the beer glasses. He tossed them in the air, caught them, filled them up, set coasters down on the bar, and served the grandpas, the punters, the customers their beers with a cheery 'Zoom bowl!' or 'Zoom bowl, Mitterand!' The left side of the bar was speaking in Polish, the right side in Czech, and over by the toilets in Slovak (but Dianka wasn't about to say hello); beyond that there were Greek and African mafias, a few Romanians and one unbelievably beautiful Russian. But the scene was still much smaller than in Vienna. Everyone wore elegant and expensive clothes here too they were well groomed, decked out in gold, with shiny shoes, fancy cigarettes and cigars, and one boy ostentatiously drove up in front of the bar in a red convertible.

'Well then, I'll just have to find myself a customer and someone else for love . . . so I'll have a place to sleep, at least for tonight. Or else a customer for the whole night. But I should see what kind of ice cream they serve around here . . .' The grandpas in the bar were showing considerable interest in Dianka. 'Well look at all those tarted-up scarecrows! And here I am in my unwashed Levi's, even more unwashed than me, but they'll put up with me because I'm new. You're only new once, and you can only hike up your price once too!' Dianka recognized some of the escorts, they'd been in Vienna and suddenly disappeared, but they all ignored her. Clearly they thought they were better than her, they'd got here first.

The faces at the bar all looked fairly repugnant, but Dianka knew from her own professional experience that a person's face had nothing to do with their character, the flesh tautened or slackened regardless of what was happening inside. Some grandpa's lips might droop at either end in a permanent scowl, but inside him lived a fellow as happy and carefree as a boy. Dianka, on the other hand was inhabited by a lazy old bitch, like a worm inside an apple. She really needed to pee, but she was afraid of going to the toilet in case one of the mafias had plans to send her packing, to attack her in there, scare her shitless, slash her face, shave all her hair off, and throw her out on her arse. They probably wouldn't do it right in front of everyone, but wait and follow her into the conveniences.

Who should walk in then, to Dianka's good fortune, but that Polish guy Michał, the charmer, the one they all called Eleven-Inch since he was always bragging about how well endowed he was, the one from Vienna to whom she still owed money. Good God, first Norma in Munich and now he here? Was anyone left in Vienna? The Pole shot Dianka the same disapproving look he'd always give her in Austria, like 'Seriously? You're eating ice cream again? Girl, really . . . Stop eating ice cream already!'

THE POLE

'Dianka, you silly whore, stop eating ice cream! Don't you know it makes you fat? Your body is your instrument, you need it for work! Ice cream is made of fat, sugar and salt, and the stuff they have here contains all kinds of artificial colours and flavours and thickeners . . . I mean, you look great now, but you'll need your looks to live on for the next five or seven years, and this crap will come back to bite you. Every scoop, every ounce of whipped cream!

'Lord have mercy, today must be a holiday. The first time in its fifty years this bar has ever actually sold ice cream! Can you believe it? Well, enjoy it, or as they say, *guten Appetit*. Lovely to see you, my dear, it's been a minute, hasn't it? *Arbeiten*, Dianka, *arbeiten*! And you actually listened to me and came to Zurich! Even if your lips are all crusty and blistered, your face and arse are truly scrumptious. That succulent arse of yours more than makes up for any temporary lapse in grooming! And just so you don't start undercutting the market, I got the lowdown from the Polish mafia: a blowjob in the toilet costs a hundred francs, the base rate for going home with a customer is two fifty, anal starts at five hundred and can go up to a thousand, and the same goes for a full night of anything. And if today is your first day, you have to charge double! Anyway, come with me to the toilet, evidently it's dangerous to go by yourself in a new place, ha ha. Come on, I'll tell you the rest in there, how things are here. Get up, no one is going to eat your ice cream while you're away. Well, OK, the boys might spit in it, so hurry up and finish.

'Just look at these bathrooms—marble walls, black-and-gold urinals, lights made of Swarovski crystal, come on, let's go in the stall. It's paradise here, Dianka, simply paradise!' The boys were telling me: Switzerland is tiny but they have more money than the whole United States, and although there aren't that many customers about, they're impulsive and they'll hire you again and again. Other than Geneva, the cities are too small to have hustler bars, but there's Davos—it's a mountain village, but once a year they have the World Economic Forum, which is a total gold mine for us. The hotels there are the most expensive in the world then, but the boys all piggy-back on the businessmen! There's at least a dozen ski resorts where rich people come from all over the world, like Sankt Moritz, Corviglia or Davos Klosters! Or you can make an outing to that hick town in Liechtenstein, Vaduz! Anyway, babe, this whole country is a backwater, but do you have any idea how much money they have? Oh, and I would suggest you not steal anything. Zurich is teensy tiny and all the customers know one another, they gossip about the escorts and share recommendations. Once you steal something, no one will want you.

DIANKA

He joined her in the bathroom and Dianka stood transfixed by the kitsch inside: black marble and granite, gilded columns, gold urinals, all of it dripping with urine and covered in filth, and in the corner someone had left an unfinished glass of beer. Looking at her from the mirror was a totally fuckable but alarmingly dishevelled twink who, despite her long eyelashes, had pimples on her nose and greasy hair. The minute she made some money she'd have to get her hair done and a facial!

While peeing she also discovered that her willy had not been left unaffected by the past twenty-four hours without a bath and journey from Munich. She held it in her yellow, cigarette-stained fingers and tried to figure out what to do, because unless she ran into that nutcase from Vienna who was into scat and getting kicked with cowboy boots in the bathroom, she wouldn't have a chance. If only she were like the Pole! He barely just got here and already knows everyone, feels right at home, slapping the backs of the other boys, he already knows which customer pays how much and for what, he probably even knows how to do the sex-with-socks thing! Rattling on about cities she's never heard of or even where they are, probably in hell. Christ, he already speaks Swiss German. Or at least he acts like he does.

THE POLE

I was awakened by the moans coming from the bed next to mine. Pavo had brought a punter back . . . A little rude of him, fucking in the room while I'm here sleeping, innocent as a babe. Slowly I opened one eye. But no: leaning with his hands on the bed and wearing nothing but his boxers, he was doing some kind of exceptionally brutal, painful push-ups. I burst out laughing. Outside the window the whole city was reverberating with the sound of bells, one after the other: boom, boom, boom, boom, boom. I don't know why, but the sound of bells always made me wistful. I looked out the uncurtained window at a bare wall.

We would freshen up in the awful, putrid and dripping-wet bathroom in the hallway and go to work. It was so convenient, I just had to communicate with Pavo so we didn't bring our tricks back at the same time. Your turn, my turn. As long as I'm still up there, stay here with your guy and wait. 'Ein Moment, bitte, mein Herr, langsam, langsam aber sicher, in zwanzig Minuten gehen wir nach Zimmer, aber jetzt noch ein Bier trinken, etwas sprechen . . . Jetzt mein Freund ist in Zimmer . . .'

But as if out of spite, my first customer that evening wanted me for the whole night, and at his place. He whisked me out of town to somewhere near Zug, but as he was paying handsomely I went. They were all the same here: clean-smelling, cultured, well dressed, with expensive cars, clean, everything clean and fresh-scented, Laura Ashley home decor, espresso machines, everything first-rate. You expect to haggle for an extra fifty, but he ends up throwing in two hundred, along with a cake filled with rose-petal jelly for the road . . .

When the guy dropped me off at eight the next morning in front of our hotel, I immediately discovered that Pavo had been busy making hay while the sun was shining (or not shining, as it happened). There at the reception was my suitcase packed and waiting, and the Arab guy was shouting to me in his broken English over 'Lambada' something about a brother: 'This not brother!' Whose brother was he talking about? Did he think Pavo and I were brothers? But I quickly realized he was saying 'brothel'(!) and that Pavo had brought half of Zurich back to our room, jizzing all over the bed, naked grandpas creeping down the hall to the bathroom . . . 'Prostituten verboten! Du Schwulen, prostituten, nach Strasse gehen!' he informed me, as if I didn't already know.

In all the commotion he forgot to charge us for the room, so we got a freebie. So much the better, especially since I hadn't even slept there and Pavo certainly hadn't slept at all. After my night with that guy outside Zug I was pretty set for cash, so I yelled at the Arab concierge in Polish how he should take his stupid 'Lambada' and go climb up a tree, grabbed my suitcase, slammed the door and headed to Milano's near the train station for my favourite sandwich and coffee.

Carrousel wouldn't open for another six hours, and it would be twelve hours before it was worth going in, so I left my suitcase in an outrageously expensive locker at the train station and took a walk down Bahnhofstrasse, looking at all the hideous lucre in the shop windows. Watches, gold, everything made of gold, gold nail clippers, gold scissors, gold keychains, lighters, pens, toothpicks . . . Like King Midas, some people need everything they touch, even the most banal everyday utensils, to turn to gold. Because nose hairs must be removed with gold tweezers, to use any other utensil would be a disgrace.

Suddenly I was reminded of that gold rush back in Vienna, which for a time had all the boys in its grip, and from what I'd seen so far, all of Zurich was in its grip too, the affluence climaxing all over Paradeplatz, where I was drinking the world's most expensive *Kaffee* and eating the world's most expensive *Kuchen*. Maybe it was all that underground gold that made the *Kaffee* and the *Kuchen* so expensive, as if they'd been infected with wealth. Perfect ladies glided down the streets, perfectly accoutred in Louis Vuitton, their little dogs on Louis Vuitton–monogrammed leashes, Louis Vuitton–printed scarves around their necks and Louis Vuitton–stamped handbags attached to their wrists by what appeared to be gold handcuffs so no one could steal them. They lit their gold Louis Vuitton cigarettes with gold Louis Vuitton lighters, they probably even shit gold turds proudly sporting the Louis Vuitton device! They came to the centre around noon, discharged one transaction at the bank, sold a few shares of this or that stock, and that was that—after all the hard work it was time for coffee and then a bit of shopping.

The most wonderful thing about that street was the smell: coffee, cigar and pipe smoke, Chanel no. 5, fresh rolls and croissants, chocolate . . . There was a life-size cow made of milk chocolate there. Some kind of installation art piece for Milka, feeding the world with chocolate; you could go up and spoon out a piece of the cow for yourself, so I went again and again and fed myself with chocolate cow the whole day. Even after I went to the lake and sat on a bench watching the mountaintops, I would go back to the cow for fillers because everything is in walking distance in Zurich. (I even wrapped up some cow in a handkerchief to save for later.) What these people couldn't do with chocolate! Normal countries made hollow Santa Clauses out of it for Christmas and hollow bunnies for Easter. But in Switzerland, just as you could have anything you wanted made of gold and with a Louis Vuitton monogram on it, you could also get anything made out of chocolate too. Especially anything that represented Swissness: Swiss Army pocket knives, Milka cows, Swatch watches, Matterhorns, trolls, gnomes and chocolate mountain huts with chocolate shutters on the windows . . . You could literally stuff your face with Switzerland and all things Swiss. So I ate, like Dianka ate Mövenpick crème-brûlée-flavoured ice cream, I devoured that chocolate cow and those chocolate pocket knives, until I was sick . . .

Later, I dragged myself around Zurich, all that milk chocolate sloshing around inside me, and although I won't get a Nobel Prize for recognizing that Zurich was a city of contrasts, it wouldn't be right not to mention it. The richest neighbourhood was Zürichberg; and as is typical for richest neighbourhoods anywhere, it was also the saddest, the emptiest and the least hospitable. If a car

emerged from one of the underground garages there and happened not to have darkened windows, you might catch a glimpse
of the driver's face, which always looked serious and preoccupied,
not like faces in the slums, where everyone is smiling. So many
obligations, loan payments, deadlines, insurance policies . . . I
marched down Langsstrasse too, a street of shady deals, red lights
and dodgy tanning salons, a street of crocodiles. I ran into a whole
nest of junkies, but it was so horrible, and there were so many of
them, I immediately ran away to some park, where I pulled out
the handkerchief and ate the last bits of cow.

I was tired, queasy from all the chocolate, and I really needed to
eat something substantial, a proper breakfast (the mumsie in me
had awakened and started scolding me), but the chocolate had
ruined my appetite. Most of all I just wanted to lie down, but I
wouldn't find a bed before nightfall and I wasn't about to lie down
on the street. I decided to go to Apollo Sauna, which was in
Niederdorf, just down from the train station, the same neighbourhood as Caroussel and fifteen other gay bars, so I could take a long
shower before the night and maybe pick up someone with a flat
to go to. The sauna was very kitschy, ugly plastic statues of Apollo
everywhere, white plastic columns with lightbulbs inside them,
lamps with fluttering red rags inside them meant to look like flickering flames, beefed-up queens behind the bar, their bodies waxed
and nipples pierced, overpriced beers, men's bodies stripped of
their Patek Philippe and Louis Vuitton, naked except for numbers
scrawled on their wrists, unexpected abrasions on their arses, the
sudden rash. This was what I shelled out thirty francs for? Once
again, old American pop songs served as a soundtrack for the
moaning and groaning. Televisions everywhere were playing the

same porn video, but with no sound, some kind of gay version of *Star Wars*. I wrapped my towel around my loins and took a seat on the lounge chair in front of the television, so it would look like I was watching it, when actually I was sleeping.

THE ROMANIAN

Of course my peace was immediately disturbed by some mal-nourished moron whose eyes were rheumy with the bitter knowl-edge of life as a migrant. You could see immediately they were from Eastern Europe and a hustler too, but I wouldn't have spent one rappen on that bag of bones. Romania plopped down right on the edge of my lounger and started up in fluent German about how I must be new in Zurich, how they'd seen me yesterday in Caroussel, how they'd been living here for ages and were in a rela-tionship with a doctor, Hans Ludwig his name, but they had his permission to sleep around sometimes, the doctor was resting in the dry sauna now but would be along any minute, and did I have a place to sleep? All the while they kept turning around one bony finger a ring made of gold, though no doubt it was fake gold, a fake, ugly, Gypsy, Romanian ring.

Later it really did appear that the guy, Andrei, was together with the doctor, but Hans Ludwig was more like his pimp, because he was always there with him in Caroussel fixing hookups for him with other guys. It turned out that helping me (although nothing good ever came of it) was Andrei's passion. I had only to find myself in some predicament for him to turn up with his doctor and their advice, prescriptions and worried faces. Once when I had earache but no health insurance, the two took me to hospital and wangled something so I was admitted without insurance.

Anyway, Andrei had been living in Zurich for many years already and was a bit of a Samaritan. But such an ugly one, pale, freckle-faced, and pathetic in a Protestant way, bags under his eyes. Then he slipped a hand under my towel and looked at me like a frog trying to seduce a prince. Girl, please . . .

'. . . I mean, if you don't have a place to stay, maybe we can help, help you out, Hilfe, gay Hilfe. We must look out for each other, no? We Eastern Europeans, shaking hands across all the borders and divisions . . .'

Sure, but wash your hands first, please, especially after groping me under the towel . . .

'So there is this one gentleman, an elderly man who lives a bit outside the centre, in Witikon, but it's an easy connection with the S-Bahn and only thirty minutes. This man may be old but he is very, very cultivated, and has had quite a few boys live with him already, not so much for sex as for the company, someone to be nice to him'—Andrei started to caress my arm—'to give him a bit of human warmth, a substitute family . . .'

Mmmm, no thanks, I'll stay at the Hilton! I wasn't ready yet for a terminal situation but I thanked him politely and said I'd need a few days to think about it. I figured I'd keep the old guy as a fallback in case I didn't find anything else. What I was looking for was the exact opposite though: a young guy with a flat right in the centre, who would head out to work in the morning and in the evening come back and immediately fall asleep.

Later, Andrei, with that worried expression on his face the whole time—honestly, he never smiled!—began dishing out advice, evidently thinking it was my first day at the rodeo. Pathetic really. He said they'd watched me yesterday, he and the doctor, and how I wasn't doing it right, my clothes were too showy, too expensive (excuse me? and what were the other whores wearing?), how I should dress like young people, in sweat pants and a hoodie, with a skateboard, not like on Dynasty. Here, I had to agree with him, because rich guys didn't want other rich guys, they wanted a boy. But I still had an entire wardrobe of gold from the gold-rush days back in Vienna—rings and chains, bracelets and wristbands, half a kilo of gold! It was shimmering on me now in the fuzzy porn light on the TV, against a dusty backdrop of backlit artifical palms and fluttering rags simulating flames in a fireplace. He wasn't completely immune to the charm and beauty of gold either, twisting his Gypsy ring while continuing to warble on about how drugs were a grosses Problem in Zurich and AIDS was a grosses Problem and Satanists and a serial killer at large who was having a field day with hustlers from Eastern Europe, since their families had no idea where they were or what country, nothing, so who would come looking for them?

I went to the tanning beds and sunned myself without taking off any of my gold so I could look like a mafioso, tanned everywhere except for around my neck where my gold chain was or on my fingers because of the rings. Oh and G-string lines too, so I'd stand out. Then I went to the showers. But the whole time I had a bad feeling that this wasn't the last time Andrei would turn up in my life like a deus ex machina, with his aspirins and prescriptions, and that I'd eventually end up staying with that codger out in Witikon . . .

Some grandpa was jerking off in the showers, rubbing and pulling his willy out of its nest of grey pubes. Consumed with desire, lost in his libido, tongue lolling out of his mouth, eyes rolling upwards. He devoured me with his gaze, but I just rubbed my fingers together as if to say, 'Hi, I'm a taxi, if you want me I'll turn on the meter now, night fare.' He looked at me reproachfully, like the kid in the tram who wouldn't yield his seat to an elderly passenger, who now had to stand. In order to help him come to a decision and fork over some of his pension, I started soaping up my crotch so my Eleven-Inch would rise and show itself in all its splendour. He stood there in shock and began pinching his nipples, which dangled from the ends of two pendulous, sock-like breasts. But it was very clear he had no intention of paying. So I made a show of rinsing myself off and then as punishment wrapped a towel around my waist, shutting down the candy shop, and slowly walked to one of the private cabins with beds and TVs playing porn in them. If he didn't follow me in, I thought, lighting a cigarette, then that would be that, and in the sultry, damp air of the sauna the cigarette had the strange taste of betrayal. Everything I knew about the psychology of elderly queens told me he would succumb and be along any minute. But no—he didn't come. Maybe he actually didn't have the money.

I went to the bar and ordered a whisky on the rocks, sat on a high bar stool, smoked and kicked off another night of boozing, because I always spent the hours between six in the evening and sometime the next morning in a state of greater or lesser inebriation.

The wallpaper on the bar's computer had an image of some naked muscle queen on it, because everything had to scream gay, gay, gay, it couldn't just be a picture of mountains or something. Even the wall clock had to allude to everyone's favourite theme, here in the form of a rolled-up condom for the face and two rotating sperm cells for the hands. Which was what made it so boring. Sexual desire was one thing, I thought, but that wallpaper on the computer was about something else. After half a drink though, it stopped being so important. I decompressed, lit up a Camel, and thought about how the best thing about this job, being a prostitute, was that you never knew what the night would bring. Would you be a millionaire in the morning? Would someone drive you all the way out to Zug? Would you sleep in a chalet near Schaffhausen? Or maybe someone would try to murder you (in a car park on the way to Chur)? This unpredictability, like playing a game of roulette, gave me butterflies in my stomach, pins and needles in my legs, and shivers up and down my spine. Other than that, I could say with certainty that on a given evening I might have anywhere from one to fifteen tricks which, despite it being labour, sometimes involved some really amazing sex. Sex is so strange: one day you're with a total beefcake but you can't get it up because his body and looks promised too much, far more than the sex could deliver, then the next day you get an ugly, old hunchback who leaves you quivering in ecstasy. Maybe this job would make me a gerontophile? That old queen in the showers, for instance, was kind of a turn-on and I was super disappointed when she didn't come shuffling after me.

So who knew what the night would bring—it was a mystery and that was the most beautiful thing about it. I'd had situations

I never could have imagined or foretold. One thing I can say, I've met a lot of interesting people in this profession.

There was one dude who had massive balls the size of apples (apparently there's a whole subculture of people injecting silicone in their testicles). A millionaire who collected designers' socks then framed and hung them by the thousands on his walls. A fat bald taxi driver with gold rings on his fingers—he would take me off-meter to his flat, which was full of aquariums, a pleasant hobby he was clearly no stranger to. A melancholic and sad American who always looked like he'd just been told he had cancer, and when I went with him—we had already got to his place—he called it off, paid me for doing absolutely nothing and told me to get the hell out. A little Goth dude, probably eighteen, all in black, long purple-black hair, cigarette lighter with a skull on it, black Davidoffs . . . All kinds of people pay for sex, if they're desperate enough.

It really sucked that I didn't have a place to live. That's always a problem in a new city. You have to hook up for free with someone who might fall in love with you, then wait until he asks, 'So where do you live? Do you even have a roof over your head?' Then you just need to lower your eyes and look glumly at your drink and blush a little, as if you're embarrassed to say. Then the guy will get more and more concerned and (correctly) surmise that you're homeless. You might tell him that you do have a place but make it clear you're just saying that so he doesn't worry. Then suddenly change the subject. 'Such wonderful weather we're having, and the franc has been so strong lately.' Don't be afraid if he doesn't come back to the topic, you've already planted the seed.

Those who underestimate the skill and knowledge needed for carrying out the difficult profession of prostitute are sadly mistaken. The expertise required to work with the elderly in their infinite variety, some of them exceptionally vicious, stingy and mean; the talent for sussing them out within the first ten minutes of conversation, finding their weak spots, their complexes, their dreams ... You need, for example, to have a sense for who can and must be negotiated with regarding payment and who is so averse to haggling that he'd sooner just drop it. The ones who pay really well, more than a thousand francs, and even throw in a bit more because showing off their wealth in front of minors is more gratifying than the sex itself. But don't even start negotiating with them! 'You know, all this talk about money ... I think I'll take a pass,' they'll tell you, and the bird has flown the coop. And so on. Dianka, for instance, would never figure this kind of thing out. By the way, I wondered where she was staying. Maybe she could be the one to marry that elderly gentleman from Witikon.

There are whores, and there are whores. As always, the quality of the service has nothing to do with how hot they look, but with their intelligence, tact and sensitivity. Customers are already stressed enough when they come to us with their ugly looks, their ageing or obese or anorexic bodies, with their haemorrhoids and varicose veins and false teeth, their combovers and toupés, their erectile dysfunctions, their chronic halitosis and unretractable foreskins drooping like the dugs of old women ... To us, because of the contrast, it all looks even worse. But they're so hungry that in spite of everything they overcome their shame, they come and put themselves in the humiliating position of the customer, the punter, the john. Some boys have no tact at all, however, or empathy, and they're incapable of chatting with a trick about things that might be of interest to him (things that are objectively uninteresting, by the way, about boilers, or the quality of cement, all their bragging, memories of the war that didn't happen here, etc.). They refuse to let grandpa walk out of the bar first, or to open the car door for him, or help him off with his overcoat. And he needs to be listened to (because who would listen to his nattering for free?), he needs to be fawned over, to feel important. With me, from the moment we've agreed my price, my customer may as well be the Queen of England, and hell will freeze over before I take a step in front of him, I always stay two centimetres behind. But some boys are so cheeky they even laugh about his varicose veins and haemorrhoids to his face! And then they're surprised when the customer doesn't ask for them again. I always say, when meeting a customer for the second time: 'Say what you want, tell me I'm too expensive, but you can't say you weren't extremely well serviced, that you weren't satisfied, or that this equipment isn't first class.' 'Nein, nein, das kann ich nicht sagen . . .'

Lost in such thoughts, I somehow managed to knock back three drinks, smoke ten Camels, eat one of those ridiculously overpriced toasts, and I could have kept sitting there until morning if I hadn't had to work, to gratify a whole Reich of emotionally needy grandpas who were already spritzing themselves with breath freshener, pulling out the shoe trees and calling for a car. . .

I grabbed my toiletries from my locker and took another shower. I brushed my teeth with Elmex toothpaste, washed my hair with Ryf of Switzerland shampoo, dried it with the blow dryer and styled it with gel and hair spray so it would hold, so even after one arsehole after another had messed up my fringe

while we were fucking, I could still look presentable and keep raking it in. I looked in the mirror. I looked like a cartoon boy, a
Japanese manga character. I winked at myself. My cheeks were
rosy from the whisky, but it would be many years before alcohol
took its toll or cigarettes turned my teeth yellow. For now, I could
get away with everything. I pasted on my false eyelashes. In the
darkness of a night club, the grandpas wouldn't be able to tell them
from real ones and they would still make an impression. I brushed
foundation on my cheeks, then rouge, and gayed myself up, blushing like a pervert. I extended my sideburns a little with black eyeliner and accentuated my eyes and eyebrows with mascara. I
perfumed myself with Dior Fahrenheit, smeared lip gloss on my
lips and spent a good while perfecting the artistic disarray of my
hair. It had to be like stage make-up, exaggerated, since guys
judged us from a distance, often from seven, ten metres away, and
the artifice only became apparent when you were in the lift from
the underground car park up to the sucker's flat, so far too late for
him to call it off. Sometimes the light in these lifts was so hellishly
bright, and your foundation had started cracking and the eyeliner
smeared. In the bathroom at Carrousel, sometimes you'd have
three boys in there at the same time fixing their drawn-on moustaches and so on, but after the eighth trick it would all be running
down your face anyway . . .

I repeated my Ten Commandments to myself:

1. You are your own creator.

2. You are your own god.

3. You are only in it for yourself.

4. You shall not make sacrifices for other people or for
   society.

5. You are alone. No one else has access to your inner life.

6. You are evil. As far as possible, steal, lie, use any means available to become rich.

7. Save your money for luxuries and expensive trips, because rich people only love boys like that and invite them on their yachts.

8. Never trust anyone, not even Pavo, NO ONE.

9. Every now and then celebrate your own luxury HOLIDAY.

10. Do not harbour compassion for other people's weaknesses, only your own weaknesses are interesting.

11. What you care about in life are sex and money. In this profession, there's no need to choose between them, they go hand in hand.

12. Talk with people, smile at them, act like you are part of the same world, but know that in reality you are better than them, you are completely independent, you do not care about their problems, at any moment you are free to sell them out.

I made a face at the mirror à la Alexis Carrington. I saluted myself and walked out, soldier of geriatric libido. It was late autumn, leaden skies, and a Saturday, the day for partying. Hordes of drunken teens spilt through the narrow cobblestone streets. The city smelt of satiety, of food. The same smell exuded by McDonald's in every corner of the globe. I walked into the centre because that overpriced toast wouldn't be enough for the whole night, which would be a long one, extremely long. And McDonald's back then was still a huge attraction, a fancy restaurant. I ordered one of their most expensive deluxe combos, grabbed the tray and started climbing to the upstairs dining area. Suddenly, fuck, I slipped in my new shoes with their slippery leather soles and everything tumbled all over the steps. I looked around to see if anyone had seen what happened, quickly cleaned up and salvaged what I could, and hurried upstairs with the tray, mortified. I holed up in the farthest corner, next to a pool full of brightly coloured ping-pong balls for kids. Suddenly I see one of the employees coming towards me. That was it. They'll make me pay for the mess I'd made on the stairs or for something. But what a surprise. He asked me what kind of combo I had ordered and whether I'd been drinking Coke or Fanta, because they wanted to replace my meal free of charge. You can take the Pole out of Poland, but you can't take the Poland out of the Pole. I even got a free ice cream as consolation for the mess I'd made.

'So, so . . . So ist das Leben . . .' My first customer that night wanted to have wool sex, but not with me, I didn't understand why he even wanted me there. He had white dressers in his home, all full of fuzzy, white, mohair stockings, berets and baby blankets. I watched, fascinated, as he pulled out those sterile white woollens and rubbed them on our cocks. Well, whatever, the customer was weird but harmless. Still, I refused to put those wool socks in my mouth. He paid three hundred francs and gave me thirty for the taxi. Which I returned (I'd paid five).

The second customer had a foot fetish, something I was already familiar with. I had to masturbate him with my feet, which was a cinch. But when he tried to do the same to me, I had to get a little aggressive and push him off me, as he had athlete's foot, something I had zero interest in catching (and I swear it took me forever to figure out how to say 'athlete's foot' in German . . .). In any case, I needed my tool for work and had to take care of it. He paid four hundred fifty and gave me a ride back to Carrousel.

The third guy was your typical guilt-ridden inhibited daddy. He wanted to have sex in his car, which had a baby seat in back and a pair of women's sunglasses on the dashboard. We drove up to the top of Zürichberg, to a little wood where everyone went to do exactly the same thing. He made the funniest squeals when I licked his nipples. He paid me three hundred and, of course, drove me back.

Number four was a quickie on-site, right in Carrousel, in the toilet, a hand job for two hundred.

Eventually it was time to start looking for a place to spend the night. To be honest, I really just wanted to be alone. I had enough for a hotel. Around three I stopped drinking alcohol and began ordering coffee, to which Mario would add a little chocolate penis wrapped in foil. And out of my utter exhaustion and endless screwing (even though I'd switched to coffee, I continued making the rounds, shooting less and less each time until all I got were dry orgasms) I made a mistake: I told Andrei, the one from the sauna, OK, you can take me to that guy in Witikon tomorrow. It was a temptation too big to ignore because it was free housing. Later I would learn that when you're offered something for free, put as much distance between you and it as possible . . .

For a while, as if in a somnambulistic dance, I kept making the rounds and coming back, because word had spread throughout the entire bar that the new guy was packing. 'Eleven inches!' 'Biggest cock in Zurich!'—I heard them whisper reverently when

I went to the jukebox to throw in five francs for Michael Jackson's 'Bad'. Or another five in the cigarette machine for a pack of Camels. Or three in the machine for pistachios. Five francs for condoms from the machine in the toilet. There was this one ugly and pretentious Greek queen, flaming to high heaven, who glared at me like a wolf and once came in after me in the toilet and tried to scare me off since I was taking away all her customers, but I just smiled sweetly at her, grabbed her by the neck and shook her up a bit, scratched her face so she'd have a souvenir and left her there, bellowing after me.

Although it was against all the rules, there were women at Carrousel too, really odd ones. They weren't trans women, they were biological women, old grandmas. One was eighty years old and dressed like Lady Spring—little bows in her curly locks, pink earrings, a gold cigarette lighter and a diamond-studded handbag. As soon as she came in she sat down at the pinball machine, pulled out a plastic bag of what looked like loose coins and started feeding them into the machine, all the while manipulating the silver ball that was bouncing around like crazy under the glass. Later she went over to another game where you needed to get three cherries or apples in a row to appear on a screen. And she stayed there, drinking and smoking, in the same position all night, smoking, drinking, her financial situation fluctuating from one hour to the next. As Swiss law technically forbids gambling, she was playing with tokens, which she would later exchange for cash from Mario. There was always someone there next to her, chatting. Sometimes it was even me, because I was fascinated by her rainbow make-up, her five clip-ons in one ear along with an earring—she was living the life! Her pink, high-heeled slippers! I was fascinated by her long claws with their pink nail polish, the way they worked the various buttons, deftly inserted the tokens, lit up her cigarettes. Her drinks were all neon-coloured, lizard-green, fire-engine red.

Meanwhile, Dianka was sitting in a corner eating ice cream with whipped cream, which no one aside from her ever ordered, stuffing her face with Snickers and Mars Bars; she really didn't want to work. I decided to introduce her to Andrei from Romania, because I was already regretting that I'd agreed to go meet that old guy in Witikon and was thinking of marrying Dianka off to him. I was already laughing inside at the idea of her ending up with him. So I told the Romanian I was sorry but I'd found something better, right in the centre, but I had someone else for him, a really sweet, upstanding and even-tempered boy, a bit of a wallflower, quiet as a mouse, 'Wait just a moment'. I went to Dianka (who was eating steak for a change) and asked if she had a place to stay, because if not, there was a couple here (Andrei and the doctor) who knew a very cultivated, tidy older gentleman who was, however, rather lonely and, for want of company, was offering a room for free— your own key, your own room, your own pillow, all for free! And by God I actually succeeded in selling Dianka on him! Since I'd already made a round out to Witikon that night, I knew it was basically out in the sticks, where only chocolate cows grazed . . .

Eventually I found my last customer of the night. A handsome, slim man with salt-and-pepper hair, Italian features. Unfortunately guys like this often have bad breath. He was nice, though, friendly, smiled a lot, didn't try to haggle and took me for a whole night. His designer flat was a little outside Zurich but had a view of the lake, in a new, modern construction, everything white. We lay in his bed and watched the news. And somehow it turned out that all over the whole world, except for Switzerland and our bed, there was a war going on, there were bombings, there were riots. Watching news about the rest of the world had a very soothing effect on the Swiss. Everywhere poverty, everywhere someone's home is being demolished, but here they renovate their houses and meticulously replace the water mains every five years before they can even think of bursting. Roaming the room was an insanely furry white cat, a Persian, no doubt expensive. The sex was all right. It was just too bad the guy's stubble was so prickly. Bath time. White frotté bath towels, white bathrobes. We sit, the guy pulls out a bag of tobacco and I get anxious he'll start rolling a spliff. Which he does. I don't partake, I never do, not since the time I got so stoned all I could do was lie there, unable to move, not even a finger or my eyelids, a total vegetable. He smoked it by himself and we went to bed. We wouldn't get much sleep, though, because it was already four and he'd told me he needed to get up at seven to go to work. And next to the enormous white bed the alarm clock went off, the signal summoning the Swiss workers to their shifts, to their national duty to establish order and increase wealth. My trick got up, refreshed as if he'd just slept twelve hours, made coffee with his retro espresso machine and toast with his silver toaster, it was like he lived in a home appliances advert. He lit up a cigarette and again and again sighed: 'Ja, ja, Shvees life . . .'

I already knew this 'ah yes, Swiss life' of theirs. They were quite proud of it after all: waking up at seven after two hours of sleep with their 'But I have my duties. Orderliness didn't happen all on its own, you know! Why, of course I wake up before daybreak, smoke and drink coffee, take a shit and shave, and head out to sit in front of a computer in a steel-and-glass office building for eight hours!'

Then he took me in his Toyota into the centre, stuffed a sizeable wad of hundred-franc notes in my hand, gave me a peck on the cheek and disappeared around the corner. And there I was— yet again—a whore with loads of cash on her, wearing yesterday's clothes stinking of last night's cigarettes, beer, perfumes and sex. I'd landed in the centre at seven thirty, when even the cafes were still closed, the shop windows shuttered, and an Asian woman was covering every inch of the U-Bahn station with a floor polisher. So I went to the train station for coffee, lit up a cigarette with matches from Carrousel (a naked man on the matchbook, arms shackled over his head) and started dozing off.

DIANKA

And so Dianka found herself in the home of a cultivated gentleman who was very tidy, very well behaved. And very far away from the real Zurich, but an easy connection with the S-Bahn. No baggage, unless you count her sixteen years.

Witikon looked like a barracks. Identical rows of two-storey red-brick houses. Andrei and the doctor took her there in their car. They drank coffee and sped away. After they left, Dianka went to her room, which was furnished in an old-fashioned style (the bed piled high with pillows and an eiderdown, the night table covered with a crocheted doily), but it was all her own, after all that time on the streets, when the only time she was ever alone was in toilet stalls. She looked at herself in the mirror and made a dumb face, then went to the window and looked out at the row of indistinguishable houses across the street.

She fell onto the pile of cushions that smelt of old people and started thinking. How would she, fucked-up little slut that she was, ever get back here at five, seven o'clock in the morning, after seven guys, stinking of seven different brands of cigarettes, seven different kinds of alcohol and seven incompatible perfumes? All without waking up Grandpa? Because though he probably knew what his new boarder did for a living, was he aware of what that meant in practice? But what if she wasn't the first one? What if he was a serial murderer whom Andrei and the doctor supplied with boys, and later the doctor, Hans Ludwig, used their organs in his hospital, their collagen in his exclusive plastic-surgery clinic for doddering cougars from Zürichberg? It did after all seem a little shady that neither Andrei nor Grandpa wanted anything for the accommodations, not even a blow job, although she would have obliged, one hundred per cent; Dianka certainly knew how to return a favour. She gazed at the ceiling decorated with folksy Swiss flowers and at the painted dishes hung on the wall with their alpine scenes—a shepherd smoking a pipe, sheep with bells—and she listened to the noises of the flat. She could hear every step her host took. He was moving something. He's lit the gas boiler. Singing now. Oh crap, he's on his way here!

A knock on the door. It opened. And Grandpa appeared, buck naked. No underwear. No socks. His shrivelled willy wreathed with silver pubes. Well there you have it, thought Dianka. But no. He asked her in English (because somewhere back in Vienna Dianka had got the reputation of speaking English, which wasn't exactly true, although it was less of a lie than if people had thought she spoke German), if she had anything against him walking around the flat in his birthday suit, as he'd grown accustomed to doing over the years, taking off all his clothes the minute he got home, 'alle Klamotten weg'. He cooked in the buff, relaxed in the buff ... And would Dianka mind going with him for a moment to his room, there was something he wanted to show her ... He'd worked his whole life for the Swiss Federal Railways and he was fascinated by trains, their punctuality, their solidness ... Swiss rail in general. He turned his white arse to Dianka and walked down the hall to one of the rooms and she followed.

The entire room was entirely taken up with a scale model of Switzerland, replete with meticulously placed mountains and hills and tunnels and their location, Witikon, marked with a flag. And just as the Earth seen from a bird's eye view looks less sloppy than it does from the ground, this model Switzerland was even more neat and orderly than the real thing. Neat and orderly lawns lined the train tracks, and miniature Christmas trees stood perfectly spaced in forests, like soldiers on parade. Perfectly proportioned snow decked the mountain tops, and the towns were assembled of perfectly even rows of houses. And perfect rows of white Swissair aeroplanes stood ready to depart on the runways of Zurich-Kloten Airport. How did a grandpa who had only ever worked for the railway have money for things like this? Dianka wondered. It wasn't the first time she'd been surprised to learn that someone worked as a night guard or janitor, etc., yet lived in style. In Eastern Europe those professions barely earned you a living wage.

Dianka just stood in the doorway with the same look on her face that simple people get when they encounter something new and incomprehensible and don't know whether to feel awe or horror or break out in laughter. Meanwhile Grandpa was setting a few of the railway cars in motion, pushing different buttons on a special control panel, and delivering his great monologue in honour of orderliness, constancy, punctuality, clocks and of course the Swiss Federal Railways.

Dianka was bored senseless by Grandpa's use of so many difficult English words (anything more difficult than 'come here, I show you something' made her feel dizzy). She looked at the pointy, fastidiously gilded steeples of the Protestant churches to which no one went and thought about how she needed to eat something and get ready for the night. She had seen a Migros shop not far from here—she would have to go do some shopping there. If Dianka didn't watch out she might end up eating only candy, a whole box of Rafaello, for instance, or whipped cream directly from the spray can, or even condensed milk from the tube, which looked like toothpaste.

Dianka was still young enough that eating only junk food had no effect on her weight. She was Wonder Woman, despite being sixteen. Smoking didn't harm her, nor did it turn her teeth yellow, her armpits didn't sweat, and she could go without sleeping for weeks, waiting for Trashmaster . . . The 'Dianka' is a new model. Performance: eight orgasms per day, or night rather. Each of them less spectacular than the one before and increasingly simulated. Now she'll be throwing junk food into her basket at Migros, miniature bottles of schnaps, cigarettes, candy, then head out to shag until dawn. And Grandpa can get on one of his little trains and disappear beyond the horizon—a horizon that doesn't exist in Switzerland, obscured as it is by mountains or houses, which is why the Swiss are said to lack perspective.

Against the backdrop of such thought, Grandpa was informing an empty room that it simply wasn't true Switzerland hadn't suffered during the war, for two Swiss buildings were hit by bombs and until now it had proven impossible to reconstruct them exactly as they had been before the bombing, but the family still got an annuity and some other handouts, although it was already a generation ago.

The lecturer was naked, coated with silver hair, but with a head as bald as a baby's bottom. Dianka looked at his grey bush with the pink prick sticking out from the middle.

'And,' he continued, 'it wasn't just two buildings that were bombed. Those two bombs threw the entire ecology of Switzerland out of whack, an ecology we've been constructing systematically since the time of Wilhelm Tell. Our sense of order too, our belief that if something or someone takes a stand then that someone or something will stand, will withstand, or stand with. Wilhelm Tell's arrow landed in the very centre of the apple and thus came to symbolize Swiss precision, Swiss timepieces and Swiss trains, which are always punctual . . .'

But that was all in the past, now Switzerland had gone to the dogs. Trains sometimes arrived a full minute late, inflation had reached two and a half per cent, unemployment was at two percent, and what did that remind Dianka of? The franc was tumbling, Swiss firms were being bought up by multinational concerns, often—begging your pardon—by the Chinese . . . These corporations were so busy buying one another up they sometimes ended up buying the same company twice by mistake . . . For example, Nestlé bought up Milka, Milka bought Dr Oetker, Dr Oetker acquired some mineral-water brand, then Nestlé suddenly purchased the same mineral-water company although it actually already owned it.

And all of this was the fault of the foreigners and the drug addicts. At this, Grandpa stared piercingly at Dianka so she would have no doubt who she was. A foreigner. The biggest mistake Switzerland ever made was opening its doors to the world! Letting in random strangers! How easy they'd made it to come into the country now! (Here Dianka could have told him about how the Swiss were supposed to stamp her passport at the border with the date of entry and that theoretically she would be able to stay three months from that date. But since they never gave her a stamp—and, as other boys had cheerfully informed her, almost never do—if she were to be stopped by a police officer it would be impossible to prove when she had arrived—maybe yesterday? And even if they did stamp the passports, the boys knew hundreds of other ways of dealing with the problem, and the Swiss were so thick they believed everything.)

It's all well and good when they're white! But unfortunately we've become a sanctuary for all the criminals, I mean, you must be a criminal to want to be a refugee and not love your own country. Grandpa clearly didn't realize that he too could travel to another country, Liechtenstein say, and request asylum there. But he'd probably die of shame! And what did it lead to? Of course: all those junkies around Platzspitz and Kornhausbrücke! Of course: the pollution in the waters of Lake Zurich! They'd even had to start raising a certain breed of fish there, one especially sensitive to pollution, so they could keep track of their health and in that way monitor the water's purity.

It dawned on Dianka that Eleven-Inch had set her up. But she had a bit of money and could go stay in a hotel for now. In any case, everyone in Zurich had money. When the lecture was finally over and the trains had all returned to their depot, or whatever a flophouse for trains is called, Dianka got her soap and shampoo and went to take a bath. Luckily Grandpa had a bathtub. She stuck the stopper in, opened the tap and let the warm water run into the tub. The guy immediately started knocking on the door— probably baths weren't allowed, only showers, because baths were expensive: 'You mast safe ze vater!' Poor Dianka had heard this business about saving water more times than she could shake a stick at, but she never understood it; in Bratislava, you paid a token amount for water and no one ever checked the meter, so essentially water was free. She switched the water flow to shower and pretended to be showering, standing up, but then she let the shower head fall into the water so she could hear what Grandpa was up to. How nice it would to immerse herself completely in the warm water! She dove in. When she surfaced, naked Grandpa was standing over her with a troubled look on his face, turning off the water. She had forgotten to close the tap . . . 'Vater ist ferry ixpinsif in Shveetserland.'

'What the fuck isn't expensive here?' Dianka asked in Slovak, because she'd already had enough of him. She dried her hair, went to Migros, got herself some candy (although all they had was Protestant candy, no Rafaello, just sugar-free shit for fasting on), returned to the house, and there a very grumpy Grandpa said to her 'Komm hier' and pointed at the bathtub. So what? What's your point? But Dianka was able to make out from Grandpa's pantomime that she was supposed to clean the bathtub after she used it. But where is it dirty, she wanted to know, which spot?

Dianka Spencer, Princess of Wales, was standing in her pensioner-scented room before an old-fashioned grandmotherly mirror. She was wearing nothing but the G-string she'd bought the day before, but the way it rode up her crack it chafed her arse cheeks, although it cost a fortune (it was a Calvin Klein). It looked great on her, but . . . She tugged on a pair of jeans, but before zipping up she stuffed a fistful of socks into the crotch—there's your 'sock sex' for you! There probably wasn't a single hustler in the whole Germanophone bloc who didn't stuff his fly with socks or newspapers; but the whole trick depended on expertly removing it just before sex, under the pretence, for example, of going to the bathroom to douche or whatever. The worst was with the vintage car buffs out in the fields or the woods, but even then you could always go off to have a whizz. Guys were always drunk and saw the world through the prism of their own imagination. Then Dianka scrubbed her teeth in the bathroom and styled her hair with Wella SP, which was the best, professional-grade, she'd got it from a stylist at the station. She smelt great and she looked great too. Then she applied foundation to her face, covering all the pimples on her nose, that little bitty cute button nose of hers—she was cuteness personified! She sprayed some of Grandpa's Gucci eau de toilette under her arms. That's what was so great about this country, that everyone could afford everything. She smeared lip balm on her lips to keep them from cracking and the crud from building up in the corners of her mouth. Then she put on her jeans jacket.

She asked Grandpa what time the S-Bahn went into Zurich . . . She forgot that trains, the punctuality of trains and train schedules were his thing. A lot of gibberish followed, about how the 307 had recently started leaving from a different platform, which was causing a small uproar . . . How he would take the 314 . . . Aha, so basically they run all the time, Dianka thought and ran out. From the vending machines on the platform she bought a large Snickers, a coffee and a pack of Marlboro Lights (Grandpa didn't allow smoking!). She puffed away blissfully until she was lightheaded and the flavour of the smoke mingled in her mouth with the minty toothpaste and sweet caramel. The air smelt of spring and was as clean and fresh as was possible only in the Swiss countryside.

The S-Bahn pulled in noiselessly and stopped in silence at the platform. The clock with Swiss Federal Railways logo said 3:14. There was only one other passenger inside, an African who smelt of vanilla. Dianka was happy again. She was ready to get her brains fucked out tonight.

THE GUY FROM THE HOTEL ZURICH

Meanwhile, after Dianka went off with the Romanian to that codger in Witikon, I ended up without a place for the night. I sat at the bar, it was three in the morning, I had three rounds behind me and I was repeating to myself the sacred rules, what to do when you need to find a place to sleep. Here, the love story was the way to go. No money. You needed to find someone young and nice, someone who'd been following you with his eyes the whole night, then make your move. The problem, however, was that Swiss men were all unbelievable nudniks: 'Morgen arbeiten, zat's Shvees life.' But this was how I happened on one of the best—as it later turned out—customers in all of Zurich, a Swiss counterpart to my Viennese benefactor Mario Ludwig (may he rest with the angels). With some guys you can tell right away they're rich even if they don't have an ounce of gold on them. Maybe it's the suntan in the middle of winter, maybe it's the appetite in their eyes, something animal-like, almost beetle-like, the handlebar moustache or the self-confidence, what do I know . . . I'd tried more than once to figure it out. Just the sight of a tall forty-year-old with receding hairline, piercing eyes and arrogance, getting soused on champagne at the corner of the bar, was enough to make all my red lights and sirens go off at once. Get him! But here too you had to follow the rules. Don't look at him. Turn your better side towards him and stand so he can see the bulge in the crotch of your jeans (enhanced with socks of course). Let him notice you and fight for you. Hard won is doubly dear, and it tastes better too. Beyond that we have to be psychologists the minute we start talking to one of these chumps. Every one of them, as soon as he's decided he's going to pay for it, to agree to be the customer, must first hold his own looks in low esteem. He must have a defect, whether real or imagined. He's either too old or too skinny or too fat, too hunch-backed or too crippled, etc., to be able to get sex for free. Or else he's just generally repellent. You have exactly one minute, not one second more, to figure out a particular case, to pin down his neu-rosis. You have to know from the very beginning why he doesn't like himself, because you'll soon have to activate the difficult art of psychology and start telling the sucker what he wants to hear. Direct mention of his shortcomings, however, is to be avoided, so if the conversation turns to the topic of age, for example, then triv-ialize it and say things like 'Getting old is like climbing a moun-tain, you get a little out of breath, but the view is much better', 'I just like older men', 'old but mature always trumps young and immature . . .', etc. Keep in mind that despite this defect—and often it's a whole rat's nest of defects (too skinny + too old + bald + generally repellent + bleary eyed + drooling + incontinent [traces of urine and stool in his pants] + bad breath + impotent + mentally ill), he must have at least one, even minor, virtue. This is your little light in the tunnel. You have to cling to it and for a moment even fall in love with the cretin. The fact that eye colour doesn't change with age can come in handy; you can always tell him he has beau-tiful eyes. And if that doesn't work, because his eyes are too blood-shot for you to determine the colour, you can always praise his fashion sense or his brand of cigarettes or whatever. There are no customers without virtues. Even the fact that he's about to pay you a lot of money is an enormous virtue. You have to convince yourself that you adore him, value him and respect him. Remember that the guy there in front of you is frightened, ashamed of his looks, knows he looks even worse next to you, and may be embarrassed that he can't get it up or that he likes to be slapped. Laugh if you want, but all kinds of people have things they're ashamed of, and phobias . . . You're his therapist and you need to make sure that while talking with you he feels happier and increasingly sure of himself—but not so sure that he starts thinking he won't have to pay! So go ahead, treat him like he's Superman, look enviously at his disgusting belly, but if he gets the idea he won't be paying, you need to politely but firmly disabuse him of it. 'I'm so sorry, I really like you a lot, but unfortunately this is my job, I too need to pay my bills, I can't help it, that's the way of this wicked world . . . Ja, ja, Shvees life, arbeiten. . .', and so on . . .

Now let's make the shift from theory to practice. From under my ersatz eyelashes—truly a secret weapon in this line of work and in the darkness of Carrousel impossible to tell from the real thing—I espy a tall gent at the bar and am unable to tell whether he is watching me back. He's not. He's chatting with our moustachioed bartender Mario. There's still a chance of him buying me a drink, though, because a moment ago he was looking positively enraptured. They keep chatting, Mario comes over and asks me what I want, the gentleman at the other end of the bar, etc. I act surprised, as if startled out of my reverie. Who? What? Oh, how lovely! A perfect Krystyna Janda. I ask for something modest, coffee with a shot of vodka, which doesn't mean it's cheap. I want him to think I'm sober, that I won't pass out on him, although in reality I'm three sheets to the wind, having started my bender at the sauna and not intending to end it any time soon, but he doesn't need to know that. I light up a cigarette and follow Mario's eyes . . . I cast the sucker a glance charged with a few different messages: openness to immediately start negotiating, indifference, a trace of debauchery, ennui, so he won't think I'm already infatuated. I pull out the tablet and stylus I use for my various calculations and start counting up my francs, drawing penises, and writing out what to milk him for: a whole night . . . five, no . . . four thousand? But what if he laughs in my face? Who to ask for advice? I ask this one beautiful Pole who lives with his parents in Germany, right on the border with Switzerland, and often comes for a couple of nights to earn some pocket money. He tells me eight thousand is nothing and I shouldn't go lower. The dude will be sucking my dick all night, he'll be drunk, and he'll end up driving drunk with me in tow, zigzagging back to Hotel Zurich. In the morning he'll be massively hungover so I need to grab that eight grand and bounce. He's from Bern, on a business trip, he always gets completely zonked, and tomorrow he'll have to be at the bank; he's a banker.

Bank—one of my favourite words.

I went to the toilet to look at myself, pulled out my eyeliner and concealer from my Louis Vuitton bum bag, quickly fixed myself up, hair, fragrance, mouth, and all the while I was wondering what his weak point might be. Why was he paying for it? He wasn't hot, but he wasn't a total dog either. He wasn't young, but he wasn't old. Your typical emotionless English type, corporate, shaved pubes and razor burn, reeking of dirty money. His eyes protruded a little too much, his hairline receded a bit too far. He would later prove to be one of those rare customers who pay for sex simply because they're used to paying for everything, because they love to spend, because they're bankers and it's all about money for them, because they don't want to wait for someone to like them for something other than money (which might take forever) . . . The guy oozed self-confidence though. He was the White Pig type.* I knew this type, they were always condescending to the hustlers; if you didn't agree to something they'd right away ask in their iciest voice: 'Do you vant to get paid?'

The slow chords of another pop classic, Ritchie Valens's 'Donna', were playing on the sound system when I finally found myself in his orbit. I was walking towards the door as if I were about to leave, grabbing a gay party flyer from the stand, when he pulled me to him by the arm, and that was that. He smelt of cigars, perfume and alcohol, and he was wearing a Patek Philippe. Identifying the expensive brands of watches was the first thing every escort had to learn. The rabble all think it has to be a Rolex but that's not true, Rolexes are considered low-class. The best brands are Blancpain, Louis Moinet Magistralis, Hublot, Chopard, Patek, Vacheron Constantin—some of which go for five million dollars! The middle class wear Rado, Maurice Lacroix, TAG Heuer (though it depends on the model, as these can be quite expensive as well), Piaget (idem). The Swiss are so decadent, you might meet a guy with a Rado on his wrist who turns out to be a janitor in some tenement. Hublots aren't worth shelling out a few million for. Rolexes can be deceiving too; first, they're often counterfeit, and second, every other hustler wears one (an authentic one) and

---

* The WASP: White Anglo-Saxon Protestant. One hundred percent of Swiss customers. The guys with the Montblanc portemonnaies, white button-downs and gluten-intolerant dogs. Often to be found congregating in airport duty-free shops . . .

third, the cheapest ones are as much as an expensive Omega, so really, big deal. I myself own a Rolex Submariner. In any case, this guy had on a Patek Philippe, and Patek is a luxury very few can afford. Rolex for the rabble, Patek for the rich.

I figured as he was accustomed to the art of negotiation he would appreciate my being direct. In the coating of frost on his mug of beer I drew a number eight with my finger, and he drew a heart around it with his. I knew at this point we would no longer need to talk about money. His beautiful grey suit, his Patek, his manicured fingers—now I was the one with the neurosis! After five minutes of conversation I understood that the guy was fairly shallow, a player who'd escaped on a business trip, and that I'd just need to entertain him, be silly, stick out my tongue, laugh when he farted or belched . . . After an hour he suggested we go to another bar, paid my tab (which was long as a snake), put on his elegant overcoat and stood on the street. It was raining, windy. Now, well in his cups as he was, he walked down Zähringerstrasse, you could see how hammered he was, but ssshhh! Quiet! Let's go! *Richtung*: Odeon!

> Oh show us ze vay to the next vhisky bar,
> Oh don't ask vhy, oh don't ask vhy . . .
> Oh vee must find ze next vhisky bar,
> Cos if vee don't find ze next vhisky bar
> I tell you vee must die,
> I tell you vee must die,
> I tell you, I tell you, I tell you vee must to die!

So we began our tour of the elegant pubs of Zurich, ordering champagne in silver buckets, around five in the morning a grotty troupe of transvestites (a fat compère dressed like a baby's pacifier attached herself to me, dragged me up on stage and made me sing karaoke 'Strangers in the Night', while my guy was laughing himself to tears in the audience) . . . Finally we arrived at Hotel Zurich. Every city has a hotel like it. In my hometown of Konin there's a Hotel Konin, and in Zurich naturally there's a Hotel Zurich, concrete blocks both of them, but that's where the similarity ends. By the time we were shagging, I already knew a few things about him.

1. He was really into Switzerland. Everything Swiss was good, everything else was shit, and although I was with him, he treated me no differently than if I'd been shining his shoes.

2. If he was partial to the Swiss multivitamin Supradyn, for example, you weren't allowed to say that some other vitamin was better. If he brushed his teeth with the Swiss toothpaste Elmex, that's what you used too. If he moisturized with La Prairie, you did too, like it or not.

3. His view of the rest of world (aside from the wealthy Swiss) was one of tolerance, he agreed that other people had a right to live and not end up in gas chambers. The rest of the world was the target market for his bank, after all. You could push subprime loans on those people and pull the noose of debt ever tighter around their necks.

4. He was very likely a racist and fascist as well, and Poles in his mind were worth only slightly more than Gypsies, Romanians, Africans, Chechens, Russians, etc.

5. He hired escorts for the whole night but he didn't actually get off on sex, just the situation of him (the better, richer one) being the customer and me, the (lower-status) escort, serving him.

6. He was completely impotent in bed, but also completely sure
   of himself and conceited. More than his cock it was his ego
   that needed stroking.

And in reality he didn't want sex, he wanted someone to emotionally shine his shoes. I decided to make the best of the situation
and make the psychological metaphor literal. I offered to shine
his shoes. He was ecstatic. The hotel shoe polish and brush were
in the cupboard. He put on his bespoke shoes and I shined them
in the hallway right up to his ankle, satisfied I'd figured him out
and he wouldn't be weaseling his way out of paying with the 'but
I wasn't serviced' argument. He stood over me, entirely naked
except for his socks and the elegant shoes, and I was so absorbed
in cleaning them I forgot about the world. I was even getting a
little turned on when something hot and wet landed on my cheek
and ... Yes! I didn't look up, I didn't need to. There he was, naked,
cigarette dangling from his lips, peeing on me, trying to keep it
from splashing on his shoes. Yes, uh huh, do it, pee on me, spit on
me. I already extracted everything there was to extract from you ...
Your superiority, your desire to humiliate ... It's true: people very
rarely pay only for sex.

Then he told me to lick it, and when I hesitated I heard the
sacramental words:

'Do you vant to get paid?'

CAFE WÜHRE

But maybe it's not actually sex that people pay for? Maybe what I really am is a kind of midwife of their true identities, which only come out of them when they're drunk and with someone they're paying for, someone who isn't threatening? Had I unwittingly discovered the blueprint for becoming the world's best hooker? That's what I was thinking, drinking my fancy coffee on the terrace of Cafe Wühre (which of course the boys all called 'Cafe Whore'). After yesterday's rain the weather was beautiful and the waters of the Limmat glittered in the sun. The coffee was superb, creamy, with a heart drawn in the foam, and it came with a chocolate and creamer in a little tub. No doubt people here too were serious collectors of those foil coffee creamer lids. I carefully peeled off mine, which showed Alpine figures in folk costumes. Maybe I'd start collecting them too? Maybe I'd even become Swiss one day? In the meantime I'd started saving the foil lids and when I met a collector I'd show them to him, and if he didn't have one that I had I'd sell it to him.

I had a slight hangover so I took out my sunglasses. I had eight thousand francs in my pocket along with a lot of other money I'd made earlier. I wondered how Dianka was getting on with that grandpa out in Witikon. Oh right, I needed to figure out where I was staying! For tonight and tomorrow I'd actually got a room in the luxurious Central Plaza so I'd be close to work, but I'd have to find someone to milk . . . But as it was only eleven in the morning, for the moment that wasn't an option. I wouldn't be able to get into the hotel room until one. The Predigerhof opened at two, which was an absolutely ideal place to look for accommodations. It drew mostly ageing, vinegary queens who would never ever pay for sex (otherwise they'd have been at Carrousel) but were ready to fall in love with the first comer and sign over their estate to him. This was what the terse write-up in the *Spartacus* guide was getting at: 'Nice music, nice people, mainly older clientele.'

So once again I was killing time in the city, but this time I had money, so I went shopping. I sprayed fragrances on my wrists, browsed for clothes, went into a restaurant and ate all kinds of delicious treats, went to a tanning salon, bought new Calvin Klein underwear . . . Zurich, having showered in the rain, was drowning in sunlight now. Everywhere everything was old, antique, and there were plaques with information about how expensive and important everything was: in this church here, Chagall himself made the stained-glass windows for which he got a tidy sum of moolah for his old age. Next door is Safran, the oldest restaurant in Europe, where in the Middle Ages merchants came to trade saffron. And next to it is the even older Restaurant zum Stock. I'd have to con some loaded customer into taking me here someday for dinner. Here lived Lenin, and here Marx—having also apparently taken a liking to this capitalist cesspit . . . Here the ladies come to shop for colourful Frey Wille bangles for a thousand francs . . . And right next door the junkies are wading in a hell of shit, blood and McDonald's packaging, indifferently watching the businessmen hurrying past in their hand-cobbled shoes.

It disgusted me. I went to the Central Plaza and threw my shopping in the suite, drew a bubble bath in the tub, and began my spa day. Later, in my white frotté bathrobe, which contrasted nicely with my solarium-tanned body, I sat in the lounger on the balcony, with a coffee and cigarette, and turned my face to the sun. Down below was one large traffic jam, car horns blaring . . .

THE ESCAPE

I put my feet up on the other chair and it occurred to me I really was living my best life. If I were still in Konin now, having to go to school—and just think of the ones who were still there, who hadn't run away from home to find their 'real life', they were still going to school day in and day out, eating burnt milk soup in the cafeteria, overwhelmed by the pong of armpits in gym class, being indoctrinated with Polish nationalist ideology, waking up in the dark at six and still having to cram for a quiz, abasing themselves before their parents and teachers, and if they could only see me now . . . Fuck, but things are good! Look who's wearing a Rolex! Look who spent the night on the town with a millionaire drinking overpriced champagne and smoking real Cohiba Cuban cigars! At home I always felt I deserved more than Konin. I knew the world I saw on *Dynasty* was out there, somewhere, and Konin was just some shitty, second-rate knock-off world. I was so distracted seeking out this better world I didn't have time to study and always got shitty marks, my parents would scream at me, and everything came apart at the seams, me with my head in the clouds the whole time.

I decided to run away. I just happened to see an advert for a winter-break school trip to Vienna organized by something called Taizé. They were some kind of religious thing. I said goodbye to my parents for a few days but I knew I'd probably never see them again. Later, in the bus, I found a bar of chocolate in my bag, which Mama must have slipped in there for me. Suddenly I was so overcome with remorse I wanted to stop the bus and go back, I would've walked! Along with the sandwiches and chocolate I found fifty schillings in there. And there I was hurting her like that?

But it was too late! I'd been preparing for the trip for three weeks. For three weeks I'd painstakingly covered all of my tracks in Poland, so the person I was would cease to exist. No photographs of me that my parents could give to the police to aid in a search. I went out to our garden carrying bags of documents, certificates, pictures from elementary school and every other period of my life . . . I set it all on fire. I burnt my school ID card, kept only my passport. Cheerfully I incinerated my current school notebooks in which only yesterday I'd had to write down my homework assignments. It was all meaningless now! I felt purified, as if I'd just buried myself. The fire consumed my poems, stories, diaries— everything ever written by that person was now disappearing along with the smoke. I watched the flames licking my face on my school ID, tentatively at first, then suddenly the face warped into a grimace and the photograph buckled then folded in half. I threw other, less personal things into the fire as well, although I felt even more attached to them: cassette tapes, my rucksack, my pillow . . . I felt weightless. When I got home my parents' nagging ('Have you done your homework? You have a physics exam tomorrow, did you study?') was already heartbreakingly irrelevant. I was already dead. I had walked out the door and never come back. I disappeared, my parents went looking for me, placed announcements in the newspapers, made appeals on television, but I was long gone, lying at the bottom of a manhole, grinning blissfully . . . Those stories of people who left home and never returned had always fascinated me—no activity on their bank accounts, no telephone calls, as if they'd crossed over to the other side of a mirror, or walked into a blank wall and are living there still.

All night long the winter-camp Christians on the bus played guitar and sang Christian rock hits.

'And I believe in youuuuuuuuuuu . . .'

I was already in my hooker clothes, too-tight cowboy boots, G-string riding up my arse, and here came some twat without any make-up on, wearing a hat with a pompom on it, handing out holy cards. I took one, since if you congregate with the crows you need to croak like one too. But as soon as Pompom moved on, I knocked back one of those baby whiskies and tried to cruise in the darkness of the bus. At rest stops I was the only one smoking, stomping out the cigarette butts with my boots. The others were praying and singing . . . In the toilets I'd go straight to the urinals to peek at the others, wasted as I was, and the Christian youth were so naive, they didn't even think to block my view.

I felt the absurdity of it and laughed to think these holy rollers were transporting me to my new life as a harlot in a bus fuelled by holy water! I had prepared everything exactly. I recommended an acquaintance of mine, a specialist in Viennese prostitution, to be the chaperone of our group, because too few parents were available. He was an old paedophile and pimp who used to procure Polish boys in the West and exact a criminally high commission, for which he will burn eternally in hell. His name was Zbigniew and was he ever. For the past month he'd been showing me various guidebooks and gay maps of Vienna, pictures of boys in his album, unfolding an image of a life with millionaires and their convertibles, which was exactly the kind of life I considered authentic.

This took place in 'his room', because although he was in his forties he lived with his mother in an enormous flat in an old pre-war building. He had something boyish about him and this he used to lure other boys. His room looked exactly as a boy's room would look if he never stopped being a boy, never grew up . . . The room of a paedophile . . . The room revealed itself gradually. There were a lot of model aeroplanes in it, more than any boy could possibly have made while he was growing up. On the walls were posters for karate films. From floor to ceiling, stacks of music CDs and film DVDs. His closet—and here, take note—was filled from floor to ceiling with a pathologically methodical installation of empty German and Austrian beer cans and other colourful trash.

He could easily have been a serial murderer. In any case, the fact that those Taizé folks could take one look at his degenerate face—a face wasted by stage-four syphilis, blackened teeth sticking out in all directions—and not realize what he was about, that was symptomatic of something . . .

I was also able to get a spot on our trip for another young queen, someone Zbigniew had taken in right off the street, from the park, a runaway from juvie who'd been roaming wild through the cities of Poland, surviving by hooking and thieving. An absolute criminal, with pinched eyebrows and scars, young but already completely fucked up, with cracked lips, warts, pockmarks, teeth that had never been brushed. They called her Cemetery Mary at the train station in Konin, but I don't want to get into why. It would come out later anyway. And that flaming queen on the run from her detention centre or even jail—who knew?—was swishing up and down the middle of the bus handing out holy cards, the halo turned on over her head, which they'd shaved in prison for fear of lice. She was cross-eyed too, so she completely fit in with all those souls crying out as one. I nudged Zbigniew, he nudged me back. With her halo running at full blast, she was coming towards us with those holy cards, with prayers and a rosary, and when she stopped next to us, she quickly made a face that only we could see, sticking out her tongue lasciviously and rolling her eyes back, so it was unclear if her rapture was beatific or perverse. So I'd joined my forces of evil to their holy team, and if the nuns' eyesight hadn't been so impaired that they had to wear glasses as thick as Coke bottles, they would have noticed right away that something was off. But they were just surprised that such a nice boy kept going out to smoke cigarettes at the rest stops.

It was because of Cemetery Mary that Zbigniew and I were both bundles of nerves, first at the Czech border and then at the Austrian, because that idiot let us know only when we were all in the bus that, being a fugitive from jail and all, she didn't have a passport. They'd confiscated all her documents when she was sent down. And she'd never had a passport made anyway, she'd never been abroad. They would catch her at the border, no doubt there'd be a search and we'd be found out! But Cemetery Mary reckoned there'd be so many of these holy coaches full of 'Catholic youth' on their way to the Taizé youth camp in Vienna that they wouldn't even check and she'd manage to slip out of Poland without anyone noticing. And she was right. Not a single border guard or customs agent entered our bus at either of the borders.

The Taizé people were some kind of awful cult, completely delusional, Catholic jihad, but my plan was to escape as soon as we arrived, together with Zbigniew and Cemetery Mary. Completely sleep-deprived and dishevelled, we arrived at a huge car park in Vienna where literally dozens of other church groups were already parked, and all of them (ninety per cent of them females wearing headbands in addition to the nuns), were singing their religious campfire songs despite travelling all night without sleep and having only a crappy mattress on the floor in some hall or church to look forward to.

'Girls,' I said, 'These are not our people. Let's get the hell out.'

And that's the last they saw of us. There was no saving us, no matter how many masses and Bible study groups we went to. We tossed our holy cards in a brightly coloured rubbish bin with an advert for some tabloid on it. Then Zbigniew took us to the Karlsplatz-Oper U-Bahn station, where various elderly punters and young boys were circling around, sitting in a glassed-in cafe (the Aquarium), watching through the windows to see who was going into the conveniences, drinking shots. And there I was, already drinking coffee and wine, smoking cigarettes, getting drunk before noon after a night without sleep, my drinks getting paid for by some old dude with diamond rings on every finger and grey remnants of hair pasted to his scalp, and already we were having to go to some 'Polish friend' of Zbigniew's where we would sleep . . . The friend was also named Zbigniew (evidently every Pole in the West was named Zbigniew . . .). Well, there was something about this other Pole that rubbed me the wrong way. This was supposed to be the big wide world, after all, but his place was a dump, some kind of homeless shelter, vodka bottles, potted-meat tins used for ashtrays, scorched pots and pans, chronic syphilis— overall the decor was very east of Eden. Only Cemetery Mary felt at home here, it being her natural ecosystem. The other Zbigniew was fat and sat around wearing only his skivvies and a (formerly) white tank top, and I felt like I was still in Poland, only worse. So we took a nap (on the floor!), splashed some cold water on ourselves (they'd shut off the gas in that flophouse long before so the boiler didn't work), and headed out into the Vienna night. Everything we did happened in the U-Bahn stations, in tunnels and subterranean walkways, dead and abandoned subway lines, underground cafes, underground toilets that smelt like community gardens in Poland, lilacs and roses. There were pavements up above us, the people, tables and restaurants were all above us.

And so Zbigniew began showing me around the subterranean, sleazy world of Vienna sex work, all of it centred around the toilets. Cruising grandpas, hookers, deviants with lust in their bleary eyes, you only had to touch them and you were sure to catch a fungus.

What can I do? I thought. As long as I didn't have money of my own, I wouldn't be able to get away from Zbigniew and find higher-quality trade.

I said earlier that my first customer in Vienna was Mario Ludwig, our beloved Maria Louisa, but I was lying.

It's probably best if you all take everything I say with a grain of salt. It's just how I am. For example, I always introduced myself to customers with different names, I'd tell them I came from different countries and make up different stories of my life. Most of the time it was that my entire family was in prison in Berlin, Mama for theft and prostitution, Papa for murder, and that my boyfriend Christophe and I went to London and for many years lived happily together in Chelsea (here I hesitated a little because I wasn't sure if the neighbourhood was in London or New York, but I liked the name, so I went with it). But all of a sudden my life changed forever: Christophe, on his way back from America, died at sea / in a plane crash (a detail I lifted from an Édith Piaf song). And now, here I was, in Vienna . . . What a life . . . In reality, I had a boyfriend in Poland, Krzysztof, who was a complete dick and dumped me. So I really needed people to be nice to me. But since no one felt sorry for me (precisely because he'd thrown me out), I had to (not without a certain pleasure) destroy him. Or else: there was an aeroplane crash, or a maritime disaster, or else he committed suicide by turning on all the cooker knobs in our kitchen (in Chelsea) and taking sleeping pills at the same time, since he couldn't live with himself after treating me that way. Or, when I was really pushing the gallows humour, I would say he'd eaten a poisonous mushroom and they found his body only a week afterwards, we had decided not to see each other and he'd ingested that crap out of heartbreak. When they broke into his flat, his body was entirely decomposed, green, bloated with gas, a greyish bit of the white mushroom was sticking out of his mouth and the discoloured rest of it lay beside his arm . . . Killing off this person from my past seemed like it would never end. Staph infection, necrosis due to a botched amputation, rectal cancer, dental angina with complications, organic meningitis resulting from despair over my leaving him (an illness that often served as emotional motivation in French and Russian novels of the nineteenth century), although it was he who left me . . . The later it was in the night and the tipsier I got, the more inventive I became, as if the beer were lubricating my imagination. My stories gave rise to a kind of palimpsest of old memories, like Babcia's story about Nel getting bit by a tsetse fly in *In Desert and Wilderness*. The incident probably didn't even happen in the book, since my grandmother liked to make everything more dramatic, knowing how much I enjoyed drama. Nel started having spasms and swelled up, grey spots appearing on her face (or maybe that was Prince Kirkor?), and the only remedy—quinine—in the nonexistent pharmacy there in the desert was available only by prescription. The lady in the white lab coat rolled her eyes and asked for the document, although Staś had dragged Nel with him to prove she was literally dying. I imagined the tsetse fly as a kind of mad person, overweight and iridescent like petrol in a puddle, who once she came to your room wouldn't stop harassing you. Anyway, sometime after three in the morning and my fifth customer, I would break out the *In Desert and Wilderness* version of my life, in which Krzysztof travels to Africa in order to figure out his feelings for me and get over our break-up, and like Christ in the desert he subsists on locusts and hornets, which sting his tongue, and poisonous mushrooms (in the desert)—but all that was as nothing compared with the bite of the tsetse fly! It bit him and he died forever, he disappeared from my life, and now lies covered up by the sand.

Later, the story evolved. I wanted them to feel sorry for me too, without Krzysztof, since their sympathy usually only came when it was time to give a tip. So now I was a precocious child, I painted and wrote, but from a dysfunctional family (as mentioned earlier: everyone behind bars in Berlin), and sex work was my only way to survive—fate and society had twisted my arm. But after an hour with me the more intelligent customers realized I took to sex work like a fish to water and that everything I knew about Chelsea came from Liza Minnelli's songs in *Cabaret*.

Anyway, so I was lying to you about Mario Ludwig, I was ashamed that my actual first customer was such a loser. Of course I milked Mario Ludwig just as much, but that was half a year after I arrived. For now, it was my first day, following a sleepless night spent on a bus full of holy rollers, the taste of exhaustion in my mouth, sand in my eyes, and Cemetery Mary irritating the fuck out of me, wearing that rumpled shopping bag and with that stupid yokel face of hers, when I had put on my best clothes and was looking positively international. We went down to the toilets at Karlsplatz and watched the parade of grandpas who, like Mario Ludwig, couldn't even get it up. My actual first trick was one of those grandpas: stout as a barrel, red face round and flat as a plate, glasses in thick frames that made him look like an owl, wearing a fisherman's cap and a sheepskin coat as big as a tent. Because he translated for the guy in German, fixed the price and procured me in the first place, then made sure after we got back that the trick paid *him*, Zbigniew took seventy per cent! And I had to agree to it because what could I do, the jolly uncle turned out to be a pimp! And there wasn't any champagne flowing, no partying with millionaires on yachts (which would happen later in Zurich), just pulling off grandpa's crusty briefs, yellow in front and brown in the back, and pulling his little pink willy out from its nest of grey pubic hair surrounded by the red rash all over his thighs and belly ... But then I would cheer up and say to myself: 'Einmal ist keinmal', big deal, they're not soap, they're not going to wear away from being used. As it turned out, I wasn't disgusted, and in general I found it pretty undemanding, since I had something of the carer in me, working in a hospice or old people's home, I'm pretty thick-skinned and anyway I'm usually somewhere else entirely in my thoughts. In any case, I certainly wasn't there in rainy Vienna, and not in that scuzzy hourly hotel, and not with that grandpa. Yet again reality, the real reality, was somewhere else, it was always somewhere else.

I figured it would all be like water off a duck's back for me, but some of it must have got under my skin, because otherwise the following situation wouldn't have happened. My next grandpa. Bearded, he looked like an old antiquarian bookseller, which is what I started calling him. Zbigniew did a little sprechen with him in German, like, 'Look at this fresh meat, straight from untouched, environmentally pure Poland, second time he's ever given a blow job, only sixteen years old!' The bookseller took me to an ancient flat, crammed with dusty old furniture, knick-knacks, various collections of bric-a-brac, miniature animals made of glass, a cane with a handle in the shape of a skull . . . He even spoke a little English, and I was on my best behaviour, opening the door for him, exactly like I was some high-class *dame aux camélias* in Paris, and not some basic bitch from the U-Bahn station. I wanted him to give me a tip, something I could hide from Zbigniew, otherwise he'd only give me a few miserable scraps for all my work. Anyway, everything went smoothly, we drank wine, the sex was successful, the bookseller was happy, his eyes were sparkling and you could see he'd be asking for me regularly, maybe even behind Zbigniew's back. He wanted me to stay the whole night. We were lying on his big antique bed, grandpa was reading something about wartime naval vessels, and I was out like a light. Suddenly I felt someone hitting my face, boxing me, like actual punches. More than one boxer even, a jab from the left, a jab from the right! In my nose! I started fighting back, someone was choking me, so I bit their arm, scratched, punched, I was fighting for my life! Full on, either I kill them or they kill me! I remember thinking it was a matter of life or death. When I came to, the grandpa was covering my mouth so his neighbours wouldn't hear my frantic howling, and I had bitten him, hit him, scratched him, I mean I'd been fighting for my life . . . Damaging a grandpa was a serious matter, I would have to apologize, but I saw he wasn't convinced by my apologies, blood had been shed. He'd throw me out on the street now in the middle of the night, and how would I find my way back to that Polish halfway house, to Zbigniew and Cemetery Mary? I tried to have a look at his wounds but he pushed me away, which I could understand . . . He didn't throw me out but he did tell Zbigniew all about it and refused to pay, 'Well, I never!' he said . . .

Meanwhile, the two Zbigniews and Cemetery Mary were joined by another revolting queen from Koło who had a pierced nose that she kept picking. She knocked on the door with the C + M + B written in chalk on it, loaded down with five cartons of Polish Marlboros for trafficking, a mountain of tainted food for the journey, along with pots and pans, because they'd told her back in Koło how expensive everything was here and she could use heated roasting forks at home instead of buying hot dogs in the U-Bahn station, although sometimes they cost as little there as they did in Poland. I of course was having caviar sandwiches in Eduscho cafes in the centre from day one.

The new queen (Damian) had brought some Polish vodka with her, and she and the two Zbigniews immediately embarked on an especially unpleasant alcohol-, cigarettes- and sex-fuelled bender. They drank the vodka warm out of tea glasses with red plastic holders and there was nothing romantic or hip about it. The queen from Koło immediately hit it off with Cemetery Mary and they spent the whole time fucking on a little sofa under a dusty religious icon behind a folding screen, because they didn't have their own room, squealing, and the two moustachioed Zbigniews kept going in to lick and rim them, and then they switched and one Zbigniew started fucking one of them and the other Zbigniew the other. All of it with the drab aesthetic of old Polish porn (*Strictly Private, Spermopoles, Farewell Little Pussy*)—the squalid flat, the appendectomy scars, the pasty white legs and bellies. Anyone who hasn't seen those fledgling productions of the Polish porn industry from the early nineties cannot possibly fathom the depths of sadness and melancholy they convey! They cannot fathom how absolutely drab and grey colour film can be, what wonders footage of Szczecin in the sleet and rain can do for your mood, what it means to get it on in the back of a Polonez! Take *Escapade in Elbląg*, for instance. Under the opening credits we see the inside of a tour bus with a pale skinny bimbo with a long braid and no make-up speaking into a microphone: 'Ladies and gentlemen, we are now arriving in Elbląg'. Strange, rhythmical music on the soundtrack. A group of good-looking people wearing sweaters and earmuffs alight and look at the Temple of Memory in the city park. It's raining. The next scene takes place in the shabbiest flat in the block, probably not even in Elbląg. Sitting on an old sofa: the pasty white tour guide and two anemic dudes in sweaters. You can practically smell the sweat coming out of their armpits. Suddenly the braided bimbo turns to the camera and speaks her obviously memorized lines, with the unnatural diction of a poem learnt by heart: 'Now I will do a hardcore sex scene with these two men.'

First man: 'Hi. I'm Rafał and I like motorcycles.'

Second man: 'Hey, Rysiek here. I'm into scooters.'

Then the three begin mechanically pulling off their sweat-soaked sweaters and jeans and folding them with the kind of deliberate care poor people take with their possessions . . . It's a little reminiscent of getting undressed at the doctor's office. Now this cold metal earpiece will freeze us, stripped of our sweaters as we are, now we shall lie on this couch covered with a cold oilcloth. And everyone in the film really does look like they're freezing, the rain blows in through an open window, it's flu season, everyone seems exposed, mortal. The girl has a mole the size of a hazelnut on her shaven pussy.

From the TV came Disco Polo, late-eighties Ukrainian super-hits, and ads for Fa shower gel. Casper, Melchior and Balthazar were three stout uncle-types in too-tight dressing gowns and too-small slippers, with jolly faces and moustaches . . .

All my life decisions have been made under the influence of aesthetics. It's the only thing that's ever motivated me to do anything.

And so I came to the realization I was of an entirely different class and needed to escape.

The bender had entered a hopelessly chronic phase, where the hair of the dog was impossible to distinguish the from its bite. It was worlds away from the style of drinking at the Dead Dog, where—even if it was sleazy, it was still a style—the Viennese alcoholics would still be hammering shots long past dawn. I even enjoyed going there because with its stench and sleaziness the place had something theatrical about it. Today's Vienna of Mozart balls and souvenir shops was, I soon learnt, no place for people and places like that. But, good Lord, even though I loved that bar, I couldn't imagine it would be there, at five in the morning, where I would suss out one of my first best customers, my ticket away from the Zbigniews and that Polish shithole.

I was supposed to be home already (to the extent that awful dump could be called a home), and I decided to have another one. The Dead Dog was located under a railway viaduct, no sign, no swag, just the essentials, a bare-bones dive bar, white plastic tables, white plastic mugs, ashtrays, moustachioed individuals who looked like the Teutonic Knights in the film version of Sienkiewicz's novel, a range of hairstyles of all periods, the most common being the mullet, or *Vokuhila*, as they called it in German, a portmanteau word that meant 'short in front, long in back' . . . The faces there were pure Kraut, it would have been a gold mine for a casting director, a one-stop shop for all your villainous Nibelungs, Ulrichs von Jungingen, SS-men, etc. One of them with long red hair and bulging eyes, all of them grubby and pie-eyed, a slowly rotating ceiling fan, flies, a disconsolate bartender who looked like she'd had every dick in Vienna in her, overhead the trains rumbled by non-stop, shaking the beers and cups of vodka on the bar. Female hookers on their last legs were sitting there too, trans women, homeless, one old pot-bellied slapper was drinking tea, greedily ogling the alcohol all around her. Whenever anyone walked in, the apathetic moustached faces would suddenly turn as one and latch onto the newcomer like leeches, as if they were counting on him to buy everyone a round, as if the fairytale prince had arrived at last to subsidize their collective habit. The party carried on in spite of the breaking day, and without the least remorse they would still be drinking at ten, at noon and at dinner time the next evening. But the place had such a proletarian, I would even say Brechtian, allure, that I entered and ordered a beer and stood at the bar, quickly immobilized by the dull torpor around me. My mind soon filled with thoughts of the East, my native clime. I saw my mother at this hour sleeping beside my snoring father, in our flat, in our block, in our housing estate, traces of red light from the alarm clock on her cold-creamed face, the dust collecting in my room, my bed neatly made up, which never happened when I was there, and everything tidy, because now that I was gone they must have cleaned up everything as if after a dead person, no doubt Mama had set up the drying rack in there or the ironing board ... I wanted to appear in their dreams but I was afraid of the background, that if they saw me in their dreams along with these dead-dog faces, they would think I'd died and was an apparition from hell ...

Suddenly my hooker radar started beeping, the red lights flashed and the alarm bells went off: someone was giving me customer-eye. Oh no, no way am I working in the Dead Dog too, fuck that—I thought and avoided looking back. Sorry, I'm off the clock, I'm on my whore-liday, ha ha, fat chance. I still had the salty after-taste of all the dicks in Vienna in my mouth, my nipples ached from being pinched, my arse hurt. But what kind of customer could be frequenting the Dead Dog? Interesting. I looked. The guy was no older than thirty, but he was all skin and bones, ugly as sin. He was sitting at the bar in a leather jacket, his hair grey and tightly curled like a perm, smoking Gitanes, eating tripe and drinking vodka. He looked like Édith Piaf towards the end of her life, or Kim Jong-il.

What a shame, I was thinking this might be one of those early morning miracles, when suddenly a customer appears out of nowhere and totally hot; just when you really can't any more, fate sends the perfect hook-up your way, just to fuck with you. So I thought, I'll sing you a price you'll never agree to . . . And if you do, then it's fine either way, because Zbigniew won't be getting any of it. I walked out of the Dog and into the street out front, a road sweeper was advancing slowly along the viaduct. With the archetypal gesture of all prostitutes since the time of Corinth, I lit a cigarette and cast a glance around me, even if the only moving thing was the sweeper. What kind of customer would be hanging out at the Dead Dog, with all those hardcore alcoholics who sell the few bottles and cans they've scrounged during the night then come carrying the shillings directly to their watering hole? Or else it's victims of the nearby casino sitting there, the casino that ruined them, that stole their wife, job, children, bank account and credit score, and now they're collecting cans as well, which to the unaccustomed eye are never anywhere to be seen. It's getting lighter. At this hour the Vienna streets would be filled with stray dogs, rats running out of sewers, sneaking around the viaduct then suddenly whizzing past your legs. All right, Édith Piaf, get your arse out here or I'm going home, I thought to myself. It's typical of hookers to give their customers nicknames within seconds of meeting them, which they'll keep using for as long as they continue to know them.

And suddenly there he was. We shook hands and walked. Was he seriously going to drive with that much liquor in him? Before we got to the car, I wanted to calculate my fee so I didn't end up getting paid in cans and bottles, or dead dogs or bottle caps, or in play money from North Korea. He agreed to everything without any fuss. We made it to the car, and there, sitting at the steering wheel, was a chauffeur! My God, I prayed, my God, please let him be one of those rich men who, out of boredom and world-weariness, love to infiltrate the demi-monde ... To have their chauffers drive them around the slums ... To frequent the shabbiest of dive bars ... And now, don't laugh please, or, OK, laugh if you want, laughter is healthy—you won't believe it, but inside the car the chauffeur was listening to a cassette tape of none other than ... well, exactly what you've no doubt already guessed ... Anyway, everything seemed more and more unreal, all the more so because we were still just shadows of the night, while all around us it was already day and with brisk steps office workers were marching past us with the day's newspapers in their briefcases. And then we arrived at his house and it was all as it should be: rich, blasé, hundred and fifty per cent impotent, and he paid like a dream, but there was something a little French about it all, the coffee in the morning, the croissant ... If you could even call it morning, as we fell asleep at two and woke up at eleven? At last I'd found my world, a world without Zbigniews: no blackened tea kettle, no ashtrays made of recycled jam jars, no yellowing underwear or nasty cooking odours, no syphilis, no sex with fat guys on damp mattresses, no leather clock in the shape of a bespectacled owl, no velvet painting of naked women on a riverbank, no shithole! Édith

Piaf's place was so elegant and sophisticated I could even imagine now and then—by way of counterpoint—missing the bread with pork lard, the tripe stew, the vodka served in plastic cups ...

Fortunately Zbigniew had to go back to Poland, because being a paedophile he worked in an elementary school and winter break was over. Anyway I had landed on my feet, I'd made connections, met Mario Ludwig, and was pretty much set, flush with cash, without even working the U-Bahn station, I had my ads in the gay papers and sometimes popped in at Alfie's. There were still two Poles working there, one extremely handsome hetero named Waldemar, a typical grifter, very friendly with everyone, and his antisocial brother, who was somewhat uppity and aloof, but not so bad-looking either. The two of them worked either side of the toilet, they'd stand at the urinals playing with their willies until a grandpa walked in and they all jerked off. They said they were saving up for their weddings in Poland. Later, they brought another guy from their village with them, and I actually invested some of my own money with him, because this one was genuine trade, pure grunt, who was ostensibly indulging his bi-curiosity for the first time. Afterwards he asked me (he clearly considered me an expert) whether his dick was all right, if everything was up to standard. I told him I couldn't have asked for more ...

The Poles, who I tried to avoid as much as possible, all met at Cafe Marilyn, which was like a Polish immigrant community centre. I wasn't a big fan of those parties because I was always getting an earful about another Joanna or Aneta or Kasia who they'd carried out of Cafe Marilyn and who'd only just arrived from Poland. Or how those two over there had taken turns fucking that

one in there, and other Polish legends about dragons in Kraków . . .
The Polish bros were ill at ease in Vienna because they never
stopped being Poles, they lived their lives as if they were still in
Poland, and—like all Polish expat grunt—they worked for their
families. I had no interest in being a Pole, I despised Poles and
always gave Cafe Marilyn a wide berth. It felt to me that with his
curriculum vitae, his certificates and passport photographs and
medical-record booklets, the Pole had been wiped out that night,
incinerated in that terrible fire on our garden allotment, when I
felt like I'd gone there to hang myself, and that's kind of what it
felt like. Now there'd be a blank slate, someone without an identity
who could start all over again as Austrian, German or Swiss.

In general Vienna meant poverty, old people, perverted grandpas
and ancient, dusty flats full of equally ancient, dusty bric-a-brac.
Mornings involved going to a cafe for a mélange and a croissant
and a sandwich of egg, caviar and salmon. You could only stand
in those cafes as there were no chairs, and behind the counter were
shelves of baked goods like in a bakery. Vienna smelt of coffee and
poppyseed and fresh bread, of pigeons and subway stations and
disinfectant. The poor punters stood there in the dark muttering
'heute arbeiten' over their tiny, sugary espressos, then walked out
into the pre-dawn darkness to go work in some factory, and the
boy stayed behind in one of the stations, which was nearly dead
at this early hour, repeating the name of the station he was supposed to change trains at—to what end he really didn't know.

As often as not I would get lost going home at five in the
morning, no amount of money could get me to remember my way
back to a certain Günter I was living with then. The network of

trains and trams and S-Bahns was so complicated, and there were so many transfers, so many escalators, so many smells, of food from the underground snack bars, grease from the escalators themselves, that I stood there, lightheaded from the fumes, and people rushed past me, bumping into me as if I were invisible.

THE NIGHT OF THE GREAT SEASON

I turned up at Carrousel around five, certain no one would be there yet and I could sit at the bar and eat in peace—a ridiculously overpriced toast with ketchup, washed down with an overpriced coffee—before kicking off my routine of systematically getting sloshed and reducing my life expectancy with Chesterfields. But I was not to have a moment's peace that evening. There are days when everything piles up and congeals, fullness and height, plenitude and altitude. One of my customers, a skinny, bespectacled banker from Schaffhausen, told me that both the franc and commodities on the stock exchange fluctuate with the moon's phases and with barometric pressure too. He always checked the weather forecast and invested in stocks accordingly.

The moon was full, holy shit was it ever full. The moon hung over the sky. The moon was the colour of sperm. A circle of uneven white stains with grey discolourations. When it's full and, depending on some other factor too (I never know what it is, but whoever discovers it will be able to predict when the Days of the Great Season will occur), people go into heat. Mostly it happens during the first spring, in March. They come in and go out, drive off to other bars, drunk behind the wheel, then come back . . . Anyway, this night started with the tourists, because no one else ever arrived before eight. The first one was a fat dude from Los Angeles who kept talking at me and getting upset over how expensive everything was ('What? Five fucking francs for one fucking mineral water?!'), to which I answered, with the delectable superiority of a local, 'What did you expect, we're in Zurich, the most expensive city in the world ... Herzlich Willkommen.' It was fun cheering up the American, because until then he'd only ever been in countries where everything was cheap. Darling, I'm so sorry you can't afford our beautiful Swiss reality, coated with chocolate and wrapped in silver in the shape of little houses and roads and mountains and lakes. You'll be even more surprised to find out how much I charge for sex, so perhaps you'd better run along, back to the USA, back to your homeless shelter.

Then came a Swiss fellow who was more American than the American I'd just got rid of. He was blond, decked out in country-and-western kitsch, from his Stetson hat to his fringed and tooled suede jacket to his cowboy boots, and dripping in gold, a typical case of Gold Rush. Wisps of beer foam were stuck to his yellow moustache. He was a typical example of a customer who had no idea how hot he was, who thought he needed to pay for it, when he easily could have had a freebie romance with me plus a bonus rim job. We drove over to the Apollo Sauna and it was very nice, and I had the additional pleasure of charging him much more than I usually did, so I was twice gratified! It was all plain sailing with him, he drove me back to the bar in his Jeep with the top down.

'Dianka!'

I throw a bottle cap at her. Spaced out. She swats the air as if it were a fly. Eats another scoop of ice cream. She's clueless.

'Dianka, what the hell, the guy's been looking at you for half an hour! He's toasting you!' Another bottle cap whizzes past her.

She doesn't even look. The guy is beside himself. He raises his glass to her once more. She doesn't give a fuck.

I look at the guy sheepishly, as if I were apologizing on behalf of the escorts of Switzerland for this substandard Slovak service. He winks at me and we have a laugh about Dianka over her head.

Eventually I drag her to the toilet and give her a good shaking on the way. She comes to, no idea where she is. I point to the guy at the bar, he raises his glass to her. She looks at him like it's her turn at the gallows. Jesus, why does she always have to be such a drama queen!

'Look, you little slut, stop with the pouting and sighing. The guy didn't come here for a grumpy little princess, he came to have a good time with a young professional escort, someone who exudes positive energy and a lot else besides, so put on your happy face and go over to him.'

She looks at me like an employee in a communist butcher's shop about to lob a catty 'we're all out' to the next person in the queue, or to hang up a little sign on the door: 'Gone to get supplies', 'Inventory', 'Not here'.

I signal to the man over Dianka's head that she's a little crazy, 'diese Person ist ganz verrückt', little sleepy-head over here, her blood pressure's lower than normal people's so you're better off coming with me. Then I steal the guy from under her nose, and she doesn't even react! I can't believe it, she actually looks relieved. She leans over her ice cream with delight and floats away into her own little world. The guy and I can't stop laughing about her on the way to his car in the underground garage. He turns out to be a super customer and would go on to hire me many times after that. He paid well and always drove me back to the bar.

My groin, pardon my French, was already chafing, and the night had only just started! I would go out on my rounds and come back, comatose, with money coming out of my ears, stuffed in my shoes, the back pockets of my jeans and my jacket, basically in every possible nook and cranny on my person, blue hundred-franc notes rolled up into coke straws, good thing they were indestructible! The other customers read success and happiness in my face and that attracted them, they wanted it too! Twice I ended up on Zürichberg with car guys, one even got aggressive with me and started playing with my belt, he tried to strangle me but, as you can see, he didn't succeed. I ended up in other people's homes, primping myself in the mirrors in other people's bathrooms, perfuming myself with different perfumes, each more different than the last, so that by the end (to the extent there even was an end, it certainly didn't look like there would be), I smelt a little eclectic . . . If one of the car guys had a baby seat in back while up front the lube was tastelessly thrown in with a woman's cosmetics, I would give him a hickey on his neck out of spite so that he'd have to explain it later to his wife. During my breaks between customers I'd touch up my face by applying a new layer of make-up on top of the old one. Things were wild. I was drinking Red Bull and vodka. Until this one Pole told me it could cause a stroke. So I switched to just vodka.

It was mayhem at Carrousel, whoops and howls of laughter filled the smoky air, someone was buying everyone a round of beer, and Mario was wearing his blond wig, dancing and bippity-bopping around behind the bar, pouring pints, and the boys were pulling out all the stops . . . I looked at my new Rolex watch, it was already one. Some of the other boys had already clocked out and were sitting there drinking, laughing, eating, totally relaxed, but I was still doing my rounds. I always had to be the head of the class, even in grade school I was given a trophy with a red ribbon on it, and now I had a red ribbon between my legs, where my shitty new Levi's jeans were chafing me. Naturally they had to be tight so my meaty thighs and kielbasa would show, and of course I had to cram socks in there too, so I suffered. It was much better in summer, I'd have on a pair of comfortable cotton trousers, suit trousers of course, most likely grey, and nothing on underneath, so my Eleven-Inch had more room for manoeuvre. Guys didn't know what to do with it, they'd never encountered such an ideal specimen before. My tight cycling shorts too left little to the imagination.

Oof. I needed a break. I went to hang for a bit with the Czechs who, instead of working, had created their own Czech pub atmosphere in the corner, with beer and music. Czechs were practically indistinguishable from Germans . . . They were sitting there with their crooked smiles, gossiping sarcastically about customers, 'Look at that bugger, ya!' With me they were getting all high-and-mighty, saying how they wouldn't be coming here to turn tricks any more. And I was like, let's see how that works out for you when you're back at the train station putting out for junkies and guys shooting in your mouth for ten francs. Then one of them, this ugly long-haired queen, tells me they were going to work for Renzo Morelli. I was like, you already do work for him, Caroussel is his, that's Renzo who comes downstairs every morning decked out in gold. They just looked at me with pity in their eyes and broke out in laughter.

'Well someone's been taking the piss out of you, mate. That's not Renzo! Maybe he's stood next to Renzo once or twice, but that's about all they have in common. That bloke's the manager here, he works for Renzo. Renzo himself is far too important to come in here and drink and kick it with the boys, has anyone ever seen him here? Renzo's out in Dübendorf, a little village outside of Zurich, just before Dietikon as you're heading to Winterthur. That's where he runs his Haus of Boys Knabenhain—Garden of Boys—you can see the adverts for it in every gay mag and guide-book in town'—at the entrance to every bar there were always stands for flyers, newspapers, bar guides and magazines full of adverts—'and we'll be working there, on the phones. It'll be deadly. A lot more money, that's for sure!'

I was thinking, 'Why put my neck on the line, let Dianka be the guinea pig again and try it first', and I started raving about her to them, while planning to have her report back to me. Dianka had already told me, between my first and second tricks, about the big attraction I'd missed out on by handing her off to that grandpa in Witikon, and I thanked God that she'd gone first, like a canary in a coal mine, so it wasn't me that gagged.

But later, Mario practically had to drag me away from the Czechs' table and nearly point at the older gentleman at the bar 'who wants to buy you a drink and you haven't even noticed him'. Because that's the kind of night it was. And of course, if there was ever a night for finding out what wool sex was, it was that night.

For the time being, however, I waited in the queue for the toilets, shut myself in a stall, and decided to do a little inventory. Out of every nook and cranny in my body and my clothes, I shook out hundred-franc notes and laid them out on the toilet seat, with twenties in a separate pile, and even a single thousand. Jesus, in

Vienna you wouldn't make this much in a year, even with Mario Ludwig . . . Then I unbuttoned my trousers, pulled the socks out of my drawers, pulled down my red G-string and looked over my poor abraded Eleven-Inch. He was entirely red. One of those grandpas wouldn't stop using his teeth. And none of them really knew how to service such delicate equipment. They seemed not to understand that I needed it for my work. Did I have to put up a sign? 'Customers are liable for any damage to the equipment'? Or: 'Please leave this place as you would expect to find it'?

I wrapped it with the thousand-franc note as a cover.

'Take a whiff,' I told him, 'smell it, it'll make you feel better. Even if you don't improve any, you'll feel better. You're my breadwinner and I have to take care of you. I don't want you to worry, but the night will be long and difficult, you might have to cum fifteen times, even if you've got nothing left to give. Little glans with your hood of wrinkles. You're old. You're tired of working, like the hands of a washerwoman. The hands of textile workers in the mill. There's certainly more than one saggy Swiss arse left for you to thwack. But tomorrow we'll be going shopping! And we'll rent our own flat, without a flatmate! Why not?

The inability to come more than a couple times in a night was such a problem for the escorts that even the management of Carrousel (that is, the guy who would come down in the morning and was supposed to be Renzo) decided to add oysters to the menu. Officially that wasn't the reason, of course, but people whispered that it was the one thing that could help restore depleted reserves, and they scarfed down those oysters, but one by one they discovered that after two oysters the sperm would come out thick and white like Nivea creme, so the oysters began to sell better the later in the evening it was. Now I was sitting at the bar as well with five oysters on the half shell before me (of course everyone started to laugh and make snarky comments and gossip, 'Ja, ja, genau', etc.), I squeezed half a lemon on them, oh fuck it moved (well at least they're fresh!), washed them down with champagne and . . . back to work!

Good God, what on earth was happening! It was all criminals tonight, and the worst sort! One of them crammed money into my mouth, I practically choked, and screamed at me like me to my Eleven-Inch: 'You want that money good, huh, bitch? You want me to shove that money in you, huh?'

No idea where these people get their fantasies from, but isn't it just way nicer to have tender, passionate sex? To kiss and caress and cuddle? And all they want is to punch and pinch and fuck and slap an arse as hard as possible, to bite into a nipple, and that's really no way to treat a young man. No wonder they can't find anyone to be with!

At five in the morning, flush with cash, my pockets stuffed with money, limping and bow-legged from the chafing, I headed back to the Central Plaza, and the streets were alive as if it were mid-afternoon. Drunken whites were staggering alongside Africans and Arabs and Czechs, shouting at one another across the street, kicking empty beer cans, carrying on and singing in various languages, vomiting, throwing rubbish everywhere . . . The only stationary figures were three ancient female prostitutes, one cross-eyed, one fat and one with flies buzzing around her head, who stood like the petrified wives of Lot in the Bible or like the Three Kings in the crèche at church, and would not move a millimetre unless you dropped money on the ground.

I thought about stopping by the train station as I'd finally run out of ciggies. I'd probably smoked three packs that night already and needed more. That and coffee. Zurich's Central Station had the best coffee in all of Switzerland. While Poland was just getting its first espresso machines back then, here they were already hiring professional baristas, real artists who could do amazing things with milk froth, like draw hearts and crosses and cows on top of real cappuccino. I took a seat in the station cafe, which was elegant, with original paintings by Toulouse-Lautrec and Miró on the walls. In Switzerland, a city's train station was its calling card, not like in Poland then, where a train station was basically a homeless shelter. I ordered a croissant and coffee and opened the inevitable Milka chocolate that came with it. I carefully opened the little creamer tub so as not to damage the foil lid. Not because I collected them myself, but it was always worth it to save them, since if I had a customer who was a collector I could show him what I had, and if the fellow found something he was missing ... Oh my God, there was this guy who collected the ones with castles on them. There was a whole series of castles. And it turned out I had a castle he was missing. And to think I might have thrown it away! I made more from that creamer lid than I did from a whole night of sex. These people were capable of paying a thousand francs for that crap. The lack of a single castle (or mushroom or bird, etc.) could upend the whole natural order for one of those guys. One little castle (or dog or cat, etc.) could cover coffee in the centre every day for two years!

I was losing my train of thought and exhaustion was making me stupid. The weariness in my bones told me I wouldn't be able to fall asleep at the hotel. On top of that, I was so wound up from constantly making money that I got it into my head that the businessman across from me, eating his breakfast and reading the *Neue Zürcher Zeitung*, was glancing at me from behind it, so maybe I could get him off and rake some more in. But I caught myself and realized it was just my imagination playing tricks on me. Anyway the coffee made me need to take a shit. I went to the toilet, and when I looked at myself in the mirror, it was clear it would have been hard for him not to look at me: I looked like an old whore who'd been run over by twenty tanks—actually, if you count that handjob in the bathroom, it was twenty tanks and one small cannon.

With the greatest reverence I straightened out all the money and tucked it away in my wallet, which refused to fold shut. Then I finished my coffee, paid and stood under the electronic departures sign with the Swiss Federal Railways logo, craned my head back and looked at all the names of places where I wasn't, where money was passing me by—Cologne, Paris, Brussels and even Zurich Witikon—as inevitable as the gratis chocolate with every cup of coffee—Lausanne, Bern, Geneva, Milan, Sankt Moritz, places like Konstanz, Liechtenstein, Locarno, Schaffhausen ... 'You can't service the whole world,' I said to my Eleven-Inch, 'There'll always be money being made in places where we aren't, money that will end up in other people's pockets ...'

All I remember of that departure from reality was that I simply boarded one of the trains, not even looking to see where it was headed, I certainly had enough money and bought my ticket from the conductor, and I had my passport too, in my bum bag, the one with the 'Enjoy Coca-Cola' design, so I sat down in a window seat and immediately fell asleep . . . The rest of the trip I remember as if it were a dream. The train pulled out of the station, it got light outside, I gave the conductor some money, not quite understanding his Swiss German babbling, and I was really happy to have bought a ticket without having any idea where I was headed. Wherever I ended up, there'd be a nice hotel, a good restaurant, a comfortable bed . . . The train stopped in Basel, which made me think of basil leaves, everyone got out. I continued. Then the landscape changed dramatically—instead of posh stations, there were crooked signs written in French, there were goats grazing on the platforms, which weren't even covered, no more chocolates with your coffee, no more chocolate Swiss Army knives, nothing but a French pigsty. Or maybe this was the French part of Switzerland? I fell back asleep. When I awoke, the train was pulling into a station in some large city, I was almost certain it was Paris, because what other big cities were there in France? Marseille? But there was nothing on the platform, no signs, just a lot of people milling about, shouting as if ants were crawling under their shirts. Only then did it become clear to me what a village Zurich was. I stood up and got off the train and stood there overwhelmed by all the commotion after the peace and quiet of Switzerland, everyone running like they were in heat, Arabs with trays of french fries, Africans, Asians, transvestites, African transvestites, Thai trans women, gays with white berets and man purses, now and then a terrified middle-class white walked by clutching their bag with all their might. Assaulted by all the erotic stimuli, the delicious smells, colours, unfamiliar exotic fruits and unfamiliar exotic people, I stood there slack-jawed and didn't know what to do with this surfeit of life. I needed to pee. As it turned out, the station facilities were the last place anyone would want to do that. You had to throw in a coin and enter through a kind of barrier, but everyone was jumping over it, so I jumped over it too, not having any French money anyway.

I went to the men's toilet and stood there, frozen. In the smell of disinfectant. In a puddle of water. There were three stalls, all open, but at least they weren't empty. In the first one, an enormous hirsute Arab was standing, entirely naked except for a pink feather boa. In the second, two dainty white queens were licking one another. In the third stall a Black man wearing a beret was languidly smoking cigarettes and making faces like he was waiting for his date who was late. At the sight of me he cast an irritated glance at his watch, as if he was disappointed, he'd expected someone better, the two queens were still at it in the next stall, and the Arab was now jerking off so feverishly that pink feathers came loose and were floating about. There was sex at the urinals too. At one of them a youth with a rucksack on his back was masturbating, turning and looking to either side.

Later, when I was trying to reconstruct those outrageous twenty-four hours, all I could come up with were single shots, scenes. For the first time I had the feeling I was actually living a life, that I had finally found it, that life was no longer somewhere else. Here's me walking in the street, bags of garbage piled up on either side, together with other guys, from Africa, Asia, wearing berets, we were singing Brecht. Me at a drag show, laughing my arse off at the queen on stage who was dressed as a lollipop, or was it a pacifier. Me throwing up in some fancy urinal. An Algerian dude exposing himself in the Bois de Boulogne, he was promising to take me to Place Pigalle. He didn't, but I went there anyway.

I got in a taxi and said only: 'Pigalle!' and without missing a beat the driver responded, 'Pigalle, see voo play!' Later I spent hours circling that Place Pigalle, harassed by aggressive red neon signs everywhere and even more so by the suspicious characters herding customers into miniature sex theatres. One of them shouted at me that the porn was live, peep show, live sex and cheap. I decided to go in. It was cramped and musty with stale perfume. Like some catcher in the rye. The show hadn't started yet, a few tourists were sitting there, and the stage was maybe two square metres, the size of a bed. They seated me behind what seemed to be a partition, and immediately two female prostitutes rose up in front of me. They were old and had too much make-up on, and their breath smelt strangely of mushroom soup. They started fondling me and I pushed them away, they didn't insist, but suddenly a fat man appeared and started yelling at me in French and French English: 'You pay! You pay now!' Everything suggested I was being set up: you touch it, you buy it, now pay! There was no show. They started undressing me, expropriated my bum bag, and now my fancy and hideously expensive shoes and watch would fall prey to them too. They were digging around in the bag when one of them found my dark blue Polish passport— and I was saved: 'Eh, Vovka, he's ours, look, it's one of ours! Ona nasha, sooch poslyednyaya! Here, here's your money back. Now don't you ever come to places like this again, you hear?'

This all took place in front of my eyes while I was waiting for the train and went back to that toilet. Professional prostitutes don't have sex in their off hours and they don't pick up lovers for pleasure because sex for them is work, that's why they call us sex workers, and who works for free? Besides, sexual arousal is so closely linked with remuneration that without money being involved it simply isn't arousing . . . Some nasty old ghoul grabbed hold of my hand and led me to the urinals, she crouched down and opened her mouth. So I peed on her, to her great pleasure, but unfortunately for free, and walked out. I got on the next train to Zurich and immediately fell sound asleep. By evening I was back at my hotel on Central Plaza, and thus ended the Night of the Great Season.

DIANKA IN THE WORLD OF SOCKS

Wool: the big, dark secret of Zurich's sex life. As the city, so its secrets. Hairy, white, cashmere, in balls of yarn or in the form of socks, scarves, sweaters. Wool. You wouldn't shove it in your own mouth and chomp on it and pull at it, because the sound produced by all those little hairs getting stuck between your teeth made you feel sick. But you had to. After all, Milka chocolate didn't fall from the sky the way it did in the adverts, it sat on shelves in well-guarded shops. This was the second one today with the socks, Dianka thought, fed up, and considered charging extra—say what you will, but those guys were perverts!

And this one wasn't even hot, he was out of shape, totally un-masculine, docile, benign and pigeon-like, soft around the edges . . . A chubby, fifty-something non-smoker in horn-rimmed glasses who also didn't drink—he was having tea at the bar. What kind of sex would they have? she wondered. There certainly wouldn't be fireworks. Horrible soft sex was more like it. Tender fondling. A wee willy instead of a dick, a tush instead of an arse, a beer belly instead of a six-pack. This soft little man ordered a refill of water and tossed in an Alka Seltzer. It effervesced. He wiped his glasses clean and smiled mawkishly at Dianka.

Well anyway, if he wasn't so dumpy and creepy he wouldn't have to pay for sex and she wouldn't earn shit, Dianka thought, gratified, drinking an apple juice (for the price of a whisky) that he'd ordered for her. Other than that he looked like one of those awful stereotypical Swiss boors, and something told Dianka he lived far out of town, at least as far as Witikon . . . He probably worked in a bank too, like most customers (even though some of them looked like upper management, they almost always turned out to be tellers). If pressed, Dianka would've guessed he was a paediatrician.

Or else he had a wife and kids, and cookies on the side, baked by his old lady, the seat of his trousers carefully mended in a strategic location. Dianka wondered which of her intuitions was correct. In any case she'd accepted his more-than-generous offer. And so it began. He didn't have a car, so they took the tram. And indeed he did live far away, but in the opposite direction from where Dianka's grandpa was amusing himself with his electric train set, washing up with a basin in order to save water and delivering monologues to an empty room about Wilhelm Tell and the punctuality of the Swiss Federal Railways.

'Will you cover my taxi?' Dianka asked, ready in case he said no to head back to Carrousel immediately.

He gave her another sappy smile and squeezed her arm a little. Once in his home, Dianka looked around indifferently at yet another stranger's kitchen, clean, modern, sterile, full of white cabinets, with a bronze-coloured electronic stovetop instead of gas burners and so on. He offered her another juice, but Dianka looked so longingly at his modern espresso machine that he finally offered her a coffee. The bedroom was white too, white bed, white shag carpet. ('At the sight of that carpet I knew something was up,' she would recount later at Carrousel). On top of that, there were literally zero gadgets to steal. The typical single Swiss man (except for this one!), after bringing Dianka back to his posh pad, would get out a little box and start rolling a hashish spliff. He would take what looked like a bar of chocolate and break off a corner of it, then strew loose-leaf tobacco on a piece of thin paper, singe the 'chocolate' with a lighter, then crumble it onto the tobacco and roll up the spliff. Dianka hated them with all her might. But this sanitary dude could have at least smoked cigarettes! Instead he sucked cough drops and offered her one too.

At the sight of his flat, however, Dianka was sure that if she even pulled out a cigarette all the smoke detectors would go off and the firemen would come and hose down all that whiteness with white foam. At the thought of white foam Dianka came back down to earth. In order to speed things up, she asked if she could take a shower, and without waiting for an answer, she marched into the sterile bathroom and stood barefoot on the heated floor. How do all these modern contraptions work? No taps, nothing, designer everything and so unwieldy, and Dianka really wanted to squander some of someone else's water, because her Witikon grandpa's neuroses made her think of water as something valuable and highly desirable. She loved to take baths in the middle of the night in the homes of customers, then to return to Carrousel after a slew of tricks, fresh and clean as a rose with dew-covered petals. She bathed before, she bathed after, scrubbing her body with different shower gels, trying every kind of shampoo, perfuming herself, gargling with mouthwash, and the later it got and the more customers she'd had, she scrubbed and washed herself even more vigorously, more passionately. It seemed she would just keep getting cleaner . . .

She asked him to explain everything. The guy kindly turned on the shower (it was three buttons on a silver panel) but unfortunately barged in with her. She wasn't thrilled, but what to do, for four hundred he had the right to take a shower with her. He was chubby, pale, ginger, big arse, covered all over in ginger hair, smelt like sweat and baby oil—well, it was what it was, if he hadn't been ginger or smelt like baby oil, he wouldn't have had to hire her. Eventually they ended up in a white bedroom. Dianka walked barefoot to the bed, her feet mired in the furry white shag carpet, which was such a pleasant feeling. On the bed sat a furry Persian cat, which looked like a piece of the carpet. Now Dianka would learn what the cabinets were for. Daddy opened one of them and Dianka's eyes took in row after row of fastidiously folded, tiny, white woollen baby socks, bibs and bonnets, bottles of Penaten baby oil, a baby bottle full of milk, baby powder, a rattle, a pink potty, diapers and a great number of fuzzy white mohair sweaters. Hmmm . . . This was some kind of hybrid of the wool-sock perversion, which Dianka had encountered when she first arrived in Zurich, and another kink equally popular in the city, babysitter role play. The guy would deftly slip into a diaper (adult-size), don an adult-size baby bonnet with toadstools and gnomes and a cute little visor, with a bow-tie under the chin, stick a pacifer in his mouth, and start to cry, kicking his legs to show he needed to be changed. Well, Dianka had already mastered that one. When she saw an advert for a babysitter, she could apply. She'd slap Penaten powder on his arse until the room filled with a powdery white cloud.

But she didn't entirely understand how and why the fuzzy wool fit in the picture. This one, after acting out a few pram scenes, smeared Penaten baby oil all over himself (and really, *all* over, from his head and hair down) along with some kind of burn cream out of a round tin, after which he looked over excitedly at the fuzzy mohair sweaters.

Ick!

What do you even want from me, man?

First you needed to smear baby powder all over him, rub him down with a fuzzy mohair sweater, then shove it into his mouth or wrap it around his dick and masturbate him. While the guy was groaning and crying you could see that his childhood, his earliest infancy, the shit-and-piss stage, was the only time in his fucked-up life he'd ever been happy. Then came the exams for a good preschool, unrelenting stress, excessive demands from his folks, competition with his friends. Dianka inserted white wool into his diaper and slapped his arse until he howled like the spoilt rotten brat he was—she never could stand children. Later he wanted to drink her milk (make-believe milk!) from her nipple, so, whatever, it's not like it hurts, he might as well . . . And then, having drunk his fill, he fell asleep, and Dianka cleared her throat nervously as she still wanted to get in a few more rounds.

'So I guess I'll be moving along . . . Any chance of getting the taxi fare covered?'

The guy woke up and looked at her tenderly, like a deer.

THE GARDEN OF BOYS

Dianka ran into that slick Polish guy, Eleven-Inch, at Carrousel, and he and the Czech mafia started working on her to give up turning tricks at the bar and upgrade to Renzo's professional brothel in Dübendorf, outside Zurich. It was called Garden of Boys and would be like paradise for her, she'd make a lot more money and everything would be better. And Dianka really had had it with that grandpa in Witikon, who was always harassing her every time she helped her ever-ravenous self to a hunk of cheese in the fridge or took a bath . . .

And so the girl succumbed to the temptation, Lord forgive her, she was dazzled by all their pretty words and tinsel and believed, not for the first time, that somewhere there really was a paradise on earth, a house full of beautiful, jaded boys walking around in nothing but G-strings, smoking, channel-surfing, shaving themselves in strategic locations, frolicking together . . . (And now, once again, the Czech mafia had put Karel Gott's 'Lady Carneval' and Helena Vondráčková's 'Malovaný džbánku' on the jukebox . . .)

One of the Czechs, who was ugly and fat and God only knows what he was doing in this profession (proof there's a lid for every pot), accompanied Dianka on the S-Bahn (*Richtung*: Dietikon). They got out at a generic, well-maintained little station and walked down the streets of the generic little town with its little white generic houses with shutters on the windows. One Migros store. Bicycle racks. A branch of the Zürcher Kantonalbank. Evergreen Bar. A run-down gallery with a sign that said 'Kultur in Dübendorf'. A shop with dusty woollen tea cosies and other shitty knick-knacks on display in the windows. Boring.

They walked to one of the houses. Dianka with just her rucksack, as she was travelling light. Another Czech opened the door. The interior was the ugliest Dianka had ever seen! The first 'bar' was in the hallway, sticky bottles of different exotic liquors, an inflatable fake palm tree, a disgusting leather-framed clock, a black velvet painting of a sunset, everything artificial, alcohol empties, bottles of coloured water. A velvet painting of a naked woman riding a motorcycle, an unappetizing penis, an aquarium full of water with fake (Dianka hoped) fish and air bubbles, a ball-shaped lamp bristling with hair, the smell of something saccharine sweet . . . It was a world of the cheapest porn imaginable. In the large room, where two boys were lounging listlessly, there was another, similar bar, only larger, with high stools, bottles of cognac and Malibu, next to a fireplace with artificial fire (fluttering fabric in front of a red light bulb), a television, coffee table, various kitschy decorations featuring naked women and men. And on a leather sofa sat a fat white guy with a frizzy perm and exuberant moustache munching on pistachios: Renzo Morelli. He was sitting like he was on the toilet. Wearing only sweat pants and slippers, and of course a chain on his shirtless chest with its pelt of curly grey hair. He sat there munching pistachios, smoking cigarettes, drinking cans of Fanta and watching a nature programme on TV about the life of snakes. The furniture in the room was even more hideous than that of the bar at the entrance. It was unclear why the house was decorated as if customers would actually come here, because Dianka knew the place was too tacky and filthy for that. But everywhere there were old, grimy 'decorations': fake flowers, a metre-high inflatable bottle of Campari leaning like the Tower of Pisa.

The Czechs had run off somewhere and Renzo immediately began coming on to Dianka. So it wasn't just the backdrop that reminded her of cheap porn. If he had been elusive, ephemeral and mysterious before, now he suddenly became only too real, his girth, his drooping nipples . . . Dianka never knew how to assert herself in situations like this, and she ended up going with him, although she was seriously afraid he wouldn't pay. It was neither pleasant nor unpleasant, just boring and went on forever, and Dianka was hungry and angry . . .

After it was over, she was taken to a small and narrow room with a desk and telephone and a person of indeterminate gender sitting there, who looked to be about twenty years old. Super weird. They were wearing tight black trousers, black patent-leather shoes, a black blouse and lots of silver jewellery, and dyed white hair in a cute bob. Despite it being winter they had a very dark tan. Black fingernails and huge modern rings on their fingers, which they were using to type with on a desktop computer keyboard (all the rage back then). She introduced herself as Beat. It turned out she was a young queen, Renzo's lover, and more or less his secretary at the brothel. You could tell she was in charge of the office because there wasn't a single fake palm tree with an island attached to it or one bottle of Campari. She spoke to Dianka in perfect English, which was a bit like throwing pearls before swine, and gave her an orientation to her new job. First things first, Dianka should thank the Lord she'd ended up here. Hadn't she heard about the serial killer who'd been going after escorts from Carrousel with a chain saw?

'So we'll need to come up with a name for you . . . What is your name anyway? Milan? Hmm, well . . . We have Eros and Amor free at the moment, they're both gods of love, only one of the them is from Greek mythology and the other is Roman (I'm taking night classes, not sure if anyone told you . . .).'

The phone rang, she answered it: 'Garden of Boys, how may I help you?'

'. . .'

'Hello, this is the Garden, yes, you have the right number, how may I help you, sir?'

'Aha, yes, we do have two boys who are available for water sports, but do you want them to piss on you or you on them?' She wrote down something in a black notebook. 'Sehr gut. So, reciprocal piss play. Stallion will be serving you, he's Hungarian. Please don't forget to procure beer beforehand.'

'. . .'

'Yes, beer. Where do you think the pee comes from?'

Brrrng!

'Garden of Boys, how may I help you? Hello? Yes, Garden of Boys. Who are you trying to call? Wrong number.'

She sighs.

'Good Lord, how come these people keep dialling the wrong number?'

Out of a shiny black cosmetics case engraved with the Chanel logo she pulled a compact of Chanel foundation for men, a Chanel pomade, Chanel perfume, eyeliner (guess which brand) and a mascara (not Dior either). She made a duck face in the little compact mirror and started doing her make-up. The colours were all so subdued no one would ever guess the little vixen had make-up on. It got better. With a bronzer she made her cheeks even thinner and enhanced her cheekbones . . .

'So what will it be, Amor or Eros? I'd go with Eros if I were you, you'll get asked for more often with Eros. Amor is too common, only Apollo is worse. And anyway we already have two Apollos, which leads to confusion for the customers. Good, so I'll put you down as Eros. Could you get on the scale, please?'

Dianka took off her shoes and stood on a scale just like the one in the school nurse's office in her elementary school. Ms Secretary solemnly began moving the little weights back and forth on the rack.

'Fifty-five kilos. Don't go anywhere, we have to do your height. Five foot seven. Eye colour?' She squinted at Dianka: 'Blue. And down there, how big? I guess not so much . . . I'll put down seven, and you can make up the embellished inch with your good looks. Okay, my dear, off to remodelling with you. Such a pretty girl and so run down. Those nails really need a manicure.'

Dianka looked at Beat's beautiful nails and was embarrassed about her own, she looked at her alabaster skin and thought only of the acne on her nose and her chapped lips . . . She was sent off to the tanning salon, then the hair stylist, then the cosmetician . . . And everything was to be paid with an advance on her future earnings.

'An escort'—Beat never used the word 'prostitute'—'must always be well groomed!'

Dianka didn't say anything, she just stood and looked at her, dumbfounded, like she was seeing a ghost.

'So you're five foot seven, but I'll put down five foot eight, which is the bare minimum here . . . You're fifty-five kilos, but I'll give you fifty-eight . . . Your arse—well, you really won the lottery there, and look at that cute face. But those pores, girl, you really need a facial, and I don't mean that kind! Just look at your nails, you bite them, don't you? I'm going to put iodine on them! You really need that manicure, honey. We're professionals here . . .'

Dianka felt like she had just joined the army . . .

'So this is how it works. Here's the full-page advert we take out in all the gay papers and guides to Switzerland and even in the *Spartacus International* guide. Look.' The entire page was black except for a band across the middle that showed part of someone's face, actually only the eyes. 'I don't mean to brag, but that's me, my eyes, can't you tell? I had on some of those natural shades from Chanel. Not sure if I told you already, but I work as a model on the side. (Hello? Garden of Boys, how may I help you? Ugh, I'm sorry, sir, you have the wrong number . . .)'

'Anyway, a gentleman will ring up and order an escort for delivery, like a pizza. They pay at least twice as much as what you get at Carrousel, and we split it seventy-thirty. Why only thirty per cent for Dianka? Because that seventy includes accommodations, security (what security?), board, electricity, water . . . You'll have a mattress to sleep on, only two Czechs in the room with you. Very well mannered, very clean. There's a fitness centre and tanning salon around the corner, and it's worth going because customers like that look. In any case, I'll need the thousand francs we agreed on for your deposit. You don't have it? Well, then we'll have to take it out of your first paycheque . . .'

When Dianka was finally alone (which meant in the toilet) she looked at herself in the mirror with pride and whispered, 'I'm an escort now . . . I'm a real escort . . . And that Eleven-Inch, he's just a common whore.'

And so Dianka ended up in the Swiss village of Dübendorf, in a 'salon' fitted out with a little bar, an inflatable palm tree (with a token island tacked on), a wall mural of a sunset, high bar stools, and a TV that was always on. It's the TV she would remember most clearly, nothing but MTV, RTL, RTL2, VOX and MTV again. They were no DVDs back then for her not to be familiar with, within a few seconds she always knew what was on. Her favourites were Nirvana, the Cranberries' 'Ode to My Family', and of course Shakespears Sister's 'Stay' and 'Hello', Sinéad O'Connor's 'Universal Mother' and Annie Lennox's 'Why'. She even bought the CD of *Diva* and listened to it on loop together with Madonna's *Take a Bow* and Mariah Carey's *Hero*. She knew the commercials and the presenters so well she was bored of them. In the commercial breaks the MTV logo appeared made of water or flowers, it was different every time. The Levi's commercials were the most original. When she wasn't watching MTV, she liked to watch cartoons, especially *Cow and Chicken*, although unfortunately it was dubbed in German, so she understood fuck all. Her absolute favourites were these two teenagers, one with lockjaw and the other with braces on his teeth, who were called Beavis and Butt-Head. They mainly spent their time eating nachos and making snarky comments about music videos, basically the same thing the hookers at Renzo's did, and Dianka, being of the same age, completely identified with them.

Now and again she went with the Czechs to the gym or just to the tanning salon, which at first she couldn't quite wrap her head around. But she fell in love with it, unexpectedly and deeply, since it was early spring and the snow was still melting, and all of a sudden here was the sun, the smell of summer, of suntan! It was always the same attendant, a chubby older woman who wore only a pink bathing suit (two strips of cloth on her massive, inflated breasts), her skin tanned black, her hair peroxided white, and always sure of somehow getting Dianka. She was probably a prostitute as well, in retirement, with her savings she'd bought a handful of tanning booths for her old age. Dianka nude, without her underwear on, was pulling down the cover of the tanning booth, a miniature summer sky, when that one barged in on her, wanting to show her something, some buttons, and leant over her, her breasts brushing against Dianka's dick, what on earth was she doing?! In her long red claws she was holding a white token that glowed fluorescent in the light and saying something about sticking it in somewhere. Dianka saw only her luminous teeth, smelt the scent of sun, the fragrance of summer air and thunderstorm, of sun-scorched lawns by the poolside on a hot day, the smell of tanning oil—in a word, the smell of Slovakia, of Bratislava . . . She had the sensation of lying on hot gravel by the side of a lake, until all of a sudden the sound of lips smacking caught her attention, and that tanning salon attendant who was also the owner had somehow managed to suck Dianka off. Oh well. Then the gratified matron kissed Dianka's Slavic belly button, which was different, tied into a different kind of knot than the Protestant nub of Swiss belly buttons, and with her fingernails began scratching the sperm out, she'd already turned the timer back to give Dianka an extra half hour on the house, as a result of which Dianka spent the rest of her time in Dübendorf imagining she looked Black. And if that fluorescent-light crap got into the DNA of her skin cells, it's because back then, at the beginning of the nineties, people didn't give two shits about things like that.

But where was the sex, where was the sex, where was the money? Dianka would spend an entire day watching MTV and drinking endless cans of Coke and Red Bull, for which she'd commandeered an entire shelf in the refrigerator, eating Rafaello and Ferrero Rocher, going to the gym and the tanning salon, smoking Marlboros, but not having sex. It was a scam. She hadn't felt this clean and pure in a long time, like a saint. Maybe this was a strange convent she'd ended up in, maybe she'd become a secondary virgin. Dianka would have escaped from this nunnery a long time ago if it wasn't for her growing debt to Renzo, but how would she pay it off if she wasn't earning anything? She went to see the 'secretary', the Chanel queen, to ask her what was going on, whether anyone was even calling? Because if this was their business model, then they could fucking keep it, she'd be on her way back to Carrousel, where she could pick up a couple of thousand francs per day, and she'd pay what she owed them tomorrow. The queen looked Jewish at her, ran her Chanel hydrating lip balm over her lips and replied: 'Fine, go. Fine, it's your choice. We don't force anyone to stay here. If you prefer to turn tricks on the street and end up a common whore who in six months no one wants any more because Zurich is tiny and everyone knows one another, then be my guest. No one is stopping you. Go. Why aren't you going?'

'Okay, fine. But why is there never any sex here?'

But the queen changed the topic. Suddenly very serious and sad, she pointed with her lip balm at the door to Renzo's bedroom, and said, 'Quiet, honey, Renzo has company. And I have to warn you to be nice to him.' She lowered her eyelashes. 'His boyfriend is with him and . . . Well, don't be surprised by anything. As for your commissions, they're just not asking for you, maybe because of your profile, you're too short, and your one real asset is your face, which they can't see in the profile. But I'll try recommending you, we'll see . . . If push comes to shove you'll just go back to Carrousel. (Hello? Garden of Boys . . . Scorching with a soldering iron? I'm sorry, we don't offer that service . . .)'

Dianka hadn't been surprised by anything in a long while. In her little corner next to her mattress she had her few belongings. The silver unreturned key from Trashmaster's flat in Munich. A woollen baby sock, no idea from where. And a red toy locomotive with the logo of the Swiss Federal Railways on it, from Zurich Witikon! Also her weathered bottle of poppers, which smelt like nail-polish remover, a souvenir from Edwin.

The Czechs came back and asked Dianka if she wanted to join them at Evergreen, their neighbourhood pub. They usually went every day around five to get drunk. Dianka wasn't in the mood but she went anyway. Out of boredom. She'd already been to the tanning salon. And she'd already reminisced over her stolen swag. And Renzo had company. Outside, the wall of the local Migros store was red with light from the setting sun. She could be sitting at Carrousel now pulling in the francs. On the other hand, the pints of beer they were drinking were ten times cheaper here than in Zurich, they smoked cigarettes, tipping the ash into pretentious ashtrays shaped like horseshoes, ate pizza and bitched. They were straight, it was harder for them, and in their heads they were still living in Prague or Budvar or Brno, they were only here for work, making money for a new house or flat or a girlfriend or whatever plan they would be going back for. Dianka didn't have that. She envied them, with their other lives in the Czech Republic, where everything was real and serious, while what happened here didn't matter. Dianka had only her one life.

Since the Czechs always knew everything she asked them about Renzo's boyfriend, what kind of dude he was, because Madame Secretary seemed really panicked.

'Oh, that's Renzo's fella. That one's a heroin addict and has AIDS, but Renzo is in love with him. They use a condom when they have sex, and then he pays him for it, like it was a service. Paying his own fella for sex with a condom, even though he knows he'll be going right back to Platzspitz for his fix! That's love for you. And that dosser looks like a corpse. Hollow cheeks, you can smell death on him a mile off. But there you have it: love. Even Renzo, even a ghoul like Karl . . .'

Dianka immediately recalled having sex with Renzo, his 'right of the first night'. Yikes.

The large beers were loosening the Czechs' tongues.

'Hey mate, trade me those Calvin Klein briefs, the ones with just the string in your arse, the thong or whatever . . .'

'Those are G-strings. Thongs have more fabric on the arse.'

Dianka really wanted to trade them her G-string, because it kept chafing mercilessly between her butt cheeks and generally the thing just didn't work for her, though she pretended to love it because the Czechs paid well ...

'Sure, for a blow job,' she said.

The Czechs understood that because they were straight they had a certain attraction for Dianka. And since Czechs were all animals anyway, it didn't matter who they did it with or how, as long as there was beer and piles of schnitzel on their plates and free tokens for the tanning salon, they were happy to pay. Conversation turned to the problems in the company, how there were no customers and Renzo was ripping them off and that it was all pointless. One Czech said he'd heard they were supposed to be working in Zurich. Dianka wolfed down an Evergreen Sandwich. The regulars at this bar all looked like they'd just got out of prison after twenty years, complete yokels. Their hair, jackets, fleece sweatshirts, 'irregulars' was more like it, they were all factory seconds, even their mullets were off, but they had their own hooks on the wall for their motorcycle helmets, their regular seats at their regular tables.

Twenty-two years later, in a bar in Bratislava, a thirty-eight-year-old Dianka would blearily attempt to reconstruct that scene, the taste of the beer, the way the evening light hit the exterior of the Migros in Dübendorf, the smell of summer air in the tanning salon, the smell of the Chanel Égoïste perfume Beat always wore ... She tried to recall it all under the gentle influence of Cinzano, and the guy she was talking to gave her a quizzical look, thinking her English could be a bit more precise. And she was trying to throw herself into the abyss of the confessional mode, narrating her life to this stranger, this attractive Black man from Atlanta, because these were things you couldn't divulge to people you knew. She needed someone she'd met randomly, someone who was returning to Atlanta tomorrow, who without having taken her number would get on the plane, a plane that might even fall from the sky into the ocean and slowly sink to the bottom like a toy aeroplane in an aquarium, the scuttlefish scuttling in through the windows and around it, if there even were such a thing as a scuttlefish … And all at once she was pulled back to the spring of that year, the melting snow, 'Ode to My Family', the smell of the seats in the S-Bahn, the smell of the tanning salon, of thunderstorms, of sun. She remembered going back to Renzo's house and running into that wreck Karl, who was on his way out, and although she really tried, she wasn't able to mask her disgust. Renzo was still giving him some things, jams, toilet paper, condoms, but Karl didn't look like the kind of person who could ingest anything but liquids, and then only intravenously. What a paradox: Dianka was from a poor post-communist country, from a poor family, but she had never witnessed poverty as extreme as what she saw among the junkies here. Emaciated ghouls with long, thin, greasy hair and gaunt, pock-marked faces, sunken cheeks, nervous half-apologetic smiles, lips crusty with some kind of white residue. When she passed him in the hallway the junkie's whole face started twitching, and Dianka could smell the stench of his mouth, a vile miasma she'd never smelt before. And he was one of the privileged, one of those lucky souls who had Swiss citizenship, the dream of every boy in the Eastern Bloc! Well, he wasn't looking that lucky now!

Renzo just watched and said, 'Where the fuck have you been? You have a call!'

Dianka stood there gaping at him, not following.

'What? What are you doing here? Eros is your nickname, right? Or you think it's mine?' Renzo shouted at her and pointed to the corkboard with the schedule of assignments. And sure enough, there for the first time stood her name, 'Eros', in Beat's curlicued handwriting. She hurried to her to find out the details.

The guy lived somewhere at the edge of the world. Dianka would no longer remember where exactly but it was definitely somewhere in the mountains. She changed trains three times and arrived at sunset in some village whose name she'd written with a pen on her hand and kept checking the whole way. Another Witikon, Dietikon or some other shitty name. But no . . . This one was called Schönenberg. And Dianka was no stranger to the direction, 'Cham und Zug', but when she got out she was stunned. The station was so tiny it didn't even have a roof, just a clock, an electronic arrivals-and-departures board, and luckily for her a vending machine with junk food in it, so with her nerves frayed as they were she bought two Twix bars to calm down. She looked around. There were fields everywhere. Sheep were grazing right next to the platform, clanking bells around their necks. The village (a few dozen houses) was somewhere down the hill, in a kind of valley, and was barely visible in the fog. But the air was amazing, like in the mountains. It smelt of spring, of grass in repose under the snow, and of course of cow pies. She put the Cranberries on her Discman, took a deep breath of the resinous air, and headed down the dirt road to look for the address she had written on her palm. It was ten o'clock, and Dianka was hoping she could wrap up within the hour in order to catch the last regular S-Bahn back. So she walked, singing 'Ode to My Family' to cheer herself up.

Everything was like in the real mountains (probably because these were real mountains), there was even a babbling brook of crystal-clear water running alongside the road, and Dianka stopped to scoop some out in her cupped hands to drink, but as she kneeled the slick soles of her city shoes slipped and she slid into the water! 'Fuck!' she yelled, and crawled out, completely soaked and with hands scraped up since the brook flowed through a kind of gutter made of stone. And now she was walking, dripping, towards the lights, so she could get it over with and quit tomorrow and go back to Carrousel, she'd be sitting there all chill at the bar, eating a big bowl of ice cream, drinking gin and not giving a flying fuck about anything! The village was completely dead. White houses with wooden beams embedded in the walls, which they call 'half-timbered', admonished her with their Protestant shuttered windows, because they were inhabited by people who got up at five in the morning, had already been asleep for hours, and never, ever ate ice cream with whipped cream on top, just crusts of wholegrain bread, grasshoppers, Pandoras's boxes and tsetse flies.

And yet, one of those rustic mountain Protestants (with the belly button cut the other way round) wanted ice cream that night, and there was Dianka, walking around like some kind of pizza boy delivering only himself. She felt stupid—at the bar, where the customer could see her in advance, she could tell if he was into her, but now the guy was getting her sight unseen, based on how Madame Secretary had described her, which was probably whatever he was looking for (e.g. 'Does he have blue eyes?' 'And how!'). The address on her palm had got blurry from the accident in the brook, and after trying to work it out for a long time under a street lamp Dianka finally figured it had to be Riedstrasse 16. A small, unassuming house. There was a red Volkswagen parked in the yard, old but well maintained. Everything was clean and modest. She went into the yard and rang the bell. A grandpa opened it. Fat, old, oof, bin isch hier rischtisch, she wondered, and looking him in the eye, said loud and clear, 'Gris Gott, isch bin Eros.'

Then she smiled like a banker offering a lifetime of credit. The grandpa just stood there. From behind him came the stench of something burnt. He looked at her glumly.

'Hallo! Griss Gott. Bin isch Eros . . . Garden of Boys . . . ?' Dianka repeated, but with less conviction now.

He was saying something to himself under his breath, only his lips were moving, as if he were praying, when suddenly he awakened with a start, and if he didn't start screaming in his awful Swiss German and punch Dianka so she tumbled off the doorsteps! And if a dog didn't start howling just then, though at least it wasn't a poodle! 'Schwule!' he screamed, that word she'd first heard in Vienna. Now she wandered around, still wet, beat up and shamed by that village, looking for a payphone to call Beat and ask for the address again. And miraculously she succeeded in finding a phone at a local Mövenpick cafe, miraculously Madame Secretary deigned to answer the phone at that hour, miraculously she made it to another street and another grandpa, who was equally morose but at least he reacted appropriately to the code word 'Eros'.

Which meant not everything was normal there either. The old codger opened the door, he had a cane, and Dianka started right up with her 'Guten Tag. Griss Gott. Isch bin Eros. Aus Knabenhain.' But now completely half-heartedly and with the smile of someone just waiting to be punched.

Gramps let her in without a word, so she charged into the musty hallway, took off her sneakers, looked at herself in the antique mirror and entered the room. She asked the old man if she could use the shower, but he didn't say anything, just pointed somewhere with his cane. Deaf-mute? No ... mute and blind (he wasn't deaf). So Dianka's anxiety about what to do if he wasn't into her was unfounded. For one, he was blind (first time with a blind person!), and second, he'd already ordered from Renzo anything that moved: Athos, Porthos, Aramis, Hermes, Drakkar, Švejk and Karel Gott—half of Bohemia had already been here, in and out. And since they'd been here and he was blind, it probably wasn't worth stealing anything, she thought and got down to work, she really wanted to make that last S-Bahn back.

She took the cane from the elderly man and put it away, helped him take off his sweater, his somewhat under-laundered undershirt, his baggy trousers, long johns or tights, briefs, socks, and let's shake a leg, the last S-Bahn won't wait! She felt a little like a social worker or physical therapist. She already knew what kind of sex she could look forward to, sex in name only, no erection, no nothing, just a frenzy of groping, and what did she expect when the guy couldn't even see his own willy because of his pot belly. And even if he hadn't been fat, he still wouldn't have been able to see it because he was blind. Whatever, this was all par for the course, you needed to go through the motions so you could cash in later. So she went through the motions, tenderly squeezing the remnants of his manhood while staking out the house for swag. But his Alpine abode had nothing valuable in it, it was all shite, a shithole chalet. Next to an old-fashioned bed a radio garbled the weather report in Swiss as well as rates of the franc, gold and chocolate. The guy groaned as if he too felt obliged to pretend he was having a great time, and Dianka thought about how frugal old men like him often liked to keep their money in a piggy bank, like that guy in Vienna who'd saved her life from the grave.

Later she tried to puzzle out how he, the grandpa, had managed to call Madame Secretary and ordered him if he was blind and mute? Somebody must have helped him. He couldn't even read the phone number on the advertisement. But this of course was a country with a high standard of living and grandpas like him had boys at their beck and call.

The problem with sex with the impotent was that there was no obvious conclusion, no orgasm as with healthy males, just a prolonged groan that to Dianka sounded like a siren for quitting time, but it wasn't, and it was starting to seem like there would be no end. So she decided that at least she could cum and hopefully when the grandpa felt the warmth on his face it would count. Normally a job ended when the customer came, after which they would usually zone out and lose all interest in the escort. Escorts complained about how rude it was, but actually they were glad for it because then they could save their sperm for the next guy. There were other customers, though, who didn't count it if the boy didn't get off. With the impotents you never knew how long the fondling would go on. So Dianka summoned images of the Czechs who'd paid her for her drawers with somewhat uncomfortable sex and shot her ample load all over the old man's face. It looked pretty funny because grandpa hadn't taken off his glasses, those black glasses that blind people wear and that made him look like Wojciech Jaruzelski, and now they were white with spooge. A little bit got in one eye so he removed the glasses for a moment and Dianka saw something she wasn't supposed to see—the eye sockets themselves, two awful craters.

She walked uphill through fields on her way back to that country S-Bahn station, but with money in her pocket, because he'd paid, and handsomely too, as they'd agreed, since it was for both her and Renzo (who would be taking away her portion soon enough to pay off her debt), but why do these people overpay when they could pay half as much somewhere else? Though the blind guy probably wouldn't go to Carrousel. The Swiss loved spending money. They never procrastinated, never shirked, they always tipped, they just clearly loved to spend money—and collect it too, basically they loved anything having to do with money.

Of course (since we know a little bit about Dianka's luck), she missed the last S-Bahn and had to wait on that freezing platform until five in the morning. She decided there was nothing left to do but leave Renzo. She looked at the vending machine with the candy bars and coffee and everything, her entire métier, and by five in the morning had spent all she had on candy.

Sometimes she dreamt of all those old men, humiliated by their bodies, too skinny, too fat, a stupid look plastered on their faces by illness or age, with their double chins, their varicose veins, their haemorrhoids and drooping man-breasts. Their masculinity had been wiped out by age and hard work. They would hobble towards her decked out in prosthetics, hearing aids, artificial legs, glasses, canes, pacemakers and vein grafts, they hobbled towards her with cotton in their ears, hairs sticking out of their ears and nostrils ... It wasn't their fault, and yet they were impossible to love, impossible to get close to, their breath smelt so bad. Actually if Dianka hadn't been a whore she wouldn't have paid any attention to them, they wouldn't have existed for her, she would have partied in clubs with young people, and it was young people she would have fucked. These old pensioners groaned whenever they tried to bend over, they couldn't even tie their own shoes, and for whatever reason took pills by putting them under their tongues . . . Now they were her whole world. The thing was, they had already made their living. A young person would know what to do with those life savings of theirs, their various real estate holdings collecting dust, their bank accounts. If only one of these centenarians would fall in love with her, be into her, leave everything to her . . . she sometimes daydreamt. But later they came back to her in her dreams, brandishing the keys to their cupboards, their stock portfolios, their bank books! The aimed at her with their canes, their crutches, wheeling their drip stands and colostomy bags behind them, lurching towards her on their walkers, kissing her, exhaling on her, IV tubes sticking out of their necks . . . Dianka grabbed their hair, and a sly little hairpiece came off in her hand. The grandpas kept rubbing against her, taking out their false teeth and showing her their different asthma inhalers, and Dianka ran away from them, she ran up the stairs of an old Viennese tenement to the very top, higher and higher, and on every door instead of a nameplate there was an hourglass, and behind every door Norma and the Gypsies were looting some pensioner's flat. Until she got to the last floor and could go no further, and from down below came the sound of many canes knocking and knocking against the wooden stairs and the sound of wheezing.

'No!' she woke up suddenly, and the Czechs were there angrily muttering about something.

A line had been drawn right from the beginning between her and the Czechs, or two lines even: she was a queer and she was from Slovakia . . . Under communism, the Czechs and Slovaks had been united by force, so they hated each other as only two neighbouring countries that were identical in every respect could hate each other. Each saw the other as a caricature of itself.

But today the Czechs were bringing coffee and Twix bars to her bed, or mattress rather, and kissing her on the cheek.

'Up and at 'em, dollface, we're done with this awful joint, we're going to work in Zurich!'

'Hello? I still do work in Zurich and that's fine with me.'

'Not in Carrousel! Renzo's started a joint venture with another brothel run by this broad named Michelle. It's a super-high-end brothel on the same street as Carrousel.'

'Great. So you'll be able to pop by to earn some real money in case that one turns out to be a scam too . . .'

'It won't be a scam! We're heading there in an hour, by car! Get your clothes on and let's go!'

'Is that the place where customers go in the morning? Good Lord, whoever thought I'd be working the daytime shift . . . I really am a lazy and lousy girl! Okay, they left . . . Time to get up, at least to wash up. Where's my underwear? Did they steal it again? Zdeněk! Zdeněk! Jáchym! Václav! Petr! Where are my briefs? What the fuck, and my smokes too? I need a cigarette! How can I get up without a cigarette? Oh there they are, on the rug. Looks like a herd of sheep trampled them. When I got here I thought I knew the entire Czech mafia in Western Europe. Then more started coming, one after the other, each one prettier than the last. They have no shame! They go with women, guys, dogs . . . it's all the same to them. Me with a woman? I guess I'd do it for . . . a million, sure, for a million francs I'd do it with a girl, but no less. I said I'm getting up, Jiři! What? There's ice cream in the freezer? Oh good Lord, good thing we're getting out of this backwater. Jiři! Are we still sleeping here tonight or in Zurich? Oh no . . .'

And here, finally, after waiting for ages in the wings, powdering herself amid constant polishing and refining, Michelle is ready to go on stage. We'll come right out with it: she's the star attraction of this story. She takes umbrage at having been made to wait so long, and she's not even sure whether they're paying her, whether being a literary heroine comes with remuneration, and if so, how much and when she should expect it.

It began with a truck full of Czechs (and one Slovak squeezed in among them) that started off from the driveway outside Renzo's house (with Renzo at the wheel) like a youthful ejaculation, direction: Zurich. Poor Dianka was burning up from the heat of the Czechs' meaty thighs on either side of her, and the whole truck was fragrant with hair gel, deodorant, tanning salon air freshener and chewing gum. Even here, Renzo had to plant more tacky, dusty American bric-a-brac, a cowboy hat dangling from the rearview mirror, artificial flowers, and of course a little Jesus statuette, because no self-respecting mafioso can live without plastic Jesus. Renzo gave us a rundown of the situation: not far from Carrousel, in one of those narrow streets, lay a hotbed of hookers, female ones, streetwalkers, with a brothel upstairs. And now there was going to be a merger of our withering Garden of Boys with this institution, which was run by Madame Michelle and was orientated towards heterosexual men, the employees were all women, unfortunately. But they had expanded their services to include all kinds of kinks, and no doubt the Czechs, as always, would come in handy. But watch your arses because Michelle was very particular, and what this actually meant was to become clear in one hour.

They drove up to an old, well-maintained townhouse, rang the intercom with the camera and monitor, which they could see themselves on, just like the people upstairs could see them, and they were let in. The lift was funny as it opened on both ends— they entered through one door and were let out on the third floor through the door opposite. At once the smell and aesthetic of a brothel: roses, powder, white shag rugs, gilded frames, artificial flowers . . . Madame Michelle's establishment was large, it occupied an entire floor of the townhouse and had many rooms and salons where the female escorts with their dark complexions (most of them came from Brazil) and in varying degrees of curlers in their hair and hangovers inside their heads were watching MTV and *Cow and Chicken*. And they had Beavis and Butthead here too, one with the braces on his teeth, the other with lockjaw, two ageing teenagers just as bored on that side of the screen as Dianka and the hookers were on this side. On that side hands reached out for a bowl of nachos, and on this side they wished they had some nachos too, but Michelle's inviting smile no doubt reminded them of the price.

The whole place was decked out in creams and pinks, or else gold. Michelle herself deserves an especially detailed description.

When they exited the lift, they were greeted by the very picture of a brothel madam. The woman was quite elderly (at least seventy), but she was tall and had long straight legs, like Barbie. She was skinny, bony, and had the greyish complexion of a smoker.

Dianka couldn't believe what she'd heard in the Truck of Czechs, that Michelle still worked downstairs, on the street. Her lips were twisted into permanent duckface, as if she were forever about to give head, and she spoke through this pout as if it were the whistle of a kettle. But the best thing was that when she spoke, this rusty old Barbie had a man's voice, very deep and raspy, her vocal chords wrecked. On the other hand, she had everything she needed: enlarged boobs, long blonde hair, long legs, and you could imagine that after spending seven hours in front of the mirror and with the exceptionally dim light of the streetlamps working in her favour . . . Who knew? Who knew what some horny, drunk cis-het-male might see when his imagination was doing the looking . . . So she opened her dressing gown down to her thighs and in pink slippers with pompoms on the toes and with earrings shaped like little moka pots (yes, stove-top espresso makers!) dangling from her ears, she led them into the salon. Dianka couldn't keep her eyes aways from her, she was utterly enchanted.

All in all, nothing had changed except that now Dianka watched TV in the company of the Brazilian and Asian girls who worked for Michelle. Whose primary characteristic, aside from an ability to transform herself into Barbie, was stinginess. She would put chocolates on the table, but no one ever ate them since they all knew that somewhere there was a hidden list of rules for the establishment that undoubtedly included the price of the chocolates. If you wanted coffee, you gave Madame six francs and she made it for you. And when a customer once came for boys and not the ladies, she served him herself!

Michelle was somewhere halfway down the road from human jalopy to Barbie when the intercom rang. The monitor lit up with the image of a rain-drenched little daddy on the other side of the camera. She let him in and put him in one of the rooms, then came over to us in the salon, wearing nothing but her shiny knee-high boots, and called everyone over individually to go talk with him, pointing with her long, fake-fingernailed finger, so he could choose someone. The guy perched on the edge of the big bed and asked each one if he had hair on his chest, what kind of cock he had and so on. But then he didn't choose anyone, as he had already wisely asked Madame how much it would cost. Exactly the question she was waiting for. Two thousand. Well, that includes the hourly room rental, the bathroom, the condoms, the paper towels and use of the bathrobe, which had to go to the laundry afterwards . . . So the guy said he wasn't interested and made to leave. But at that Madame pointed to the list of rules and prices. The guy spoke English, which had never been Michelle's forte, and besides, she came from the French-speaking part of Switzerland, and everyone knows how the French are at English, but she began to explain to him in her low, masculine voice, which shot out of her mouth like steam from a kettle whistle: 'You sit here. Outside, it rain . . . I pay for ze heating here . . . You sit in dry . . . You have one cola, one cola ten francs . . . You talk with boys, you touch boys, now you not take boys? You must to pay one hundred francs, I give you special price . . .'

And if the guy had any objections, Michelle would sick this one really muscly Czech, Jiřík, who she lived with, on him. (He worked at Carrousel too, and called her his 'Old Lady' behind her back.)

So whatever decision a customer made, Michelle never lost money, she always managed to sell that bubble of heated air. She herself would sit at her mirror until ten in the evening executing her transformation, and although Dianka never earned anything in Michelle's brothel either, she never spoke in retrospect of her time there as having been wasted.

She would watch in fascination. Michelle (who had been a hairdresser) would blow up her wet thinning blonde locks with a hairdryer and mousse to massive proportions, a storm of blonde to anyone who saw her on the street. For now however the wisps were pulled tight into a little bun, and Michelle was working on her sallow, solarium-blackened face, ugly as sin, a duck's beak where lips should have been exuding the voice of a woman whose diet consisted of gonads, the sperm of wild males, steroids, hormones, testosterone, whey protein shakes, men's underwear, machine guns, jackhammers and anything else having to do with men. A low, raspy voice speaking pretentious broken English in a laboured Swiss accent that always sounded like someone with a huge chip on their shoulder very smugly lecturing anyone who'd listen.

THE LAMP

The Swiss news—the dullest news in the world since nothing had happened here since time immemorial and nothing ever broke—was making mountains out of molehills again by way of killing airtime, and Dianka was eating chips, which no one else was touching, although she had an inkling as to how much she'd have to pay for them ('I give you special price . . .'). Anyway, the lead story of today's news, as it was once a year, was about indoor lighting. Evidently there was an enormous crystal chandelier, the pride of the city, hanging in the Opera. And once a year this chandelier was carefully lowered on a rope down to the floor so it could be cleaned. That alone was a reason for the photographers and camerapeople to show up. A hanging lamp! Like every year, the chandelier would be lowered from the ceiling to the ground floor and each crystal would be individually cleaned with a special fluid! Specially formulated by scientists from Zürich Universität! The great chandelier must have been front-page news for at least three days. And they were rehashing its history on TV again: when and by whom the gigantic lamp had been designed back in the nineteenth century and all kinds of chandelier trivia, like how much it weighed, how many crystals it had, and the distance its crystals would cover if they were laid end to end (like, from the Opera to Witikon) . . . When they were done with the lamp, the man with the glasses started telling us about Milka's new marketing campaign: chocolate cows grazing on Bahnhofstrasse! Exactly like last year! (But not a word about the junkies literally 500 metres away.) Then there was a story about the new public toilets design competition, which a record number of artists, designers and architects had entered. Zurich was inundated with proposals for the most postmodern privies, futuristic facilities and revolutionary restrooms, bathrooms alluding to Bauhaus and Brutalism, Dadaist urinals, latrines in the shape of Swiss Army knives and Rolex watches, lavatories that looked like cows ... There were even more proposals than there'd been for the Kirchner Museum in Davos!

The hookers were happy to be living and putting out in such a beautiful and prosperous city. Meanwhile Michelle was painting her whole face with a light foundation, then she sprayed it with fixer, and drew her eyebrows on somewhere completely different from where they actually were. She glued on her extra-long eye-lashes (lashes are hard to see on the street and a hooker needs to charm her trick from at least ten metres away), masked her double chin with contour and clear fishing line and redrew her mouth with lip liner at a remove from her actual mouth, completely ignoring her beak-like lips ... Dianka couldn't take her eyes off her. The chandelier! The chandelier! The chandelier on TV! When she turns into a diva! And that video they were always playing on MTV of 'Why' from *Diva*, where Annie Lennox sits at her vanity gradually turning herself into a star, but what a different star she was from Michelle! And yet ... Michelle's transformation seemed to mimic the video ... In the one, Annie was putting on the diva's feather headdress, here Michelle was snuffing out her cigarette with a lipstick-covered cigarette holder ... Once, on a school trip, Dianka had gone to the opera in Bratislava, and the lady appointed her to present the singers with flowers. Dianka was terrified, but happy, walking on stage through the applause from one singer to the next. She gazed dumbfounded at the eyebrows on their foreheads, at their lips on her nose, at their wrinkled breasts, the digital watches on their wrists and the plastic diamonds on their fingers. But they didn't hold a candle to Michelle! Sometimes she did her own hair, but more often she would wear this spectacular wig (though not so spectacular that it was obviously a wig), and throughout the entire transformation, she chain-smoked cigarettes, leaving red smears on the cigarette holders.

At the end she would don a shiny black plastic miniskirt, black knee-high boots, a tight black leather jacket, a string of enormous pearls on her contoured cleavage, and a silver fur muff, grab her gold purse and head downstairs. Why did she still work the streets, despite being the madam of a luxury brothel? She did, of course, always bring them here, to us, upstairs. But after sixty years of scoring in the street, it's not like she could live without it, she needed to breathe the fresh air, to watch the passing cars, to exchange gossip with the other hookers, get into fights, and more than anything . . .

More than anything Michelle loved the contemptuous looks of all the non-customers, all the daddies on their way home from the office, whipping her with their eyes—there was something masochistic about it. Downstairs she had a little niche in the wall of the house, a kind of grotto, the walls of which she'd made smooth from so many years of working in there . . . She'd stand there frozen in a theatrical pose with her feather boa or the fur, her cigarette in its little holder, and her duckface pout, so that from a distance all you'd see was a heap of blonde hair, boobs, frills, diamonds and pearls—looking good! But the theatre has its own rules and Michelle pulled in Arabs every night. Only Arab men went for her and supposedly she only charged them a hundred francs—you couldn't even get a blowjob in the bathroom at Carrousel for that. Michelle would stand in her little grotto in a cloud of perfume and earrings and smoke, without moving a muscle of her own, like an alligator. She stood there impassively for hours, watching everything through her artificial lashes, the only movement her hand mechanically bringing the cigarette holder to her lips again and again, it was as if she was propping herself up, hands on her hips. The way the street lamp threw its light on her, her artificial eyelashes cast the silhouette of a rake on the pavement when she lowered them. Now her skin was white, no wrinkles, her lips red, her eyelids silver, brows high and fine, her cleavage smooth with concealer, pearls in her ears, her pearly white hair, her pearly fingernails, her mother-of-pearl cigarette holder. She was like a wild animal playing statue of Cleopatra on stage. It didn't matter what was inside. This was theatre. This was the night. From a distance everything screamed hair and more hair, lips and boobs, feathers, femininity itself. An illusion that would continue until she opened her mouth to speak.

In the crazy spring that followed the Night of the Great Season, I bought myself a lot of new things, including a Discman. That was the era of various strange intermediate inventions: pagers instead of mobile phones (although I already had one of those) or Walkmans for compact discs. Big, heavy and unwieldy, it stopped every time I took a step, and the rechargeable battery only lasted an hour. Anyway, I would listen to Kurt Cobain while strolling on the banks of Lake Zurich. At last I was living on my own, renting a flat that cost more or less what I got from two more lucrative tricks, and it had a view of vineyards and the lake. I thought, why should I shack up with some sugar daddy when I can cover my own rent in two hours? I was sitting in front of the TV, slathering self-tanner all over my body—ears, face, legs, hands, arse—when I heard the terrible news: Kurt Cobain had died. I didn't know what to do with it, like when someone hands you a hot potato and says 'pass it on', because the other boys at Carrousel could not have cared less. All I could do was cry on Dianka's shoulder. It was immediately clear to us that this was no suicide, but that *she* had killed him. So I was listening to Nirvana non-stop at full volume.

This totally turned on the guys because they associated head-phones and Walkmans with teenagers and youthful rebellion. I soon learnt that what that Romanian dude Andrei had said to me ('you dress too stylishly') was actually useful, and why was I buying expensive things for myself when really you needed to dress like a child for these guys to be into you. I'm no Dianka, you don't have to tell me twice. I went to the Levi's store and got myself some rebel youth-wear, bought a skateboard and spray-painted graffiti on it, carefully shaved the wisps of stubble on my face and decided to let my bangs grow as long as they wanted. I styled my hair with Ryf products—available only in Switzerland—and it turned out so sleek and shiny! Other than that: no more gold and no jewellery. My watch was a colourful, retro-reflective Swatch now, my shirt a hooded rave top, my shoes yellow Nikes with oversized tongues and laces left untied. I topped it all off with a red baseball cap, and I was ready to take the city again! I grabbed some toy or other, a pink stuffed piglet, which drove the guys wild, like a cape before a bull. I didn't even realize what a fashion statement I was making!

The Carrousel, as a community comprising a small number of escorts and a couple dozen regular customers, was quite susceptible to the winds of fashion, which could change direction even twice a month. Sometimes everyone would be dressed à la Gaultier: navy uniform, white collar, white sailor caps, anchor on the brim. Tattoos, stripes, that sort of thing. Two weeks later they all looked like they were off to go mountain climbing in the Alps—done up in Victorinox outdoor wear, heavy-sole lace-up Timberland boots, leggings, knives, pocket knives, chrome water bottles, backpacks, all very L.L.Bean, all very expensive. Then suddenly the very opposite trend—after Kurt Cobain's death (which they evidently got wind of somehow) everyone started dressing very grunge, very Nirvana, with three t-shirts on and five plaid flannel shirts, all in layers, fake gold signet rings and straps. Then, like summer, the cycling shorts came back, in red of course because junk shows best through red lycra. Plus the helmet, expensive retro-reflective fingerless cycling gloves, all kinds of brightly coloured watches, cleats, knee pads, all the trappings of a luxury cyclist, just without the bike, because the bike would have to stay outside the bar and that would be a waste of an accessory.

Of course some boys were too basic for this kind of thing, they didn't get it and always went out in mom jeans and no-brand sneakers (cf. Lady Dianka Spencer). A sad sight indeed. But most of us queens loved money and hooking and were perfectly fine with fashion, although there were always a few red-faced rednecks from Poland B who should have been working construction or picking fruit or some other seasonal job. They'd ended up here by chance, blown in by the winds of chance from Katowice or Żagań, and chance had taught them that even if they didn't understand what it was all about, the money was a lot better than what you'd make under the table on a building site. So they came with their kielbasas by bus from Poland, watching pirated copies of B-movies on the monitors all night. Not a peep out of them in any language, just Silesian. I would sometimes hire these fellows myself, and not out of charity either, but because their innocence and basicness turned me on. I could see they were too dumb to play games with customers, blushing with shame as they did and prone to vomiting, they washed it all down with beer and vodka chasers, and in a year would be complete wrecks, alcoholics. I always strongly encouraged them to go back to Poland, to their girlfriends, their neighbourhoods, their football teams. But they were always afraid of returning before they'd made their fortunes, before they'd turned their ship around, because it would just be another embarrassment to return with nothing, when everyone would be expecting a new car and glitz and glamour . . . I knew these Polish grunt were shriveling up in this air permeated with expensive perfumes and the sweetish smell of quality pipe tobacco . . . They were oblivious to luxuries, to oysters, to Burgundy, it all went over their head, these were guys who could pull out their own home-made sandwiches and eat them right there in the bar, in the middle of a Friday night . . .

One time I got there at four, thinking I'd be the first one and could nab any tourists who might turn up. And there at the bar was a boy who looked no older than seventeen, blushing, clearly Polish. Maybe he was more red in the face than blushing. He wasn't pretty, he wasn't ugly, just young and strapping. And he wasn't fat either, although he definitely had some meat on his bones. He was clearly tense. It was evident he'd walked by the bar eighteen times before daring to enter, and eighteen times he'd stopped at the door until finally, throwing caution to the winds, he took the plunge. His face said 'keep your distance'—a mixture of feistiness and truculence, insecurity and fear, and pride in his leather jacket, which any of us could have bought for an hour's labour without even taking off our trousers. It wasn't that unusual for a guy to invite us for dinner of a Sunday evening just because he was lonely and wanted someone to share a meal with. In a fancy Japanese restaurant. So this Polish boy was proud of his bomber jacket, his tracksuit bottoms and his shoes, completely ignorant of whatever was then in vogue in Carrousel (it was the 'white look' that summer, which I'd launched: tanned skin, linen everything, white polo and tennis shorts, orange juice as accessory, white tennis visor, Lacoste or Ralph Lauren, everything super light, super clean, with bright, citrusy perfumes like Clinique Happy ...)

Well, I thought to myself, if I don't go, someone much worse will get to him, and then they'll make mincemeat of him in the bathroom. And it won't matter whether they use a rusty needle from Platzpitz or a golden dagger from Cartier. Especially because two exceptionally nasty mafiosi had just turned up: one from Brazil, the other Albanian. Fortunately, I hardly ever went to Carrousel any more, I was down to half-time in the demi-monde, and for the other half, well, I was a high-class courtesan now, a proper *dame aux camélias*, I hardly even fucked any more, I just strolled around with princesses at garden parties, so I didn't give a damn about some vile Balkan-Latino mafiosi turning up at Carrousel. They sure weren't around back when I got there. They were Creoles, Latinos, even those godawful Albanians, and they were all wearing white too, down to their white newsboy caps, but they were thugs! You're there chatting up a guy, in the middle of settling a deal, and you leave for two minutes to go to the toilet, to take a leak, fix the socks in your crotch (since they'd slipped down your trouser leg to your ankle and were about to fall out), you come back to your customer and one of them is standing there talking to him. You tap the chode on his shoulder, but he's like a tick, he won't leave, instead he's telling your trick how the twerp who went off to the toilet (you) is too expensive, poor quality and sick, how he might be infectious, 'AIDS ist grosses Problem in ganz Schweiz, you know', and how he'd give him a much better time for a lot less. Well, all I can say is they're quite welcome to fuck themselves, I've more important things to do!

Anyway, I went up to the kid to have a look at him. Red freckles on his face—he'll sure be breaking hearts tonight but he has no clue what his poor arse is in for! Still, I figured I should tell him about the rates, because those Latinos in their white caps would try to fuck him up. Of course he wasn't drinking beer or coffee or even vodka, but whisky on the rocks (liquid courage), Johnnie Walker Black Label, and he wasn't smoking Marlboros, but those pretentious black John Player Specials. You could see he wasn't really into either the whisky or the cigarettes, that he'd have preferred to have his LMs and beer, but what to do, he needed to boost his spirits. He was sitting in the perfect position for not picking up anything all night: at the bar, his back to me, and facing Mario. Mario winked at me over his shoulder and made a worried face, to the beat of some music from the fifties, he was wiping dry a mug—or rather a tall pint glass—sighing over and over like an old queen, 'ja ja, so ist das Leben,' and rolling his eyes . . . He was in a good mood today, which is why he placed a glass of amber-coloured Turbinenbräu on the bar before me, with wink and a cheery 'zum Wohl!' On the house.

Anyway, I took my beer from Mario along with the cardboard coaster and my cigarettes, and went over to the other side of the bar and sat down on the high bar stool next to the kid. I thought of claiming the right of the first night, the way Norma did in Vienna, and be the first to try out this fresh-faced ingénue from the Polish countryside. All the while showing him the ropes. So I grunted a little, offered to light his cigarette with my white Zippo lighter (because everything had to be white that summer), and he totally flipped out! His ginger eyelashes wet with tears! He was feral, a regular wild boy. He looked around in a panic, to the left where the entrance was, to the right where the toilets were, probably calculating that he wouldn't be able to run out into the street because he hadn't paid yet, so instead he ran into the toilet and stayed in there forever (Mario kept making his worried face), before coming back out, settling up with Mario and running off with his tail between his legs.

The kid's wildness only endeared him to me even more and I sincerely hoped I hadn't driven him all the way back to Poland B, to Koszalin, Lubiąż, Tłuszcz, Wronek or Szamotuł, that he hadn't jumped on the first Chrobot Reisen bus back to the land of Pollena Ewa. I walked outside into the spring sunshine in front of the bar. Solarium-Tan Lady across the street, in her black platform boots and black vinyl miniskirt, was leafing through some book like *Fifty Shades of Rubber* and keeping an eye on her mannequins modelling various equally naughty Bellezza outfits. The air even smelt like the inside of a tanning salon. I looked left and right and saw him—he was standing there pretending to look at the window display of my favourite antique jewellery shop. They carried things from ancient Greek graves, medieval crypts, crooked rings extracted from excavation sites, with prices starting at eleven grand, but then you'd be wearing a Teutonic Knight's ring or Cleopatra's earring, which not everyone had. But the kid didn't look like someone who was actually interested in such things.

Meanwhile, a small silver convertible pulled up outside Carrousel, one of those retro cars, a toy for grown-ups, and a hottie with a shock of blonde locks stepped out and I forgot all about the kid.

Some time passed by. The kid didn't show up again. Things in the Carrousel were getting less and less interesting. That awful Latino mafia. The customers didn't like them, because they weren't honest, and the employees didn't either, and eventually someone came up with he idea of asking Renzo to ban them from Carrousel altogether, this being peaceful and prosperous Zurich after all and not that gang-ridden Rio of theirs. They were capable of slashing a customer's tyres and letting out all the air if they hired someone else. The customers were kindly, upstanding Swiss daddies with freshly ironed button-downs and Diners Club and American Express cards, they liked their escorts without tattoos, nice and equally upstanding twinks, not those Brazilian savages straight from the favela.

Eventually, however, he came back. The Kid. He sat in the corner, like Dianka, at the very end of the bar, by the toilets and slot machines, absorbed in his beer, freckled, ginger. I should have gone over and started singing my little ditty, 'arbeiten, Dianka, arbeiten!', but I remembered how he reacted to me and decided on a different strategy . . .

He didn't know that I was Polish. I would have to pretend I was Swiss. Young and attractive, sure, but even the young and the attractive sometimes (in a blue moon) hired escorts. That was the real debauchery for us! Let's say a Swiss guy realized he was bi-curious and wanted to explore his curiosity for the first time, he might feel less ashamed hiring a prostitute, maybe because money cures all ills, especially shame. Paying for it was the thing. You pay, therefore you are. It was such a treat to have such an apprehensive customer, with all of his sixteen years, paying for it with his allowance, which he'd saved for two months! A rent boy renting a rent boy . . . A Swiss rent boy renting a Polish rent boy with Swiss money. A Polish rent boy pretending to be a Swiss rent boy renting a Polish rent boy with Swiss money in Switzerland ...

In the meantime I noticed the grandpas were already lining up for him. Not literally of course, but at least three punters were winking at him, drawn like bees to a rose bud. And he was completely blind to them, staring into his beer, rhythmically flicking the spark wheel of his lighter. I knew all three of them: one was a portly taxi driver with a fat gold ring on one finger, a nice guy but hardly a big spender. The second was an old paedophile who was always flying off to Thailand, and thanks to him my Thai Queens had been able to renovate their flat. He was the reason for their growing prosperity. The third one, who was completely decked out in gold and had a mouth full of gold teeth, was a tired, old, psychotic queen I'd rather not go into detail about. But I figured if the Kid ever even noticed those gawking grandpas, he'd probably go with the last one because simple folk always run after gold, thinking gold means affluence. Well, my dear ... If I were the new kid now and had a face like yours, I'd milk the three of them for all they were worth and build myself a stone house tomorrow on the other side of Zürichberg. Where even the rainfall costs more than the best mineral water in Poland! And look at you, throwing it all away!

In the meantime, I had to turn my attention away from the Kid to someone else who was staring at me. A new face. Thirtyish, shaved bald, in a leather jacket with an American flag on the back, protruding eyes, obviously a perv. Something about his mouth made him look like a predatory fish—when he smiled you could see all of his teeth—and it must be remembered rich people resembled animals. But blah blah blah. What was a young, attractive guy like you (me) doing in a place like this? I could ask you (him) the same question. And yet, and yet, and yet, and yet, could he, could he really, maybe . . . maybe coffee? Maybe not, maybe a gin and tonic? Not true, it's not so awful in here, it's not so hot outside. Oh but it is, it really is . . . But everything has a silver lining, as long as we know each other now, let's drink to friendship (as long as that friendship doesn't leave your arse wrecked) . . . Sure, it's hot outside, it's sweltering, and you're hot too, I see, ha ha ha. Well, maybe he's hot, maybe not hot, it's still too hard to say . . .

Suddenly he begins speaking directly, no more games with half-words. 'My name's Harry. Would you like to come over to mine on Wednesday? It's quite an interesting place, an enormous house, a palace really, up in the mountains . . .' He lacked for nothing, and all of it was somehow connected with American pop culture. Slot machines, foosball tables, every kind of whisky, even the most expensive; pubic hair from Marilyn Monroe, locks of hair from Elvis Presley . . . A collection of toy Cadillacs . . . He wasn't even particularly old or creepy, so I decided to give him a freebie, one of my 'Long-Term Millionaire Specials'. See you Wednesday then, where should I wait for you? I'll pick you up in my supercar, a sky-blue American sedan from the fifties, a museum piece, I had it completely redone with parts specially ordered from Santa Monica, where it never snows . . . Okaaay . . . I saw his ring with the strange insignia etched on it as he was raising his whisky glass to his lips. Later I'd have to describe that insignia again and again to other people, draw pictures of it on sheets of paper . . . For now, though, we just said 'Tschüssi! Bis später!' and he left, ogling me with those pervy eyes of his as he walked out through the door, as if to say, 'I'll hold you to your word that you're coming on Wednesday . . .'

I can't say I was into seeing him again, since after two and a half years in the field I had few illusions and not much excited me. But there were always exceptions. Still I wouldn't have wanted to live in the mountains and have to commute. But maybe he'd pay or else I'd manage to steal something nice, but discreetly, not like Dianka with her alarm clock from the bedside table or the door-mat.

FELIX

Meanwhile the Kid had disappeared again. I hadn't managed to find a trick that night for a decent price, I'd only succeeded in attracting the advances of a young Swiss guy with hair parted in the middle and frog lips, but super nice and smart, a designer. I wasn't quite sure if he designed clothing or buildings, but he was wearing all black, very stylish, and I was all in white, so we matched. I suggested we take a walk by the lake. So we got in his convertible and he took me to a part of the lakeshore I'd never been to before. On the beach was a merry-go-round and lounge chairs, like a mini-amusement park. I stripped naked and swam to the nearest buoy. I didn't look back, but I was excited by the idea of him swimming up from behind me any second and embracing me. I liked him. Also, he had a twin brother, he showed me his picture, they were identical. I thought: 'Well, two at once would be more happiness than I could bear.' We made love in the water and it was fantastic. Utter kitsch. The lights of Zurich in the distance, everything very Nora Roberts. His name was Felix. Well, anyway, romance is romance, but I wanted to find out what his financial status was, whether he was worth falling in love with and eventually moving in with. A few years in this business can seriously deaden your feelings and you can end up emotionally stunted for the rest of your life. But that summer night on the lake was amazing, crickets chirping everywhere, and after our swim we found a children's playground, little houses and monkey bars, and played on the seesaw, which none of my over-the-hill customers would ever have managed, but this guy could. I remember him asking me out of the blue if I liked francs (something only the Swiss would ask).

'Do you like francs?'

'In what sense?' I replied, since I wasn't sure what he was getting at, and I had several different areas of interest in the topic of Swiss currency, not all of which I felt comfortable talking about just then.

'We have nice money.'

But as it turned out, he was talking about how the banknotes looked, as he was apparently part of the group that designed them.

'But how? You're too young!'

It turned out those cartoon-like, brightly coloured Swiss-franc notes were quite new, they'd been introduced not long before, while the old ones were still in circulation. So there I was spinning around on a merry-go-round that resembled a toadstool, hanging out with the guy who designed the franc. I was thinking: 'He'll do for now, and being the designer, he must have few author's copies. Such a nice guy, a dimple here, a dimple there . . .'

'I like them,' I lied, as I didn't actually like the new banknotes at all. I much preferred old-style money, like dollars, all those flourishes, always the same. Dollars would have been better suited to the conservative Swiss. Imagine sitting in a bar from the twenties, paying with money that hadn't changed since the nineteenth century . . .

Later, we went for another swim and took another walk on the shore. I hadn't wandered around with someone like that in forever. I couldn't keep my mouth shut and among other things I told him about my new 'American' friend who had a house in the Alps and had invited me there on Wednesday. Felix asked me more about him, what he looked like, what his name was (it was Harry of course, what else was he supposed to be called?), and where exactly in the Alps his house was located. He asked me what the insignia on his ring looked like, and with my bare foot I drew this in the sand:

I looked and wondered why he was listening to my story with such a serious face, as if I didn't have men inviting me for dinner every day, to Safran, to the Odeon, to their yachts, their dachas . . . Suddenly he grabbed my hand, 'Do not, under any circumstances, go with that guy to his house in the mountains. I think I know who he is, and if it's true, then this guy is a well-known Satanist, and Satanism ist ein grosses Problem in Zürich, wie AIDS, wie Drogen . . .' I made a joke, something about always wanting to meet a Satanist, wanting to know what they're like in bed, how they're probably terrible pervs, it would be good to find out. But the way he looked at me I realized this wasn't something to make light of, here on the shore, that he was upset. He punched me and shouted, 'If you're that stupid, dummy, then go, go to that lair of theirs so they can burn you alive, no one will bother to look for you!' Only then did I understand that the Satanists were for real and not just another gay faction like the leather daddies or rubber queens, that they really might murder you during a Black Mass. Oh Lord, did I ever freak out then! I'd always thought it was just some nonsense, those pentagrams, upside-down crosses, triple sixes, praying the rosary on anal beads, but it was deadly serious!

It was morning when we got to his place (just a puppy but already a homeowner!). I was asking him how it was possible that in Switzerland I'd go home with a janitor or cloak-room attendant and there'd be a high-end Bang & Olufsen stereo system there. Or with someone on unemployment and he'd have a Bang & Olufsen too, as well as glazed windows and underground parking, things that in Poland only bank presidents had. And how did bank presidents in Switzerland live? Well, it turned out they lived in old castles surrounded by golf courses. And as for the unemployed, the minimum wage was so high that regardless of the job you used to have, you could live well. But it was misleading, because after getting fired the person would continue to receive the same salary for at least a year, but then it would stop and they'd be caught with their hands in the cookie jar. And that was basically like communism.

I lay on his bed and had a post-coital cigarette while he laid out his collection of matchboxes on my naked body, matchboxes from every time and place imaginable, with inscriptions in Chinese and Arabic and pictures of black cats on them, he even had some ugly Polish ones, which he actually said he liked (weird) because they were well designed. There were matchboxes with black-and-white nineteenth-century photographs of naked plump German women striking exaggerated poses, with artificial pastries and birds in their hands ... Anyway, he put them back and started showing me (by spreading them out on my tummy) his collection of foil coffee creamer lids. I was covered in those crappy little lids when our conversation turned again to that business about Harry. He asked me to promise him that I wouldn't go on Wednesday to visit the guy. I snarkily mumbled a promise and he got upset and hit me again, sending all those idiotic creamer lids into the air like confetti. He threw himself on me and whispered into my ear how they'd kill me. Then we fucked again in a sea of foil coffee creamer lids and on a snowbank of those creamer lids, and then I fell asleep. As I was falling asleep I thought about the Polish Kid, wondering where he was sleeping now and trying to remember what his face looked like. Nice Money was already asleep too. Once again I was spending the night in a stranger's bed, without even brushing my teeth.

So Wednesday finally came, and I kept looking down the street to see if that Harry guy was driving up in that nice car of his and parking and coming into Carrousel yet. I still wasn't sure if I would go with him or not. He didn't look one bit like a Satanist, aside from his bulging eyes, but I didn't doubt that he was mental. I wanted to see Marilyn Monroe's pubic hair and those old slot machines and the pool table, but I knew Felix might be right. Harry did come, but I didn't leave with him. Calcified grandpas were one thing, one kick and they'd shatter to dust, but thirty-year-old bald beefcake in a leather jacket was something else entirely.

FASHION (CONT'D)

So I introduced the pre-teen style and the returns at Caroussel went through the roof. First, all those hookers dripping in gold, lighting their gold cigarettes with gold lighters, just looked at me like what? when I walked in, but suddenly there was a flash of light in their eyes, like holy fuck, he's right! Give them a son, the elders, the childless ones, give them a pre-teen! At first, one gold-laden ape from Greece still had an ironic sneer flickering on his lips, but it was extinguished like a cigarette when the grandpas literally began lining up for me. The ones who caught on all wanted to buy me drinks, to surprise me with a Kinder Surprise! The next day, that ape from Greece was singing a different tune, practically wearing a bib and a baby bonnet with little ducks on it, pretentiously making moues like a diva, like Augusta Poppea from *Quo Vadis* (I know what I'm talking about, we had to interpret the whole thing in Polish class). And then . . . a golden age began. I would walk into Carrousel in a wool cap (with a pom-pom! in May!), in jeans with the crotch hanging all the way down, like a skater, wearing huge headphones, carrying my skateboard . . .

The innocent garb of someone who dwells in the sweet spot between toddler and adolescent combined with my growing knowledge of customer psychology to produce better and better results in the form of a skyrocketing balance in my Credit Suisse account. At the high point I had almost a hundred thousand francs in there! For a boy from Poland, which in the mid-nineties was little changed from communism, this was unheard of! And I really was fascinated by my customers, analysing their neuroses, their dreams, which they had never revealed before, even to themselves . . . Very few ever came for normal sex, although of course they didn't know how to ask for anything else, so they came for one thing and got another. I was good at my job. I'd have a guy built like Rambo, square jaw, shoulders, but in bed he couldn't pass the nipple-licking test. He'd start squirming and squealing with a woman's voice. And it was my role to help him let himself be, with me, the woman who he really was, who lived bound and gagged inside him. If a guy was ashamed to live out his fantasies in bed with a whore, then that surely was a bad whore, I'll tell you that.

But I needed to move out of the hotel and, despite everything, I went and got advice from the Romanian and her doctor, who immediately forced one of their grandpas on me. Or rather, they forced me on him. He lived in a faraway apartment block, in a flat buried in porn on VHS tapes and video equipment. He was fat, diabetic, rarely hit on me, and was always trying to get me to feel sorry for him, 'You know, I am very, very sick . . .' But the narrative gods must have made a mistake, because this place definitely should have been in one of the Dianka chapters, the way that diabetic guy hoarded sweets. You'd open the fridge—an enormous freezer full of ice-cream bars, boxes from Marks & Spencer with twenty bars each that you could eat non-stop. He was constantly giving himself injections in front of me. Luckily I had my own little room where I could hole up away from him, charge my Discman, listen to Nirvana and look at all the new things I'd bought.

In the meantime, Dianka's joint venture with Renzo Morelli had ended with a bang, and—up to her ears in debt—she landed back at Carrousel, the only one still wearing clothes from before my pre-teen style coup; that is, she had on some designer jacket and patent-leather shoes. I lay on the sofa and the diabetic would bring me ice cream, then cocoa and then chocolate. Everything was falling apart even with me just lying there. I gazed at the ceiling and made plans. The main thing was that I still didn't have a decent place to live, and this grandpa would be great for Dianka, but not for me. The next day I met a Thai Queen in Carrousel. I started talking in English (Thai English), and asked about her friends, and it turned out that 'in one hour will be here, by car'. These were different Thai Queens, though, and a different car, but they were the same, completely the same! They responded in exactly the same way to me and my Eleven-Inch, they smelt of the same Thai food and massage oil, and with the same silly smiles on their faces they gently stroked me with their little fingers. I looked into their child-like but ancient faces, in their blank but canny eyes, and I wondered if they might not have been the primordial rulers of this planet, later overthrown, all the other races being more aggressive and stronger than they were. Maybe they were the ones who flew over the mountains and the new arrivals took them for dwarves and trolls? I moved in with them for a while, to their immense joy, and once again I was having too-spicy dinners on a mat, once again massages every day, once again the smell of incense and once again five hungry mouths feeding on my Eleven-Inch ...

And here begins Part Two of what I would call 'Tabasco Love Story; or, Gangbang Love with Thai Dragon'. Not quite the same as in Vienna, but identical. With the same car, the same jobs in laundries, in mortuaries, which they took 'for the visa', although getting settled was a completely different affair in Switzerland, where even after years of living here an escort from Eastern Europe will still feel like a foreigner. They began putting down roots as soon as they arrived, while the ones who were already here—and who knows, maybe they'd been here a hundred years already—had managed to forge ties. Their English would forever be broken, but their Swiss German (Schwyzerdütsch)—respect! Poles had the problem that after a customer had hired them, he'd soon get bored of them—why always go for the same boy when there were so many other little hotties waiting to be tried? But customers couldn't tell the Thai Queens apart and they'd end up hiring the same one every time, convinced they were getting someone different. A hundred times over they'd go for the same hooker, and each time she'd introduce herself with a different name: Rolex, La Tour Eiffel, New York City, Louis Vuitton—they emulated the Asian brothels in mimicking the language of Western consumer culture. One week it was La Tour Eiffel giving blowjobs, the next week McDonald's on all fours. There was no telling with them. Snatches of their high-pitched laughter echoed everywhere: at the laundry, in the mortuary, in hospitals and at the Kunsthaus, where they washed dishes in the cafe and ran the vacuum cleaner after hours. You never saw them, but they were the ones behind all that Swiss order and cleanliness. The table-cloths in the restaurants didn't iron themselves, the cups didn't wash themselves, and it was on their account that Zurich had so many karaoke bars, because they were crazy about karaoke, and they were my first singing instructors! We would go to this one really kitschy karaoke place, with red carpeting pockmarked with cigarette burns and a revolving stage and an emcee dressed up like Elvis, and they would always ask me to sing Eric Clapton's 'Layla' or 'Strangers in the Night' or 'Love Me Tender', because those were my signature numbers, which I could already belt out in a low enough key that my changing voice wouldn't break. They would all roll their eyes and whistle, acting out their fantasies of being American celebrities, I don't remember who was in vogue back then, Naomi Campbell for sure, but in any case they were the only ones living in that city like it was paradise. The karaoke bar was their secret headquarters at the front in their ongoing war with Switzerland. What didn't they get up to in there—they ate, trimmed their nails, sorted out their shady deals, their trade in chilli peppers and incense, I think they even used the cabins there as hourly rooms for turning tricks.

And they were the ones, sly and seemingly omnipresent as they were, who helped me advance my career to an even higher level of service. It was from them that I first heard of Club Victoria . . .

Of course, with their hair smelling of fried food they would never have been allowed in through the door, except for the fact that dust is democratic, dirt equally divided between the rich and the poor, and wherever there's a mop, there's a little Thai Queen smiling from ear to ear. The Thais all called rich people 'princes', although they were really just fat landowners. We're going to the princes to clean. The princes had a party yesterday and all the A-list boys were there in a villa on the slope, overlooking the entire lake, snow-capped Alps in the distance . . . The princes had caviar and champagne last night, they played golf and tennis, and lounged on deck chairs drinking orange juice . . . We know, because we washed the glasses . . .

From their chattering in English I gathered there was a club of rich queens who met on the property of a different club member each time, and in order to get in you had to find yourself a rich boyfriend, a long-term relationship with a millionaire! Above all, not a word to Dianka and the rest of that riffraff at Carrousel. From that moment on, low-level hooking, paid by the trick, would be repellent to me . . . To give it away for free to the nastiest, most revolting grandpa of all, but to give it with the possibility of becoming his boyfriend, of entering into complete financial association, of riding around with him to other rich people's villas! 'Villas of the rich, for free I'll be your bitch, / I'll be your free bitch for the villas of the rich!' I sang out loud, running on the shore of Lake Zurich in my tracksuit. To just give it away to someone like that for free. The grandpa all disoriented, what is this, he asks himself, could someone really still find me attractive? And he looks in the mirror and he's so smitten with the idea of being found attractive that . . . oh, the villas of the rich! I'll be your running bitch! I ran with a bottle of Perrier in my hand, outdoing myself . . . But then, you win some, you lose some, it's an investment in the future, and of course you might end up taking a loss, you might give it away to some creep for free and he just takes it and rides off into the sunset, without even falling in love with you, without you becoming his boyfriend, without him leaving the villas of the rich to you in his will. 'But nothing ventured,' I said to myself, 'nothing gained.'

Now I had my radar set exclusively to millionaires. From morning to night I went around wearing Things from the Suitcase of Mario Ludwig. I even started feeling like a carp! I rehearsed my role. A fat fish comes up, liver spots on his paws, his face all twisted from cynicism and thievery so he looks like Michelle doing duckface, he smiles the smile of a shark offering you a bad loan in pink, sugarcoated packaging. The two of you get talking, he wants to hire you, but all you want is water, transfixed as you are by his beady eyes . . . He can tell something's not right, you've been chatting for half an hour already, he's made it clear he wants to bed you and according to all the rules you should have come up with a few more or less thinly veiled allusions to payment by now, changing the subject to exchange rates, the strength of the franc, etc. But instead you just sit there mesmerized by his eyes, you hold his hand and listen, you let him talk. You really have to know how to listen in this profession. Grandpas are never especially interested in you and when they ask you to talk about yourself, you need to be brief, because they're only asking to be polite and they'll tune out your answer. What the hell does he care about you and your Krzysztof who ate a deadly mushroom in Chelsea out of longing for you. You, on the other hand, should just let him talk. Don't interrupt. First, because he rarely has a chance to natter on freely like this, as most people won't put up with it and cut him off. Second, you're just analysing data to get your computer warmed up. What he keeps droning on about, like a patient on a psychoanalyst's couch, will just be processed for information about his romantic preferences and immediately converted into the physical form of the person sitting facing him. What kind of guys is he into? Modest and shy? Confident and feisty? What about sensitive? I have to admit my knowledge of customer psychology had grown by leaps and bounds since the days of my 'Love' campaign . . .

Above all, if you meet that grandpa again and you still aren't interested in money, gifts, or even having him cover your tab, then the grandpa—who isn't stupid, he's rich after all—will catch on. He'll recognize you as a gold digger. This is a critical moment, and readers of this guide must take note. If Gramps inherited his fortune from his parents, who were arms traders during the war, that's one thing; but if he made his money himself, then he clearly wasn't born yesterday. He'll start making allusions to being together, to which I suggest you respond with: 'It's too early to think about that'. Don't take the bait. Or if he mentions in passing that he has an ex-wife, who with her pack of lawyers will have his estate tied up in court long after his death and he can't do a thing about it, then: what on earth could he possibly be talking about, all you're interested in is him.

Most importantly, I needed an overhaul of my wardrobe. Whether I really liked an item and felt good in it was irrelevant. I needed to conform entirely to Gramps's taste. Once he's dead, then I'll get the tattoo and the nose piercing, but for now . . . Gramps's tastes were formed in the thirties, and he grew up in the forties and fifties, so it was only natural that his idea of how a young man should dress should have crystallized then as well—a young man presentable enough to appear in his company in society. This was pure conservatism, of course. How did they even dress back then? There was no internet to check, so I went to the library of the Kunsthaus and looked at Taschen coffee table books about the history of fashion. My skateboard, baseball cap, earrings, dyed hair and baggy pants that sagged in back exposing my Calvin Klein underwear would all have to go. Summer was just around the corner and I decided to go for the 'country-house-tennis-court' look from the villas of the rich, which meant: a suntan, a white Lacoste polo and white Lacoste shorts, a white watch, white tennis shoes and hair parted on the side. At the bar I ordered a freshly squeezed orange juice, mainly for the colour, which went well with the breakfasts of the rich and with health and with youth. And my thighs practically black jutting out from those immaculate white shorts. Once again it caught on maybe even too quickly, because the next day the escorts all showed up at Carrousel wearing the same thing. Good heavens, here we are walking in all in white, this must be some kind of high-end joint, they must have said to themselves before entering the bar.

But by then I was already a good little boy, an aloof English boy in my Burberry coat, in chestnut and beige, in plaid.

The rest was the con. But you have to tell a guy something about yourself, especially if you start going with each other, on walks or—Lord help me—he takes you out on his yacht. It's not easy at all to build a con. Like a good sauce it's made up of many ingredients, none of which may predominate. You have to tug at his heartstrings, nudge his paternal instincts awake, embarrass him a little, and above all make him curious! The business about my ex

Krzysztof eating a deadly mushroom wasn't such a good idea. Too much information, too soon, and poisonous fungi are hardly a positive association. What if he started thinking it was you who poisoned the guy, the same way you'd be poisoning him? Avoid talk of poison! Unfortunately, instead of preparing a solid foundation for my con, I just started winging it, telling different stories to different guys each time. Each was tailor-made for a particular grandpa, but it was impossible to remember what I had said to whom. A few things, however, were constant; my name: Kamil. Country of origin: Poland. Why I was hooking: bad people.

The first sucker I tried to seduce, when he finally understood I didn't want money, he panicked and ran away. For the Swiss, to withdraw from a deal was scandalous. These guys had fewer illusions about other people than I thought. The way they figured, if he doesn't want my money, then he'll be after my things, because there's no way he's attracted to me. And so I was left standing there without money and without the customer who'd fled. I couldn't afford this, and all three mafias immediately started hassling me about how I could be offering sex for free, was there something they didn't know about, weren't there minimum rates here? For a moment there it was getting pretty uncomfortable. I decided to change my venue. The oldies went to Barfüsser and Odeon too, in fact the wealthier ones were mostly at Odeon . . . I decided to frequent Zurich's most expensive bars and cafes, especially the ones in hotels. If a guy is gay, he'll be noticing beautiful boys outside of Carrousel too . . . To think what I spent on coffee back then! Those prices were sick! You know where: Baur au Lac, Eden au Lac, Widder Hotel . . . I enjoyed it so much I started going to Davos and Sankt Moritz (unparalleled locales). When I ran out of money (but fifteen years in advance, like with the water mains in Switzerland), I'd find myself a wealthy customer to take me out. In general I was only interested in rich old men. I was climbing up the ladder. Dianka was crashing down.

And that young guy, the one from Poland, who some of the other Poles and I started calling Jakub Szela, who knows why, was hustling at the train station now. Which meant he was either a drug addict or a simply an idiot. I felt so sorry for him I decided to track him down and see how he was doing. I don't know why, I guess I felt a little guilty on his account. The problem, of course, was that an escort like me, one who invests in PR and tries to mingle with only the wealthiest clients, a regular luxury *dame aux camélias*, can't just go and stand outside the toilets downstairs at the station, together with those schmattes. The most I could do was walk briskly past them through the underpass. But as soon as I saw him I knew he was using. Nothing was left of his babyface, his rosy, pudgy cheeks were gone. His lips were cracked, the light had gone out of his eyes. He was beyond saving.

Did you know rich people like to simulate wild animals? They cover themselves in their furs as if they were boasting of victory in battle and were wearing the skin of a defeated foe. Their faces take on the grimaces of insects, moustaches curling like antennae, eyes gleaming like a cockroach's ... Eating all those oysters and lobsters, wearing all those leather accessories, their shoes, their Hermès scarves ... They were very bad, very cynical people, and that's why I felt so good around them, although I had no illusions—I knew those grandpas didn't fall in love so easily. You could see it in their mouths, how accustomed they were to cheating business partners, the way their lips quivered with cunning. Mouths that were all the more hypocritical for being plastered on a face that displayed honesty, sincerity, a genuine understanding for and interest in your problems, liberalism and sympathy for pro-family policies, as well as a passable capacity for going a little wild now and then, like spending a weekend at a spa.

If they have a long-term thing happening with someone from Eastern Europe, it's only for convenience, to have someone to serve them and suck off whenever they want. And yet, one grandpa did fall in love. But he was unusual from the start. So unusual, even my rich-grandpa radar didn't go off. More than once it had identified rich seniors pretending to be poor, rich penny-pinchers, rich socialists (laughter in the room), rich communists and rich fuck-ups, because people like that exist too. This one, though, was a rich intellectual, which was why he hadn't got laid for free in forever. But it was also peculiar that of all the rich, the boring and the bad, it was the good, intellectual one who was interested . . .

A little old man, pure and simple. Lienhard. Graphite button-down, rimless glasses, an antique wristwatch, comfortable suede shoes. Excellent English, and High German, not Schwyzerdütsch. Everyone here spoke the latter, but the intelligentsia considered it beneath them and did their utmost to use the superior form of the language. On the other hand, less educated people sometimes could hardly speak German at all. He was maybe seventy years old, but he looked like a hundred. As I mentioned, my radar set to net worth (in Swiss francs) didn't go off, and I charged him a tidy sum the first, second and third times we met. The guy kept coming back to me like a boomerang. If only I had known then! But he was well camouflaged. He didn't even have his own car! He rode around Zurich on a bicycle, so I think you get the picture.

Anyway, I eventually started to see the writing on the wall and realized this was it, there wouldn't be another millionaire for me, such was my fate that the one who fell in love with me was the guy with the bike. He rode a bike, but he was still a millionaire. Most importantly, he paid like a champ, although he was neither inclined nor able to do anything other than literally rubbing his groin against me and dry humping. Whenever it came to pay, it was as if he was suddenly seized with remorse at having hired a hooker (escorts wouldn't exist, of course, without customers), and he always gave me much more than we'd agreed, and the agreed amount was already quite a lot. What's more, the guy was an art collector, and like all collectors he was completely loony. His entire flat on Hammerstrasse was covered from floor to ceiling with paintings and sculptures, and he had cabinets and drawers under lock and key that were full of limited prints. Picassos, shit like that. I wasn't too familiar with it all, but for his sake I would hang out in the library of the Kunsthaus (where my Thai Goddesses washed dishes in the cafe) and educate myself like I was taking an exam. He had a bad conscience regarding the Poles because his old man had traded chemical weapons with both sides during the War.

It occurred to me to tell him I was Jewish . . . Which was a stroke of pure genius. A Jew, a sensitive artist whose family had suffered immeasurably during the war. I pretended I was someone who had wanted to study art history, to write about sculpture but, due to circumstances (and my society, naturally!), had had no choice but to do this kind of work instead. But for all that, the character I was playing was a perceptive, insightful soul, someone you could talk with over gin and tonics about every dash or line in a Max Beckmann lithograph. So there I was, sensitive, subtle, ready to be saved, 'uplifted'. Lienhard didn't bring up the subject of 'uplift' until we'd met at least ten times or so. And I was unresponsive . . . Who on earth could want to lift someone like me up? Up where? People like that don't exist in this cold, cruel country . . . And I began to cry—I told you I was an actor—real tears. Which I'd never had a problem with. Even in grade school when I was in the drama club, when I would take part in poetry recitation and song contests, I almost always burst into tears on stage, and the jury just ate it up.

In fact, I was in no hurry to be 'uplifted'. I loved my job, the convergence of sex and money, two great forces of nature that keep the wheel of history rolling along. If he had come up to me the eleventh time, for instance, and said, 'Now I am going to uplift you. Stop going to Carrousel. Here's a monthly stipend from me. Now go back to Poland and study art history,' I would not have been happy at all. And then of course there was the fact that I didn't even like him. He was the polar opposite of me. Fortunately, he belonged to Club Victoria, and I convinced him once to take me to one of their gatherings.

'We'll go with Max,' he said. 'Max will pick us up in his Rolls Royce' (impoverished as we were, we didn't have wheels of our own). It was a Rolls convertible, and maybe one of the Carrousel crowd would see me in it.

During three years of whoring around in Zurich I must have met a hundred millionaires and they were all cut from the same cloth. The boring sports they played, like golf, yachting or tennis! They played them like they were being forced to, so they could buy more sportswear and join another sports club. Maybe one of them just wanted to go swimming in a lake (that would be me!), but no—it had to be golf. Their gigantic houses, their enormous beds, their colossal refrigerators, their mammoth televisions—all of them far too large to be convenient! Was it convenient to walk half a kilometre from the door to the bed? Not one, but fifty luxury watches, as if they didn't know that while one might make you happy, fifty were fully depreciated. (I had fifty watches of my own from the Suitcase of Mario Ludwig.)

All in all, it was fine that Lienhard was a grandpa on a bike. We would take the train to Basel to attend art auctions, bidding like mad on the Goyas, and during cigarette breaks the paparazzi would take photos of us. I thoroughly enjoyed it but my delight awakened only terror in him. How could anyone be so shallow and empty! At one of the auctions I ran into a 'princess' I'd met at Mario Ludwig's wake. We exchanged a few pleasantries, chatting about the relative worthlessness of Salvador Dalí's late prints, given that they were machine-produced by assistants and all he did was add his signature. That's why they were so cheap. And what do you make of the Picasso? Glass of champagne? No, no, I'm with the car. Ach so! Tschüssssi!

We travelled all over Europe, hunting for new and interesting works of art, oftentimes purchased directly from the artists. I felt very odd when I had to take Lienhard around Krakow and Zakopane. Showing him Kantor and Hasior. It transformed me into a cultivated gallery lady explaining Witkacy's portraiture to her clients in English. We succeeded in discovering and buying a few artists we hadn't heard of before, like Krzysztof Kamil Malewicz, Łukasz Korolkiewicz or the then-relatively-unknown Wilhelm Sasnal. But that is an entirely separate story, which I shall tell another time . . .

DIANKA

Dianka Spencer may be the queen of the people's hearts but definitely not of their pocketbooks. Our connoisseur of gadgets from Kinder Surprise eggs knew that this time there would be no getting back on her feet. The Pole wouldn't lend her money, there were no rutting johns to be found on the street, and she was banned from Carrousel. The Pole was clearly on the make these days. She saw him once in an open-roof Rolls Royce, and he saw her too and barely waved. He'd started dressing like a good little boy from an English novel. He was definitely up to something.

She knew that sullen Romanian queen Andrei wouldn't appear out of nowhere like a genie from a bottle because he almost always went to Carrousel or Apollo Sauna, where she couldn't afford the entrance fee. And she wouldn't be running into any lonely bankers ready to pay for a little company over Sunday dinner, or even to invite her to dinner without paying. She knew that no matter how hard she looked, there was little chance of stumbling on a Cartier watch some hot-headed businessman had lost on the street . . . Businessmen didn't lose luxury watches.

It all started with her debt, which for Dianka was completely fictitious. When she left the Garden of Boys and went back to freelancing at Carrousel, the Czechs came after her, including that muscle bear Jiřík, Michelle's boyfriend, and showed her how much she owed Renzo and how much she owed the Old Lady, and

for what—water, light, coffee, electricity, washing the towels, providing air that smelt of pine needles and cum . . . But all she had
to her name was ten francs, and you'll never guess where she got
it. Jiřík couldn't believe it: the Old Lady herself had lent it to him;
the little Slovak had so utterly charmed old Michelle that for the
first (and no doubt last) time she actually lent someone ten francs!
The Czechs were amazed and in awe and kept repeating the news:
Michelle lent someone money, the Old Lady lent the Slovak
kid money, how unbelievable, wow, respect! Dianka was utterly
fascinated by Michelle's metamorphoses, which took all evening
accompanied in the background by the brainless laughter of those
two unpleasant teenagers, Beavis and Butthead. And Michelle
loved it, at last she'd found a worthy audience, so she let Dianka
comb her hair, and she let her see her pussy and tits although
Dianka wasn't interested and hadn't asked. She taught her how to
give a blowjob, a talent that must be learnt because no one is
born with it. And when Dianka packed her suitcase and left the
brothel, Michelle pulled out from her black lace bra a crumpled
ten franc note and lent it to her. At first Dianka wanted to hold
on to the money as a keepsake, but as it turned out lean years were
on the way.

In a city where everyone just wants to lose weight and insists
on doing without, lean years had come for Dianka: Special Offer!
Special Offer! Now every low-fat soup comes with a free appetite
suppressant! To top it off, the ATM accepted Dianka's card (she
was sure she had another ten francs on it), only to imperiously
inform her that it would be retained. Danke schön very much!
The flap shut ceremoniously like a curtain, and no amount of
pounding her little fists against the machine would help.

Dianka had no money, and those with no money were unwelcome in Switzerland. God was no friend to those with no money. Only a rich man would find money on the street, he'd won it, it was his present.

She was unwelcome at Apollo Sauna, unwelcome at Carrousel, unwelcome at Odeon, unwelcome at Barfüsser . . . No more porcelain smiles and friendly faces shouting 'Grüezi!' (Swiss for 'hello!') . Dianka might have rallied one last time if Eleven-Inch had suddenly sprung up in front of her with one of his lectures ('arbeiten, Dianka, arbeiten!'), but the Pole never showed up.

Without any money, the discourse of chocolate collapsed like a deflating balloon and trailed along behind her on the cobblestones, snagging on whatever it could. The lights, the merry-go-round, had all shut down, and as if to spite her the chocolate cows on Bahnhofstrasse had disappeared too, they were there just yesterday, today they were gone. Even the really nice customers, when she ran into them, would listen to her tale of woe, then suddenly excuse themselves, they had somewhere to be, and wish her the best of luck. All those people who had been so friendly just yesterday were acting so mean now. Like when Dianka ran into a Swiss queen she knew and started talking in English, and the queen just answered in German. Dianka didn't understand. So finally she switched into English: 'You are already enough long time here to learn German. If you vant to live here, you must to learn German . . .'

As if Dianka didn't have bigger problems to think about. She knew that a convertible redolent with Asian food and gospel music wouldn't be coming for her any time soon. The Thai Dragon never came for her anyway, her cock was too small for them, size queens that they were.

One time, homeless Dianka ran into this one really nice former customer of hers at the train station: thirty-eight years old, slim, rich, freckled, and he had something boyish about him (although Dianka didn't know how studied that boyishness was)—the 'helpless' look of a Meghan Markle, the carefully disheveled hair, the expensive shirt, the elegant cufflinks . . . Always so nice, always on time, he was the guy from the advert. Just a big kid, and loooook at that pudding he ordered! He was a banker, and how! And then there was his studied, disarming demeanour, like in a travel brochure: a dash of boisterousness, a dash of impishness, combined with the confidence that once anyone entered his orbit their worries would disappear . . . And now, of course, homeless and the worse for wear, Dianka ran into him at the train station. He was just walking along like an advert for the Swiss Federal Railways, a box of Merci chocolates in hand (as if he were on his way to give them to a traveller), as if he were meeting Dianka here on a date, he saw her, cracked a smile from ear to ear, his artificial teeth beaming, and turned on his charm . . . Dianka got him to have coffee and cake with her, she knew he was too invested in being nice to say no . . . His eyes welled up with an understanding as deep as Lake Zurich for Dianka's problems, and for all the world's other problems too, including the starving children in Africa. He was the very picture of concern, and at the same time had a certain aloofness, after all, he was all that was standing between those problems and us!

With Africa, for example. He'd adopted a virtual child from Africa who he'd never met in person and had no plans to, but it was just one. He could just as easily have adopted ten, since all he did was transfer a small sum of money to the foundation's account every month and it's unlikely he even felt it in the pocket. But you have to know your limits, where your boundaries are. You can't save everyone.

He ordered her coffee and ice cream, and Dianka had a feeling of déjà vu, because when she'd arrived here from Munich over a year earlier, with nothing but Trashmaster's key in her pocket, she'd right away met some other guy who took her to this same cafe for coffee and ice cream . . .

So Dianka, taken in by his niceness, began to recount her trials and tribulations, intending to ask him at the end for a small loan, something to cover some new clothes and cosmetics, a hotel room, to help her get back on her moneymaking feet. He was having a hot chocolate (boyish, no?), and when she paused for a moment to roll a cigarette, he started in with how bad things were going for him, too. Because complaining is always best when it's done in company. When the neighbours come together at garden parties, they immediately start griping about Switzerland, that's their bag!

'Things are bad, it's getting worse and worse! Not just for you, it's the same all over Switzerland. I mean, the Switzerland you came to doesn't exist any more. Did you see what just happened in Berne and Basel?' Dianka hadn't seen because her little abode, the train station, had no televisions in it. 'Right? Everything is getting so expensive, you have to have three jobs just to pay the gardener! And then it turns out your dog is gluten-intolerant and you have to pay for special, gluten-free dog food . . . Taxes . . .'

So Dianka had her troubles, he had his. Biting into the biscuit that came with the ice cream, Dianka told him she wanted to trim her nails, if someone could just lend her clippers. Taking a sip of his Perrier, he told her he wanted to sell his boat, because who can afford to keep a yacht these days. For what he paid in insurance for that yacht, he could feed an entire village of Blacks down there, in beautiful, far-off Africa. Dianka felt like an African child herself and wished he would adopt her, why go so far away when there's misery right here in front of you? He, on the other hand, had just lent a painting to a museum, even though it still belonged to him, it was in a museum now, because he couldn't afford the million francs in taxes every year.

Somehow the two were actually on the same wavelength.

And then a miracle happened, Dianka succeeded in getting him to invite her to his place. Now. Right now. He wanted sex. She was happy to oblige, of course, as long as she could take a bath. And he was so nice he wouldn't dream of refusing her. Moments later, Dianka was in the underground car park, getting into his big, streamlined machine. They drove up to Zürichberg, taking the road she knew so well now, sweltering heat outside the window, in summer Zurich was like a Mediterranean city, another Dubai, inside the car it smelt of vanilla and money, and he was wearing dark sunglasses, while Dianka gouged the skin between her fingers and found something breeding in there, tsetse fly spawn. Once again they were driving up his driveway, into the yard and the underground garage, they took the lift up, to the living room, in the bathroom were five washbasins in a row, as if the world were paying Dianka back in spades for the privation of just one of the last few weeks ... Now she could shit to her heart's content and wipe herself with moist toilet paper, oh no, no more snickering over these bourgeois inventions the way she did at Jürgen's in Vienna, she knew their worth now!

She opened the taps of all five sinks at once, recklessly, wastefully, after all it's not like we're still living with that 'model-train grandpa' in Witikon. Wastefully she let the water flow into the bathtub, pouring sumptuous oils and salts into the bath, and soaked herself ... She washed her hair with now one shampoo, then another, then a third, a fourth even. She submerged herself. She drank cold water straight from the tap, it was mineral water after all, from the Alps. Dianka Fish. Dianka Hydro-Riddle. A Fish Named Dianka. Now we'll have ourselves a shave with his electric razor ...

An hour later, fragrant with Cerruti 1881 and Chanel Pour Monsieur and Dior Fahrenheit, attired in a white terrycloth bathrobe, Dianka walked into the garden, where there was a swimming pool and a golden blond sunning himself, a glass of orange juice beside him. The blond smiled at Dianka with a stereotypical artificiality, the genteelness of the upper class, and there was Dianka, lying on a beach chair in the very same garden that had lost its gardener, the gluten-intolerant dog rubbing up against her legs, gnawing on his gluten-free bone ... And then she was summoned upstairs, where the nice guy was lying naked on a white bed stroking himself, unaware of the pubic lice he was about to catch. Dianka would have given a lot—and given her meagre assets, that meant she would have given everything—for that day to last a whole night, which meant having a bed to sleep in, but unfortunately it was just past noon. Following intercourse, it was politely suggested to Dianka that she leave, a hundred-franc note stuffed into her palm. (A hundred francs! If she hadn't needed it, he would have given her five times that!) I'm sorry we can't give you a lift back, but we'll call you a cab (there goes fifty!). 'Bye bye! Tschüssi!' Hookers like you always manage somehow, little sluts like you always land on all fours!

Dianka slept at the train station. Dianka slept in the gutter. She didn't brush her teeth, although she was living in the Kingdom of Elmex, but she did dream of customers fragrant with air freshener, bankers sitting on the toilet with their boxers around their ankles, reading the newspaper, their genitalia shaved, with their rashes and razor burn. In every stall a forty-something banker was sitting, reading the exchange rates, enthusiastically holding forth about chocolate, chocolate cows, chocolate army knives and Supradyn, the Swiss multivitamin ... Of course, those bankers' willies were all shrinkage, pale, made of gooseflesh, like feathered chickens. But who cared, once he took out his contact lenses and put them in that special solution, Grandpa couldn't see a thing anyway ... Dianka dreamt of those people with their shoe stretchers. Those people with their complicated coat racks and garment bags. Those people and their trips to Poland, chartered so they could have all their healthy but slightly yellowing and crooked teeth knocked out and replaced with pearly-whites so white they were grey. Those people and their duty-free shopping trips to the Republic of San Marino. Those people and their fucking wine cellars, their bottles of wine reclining in their wine racks.

Those people and their Mont Blanc fountain pens.

You people with your massive goblets with only dregs left at the bottom.

You people and your too-sharp knives in their special cases.

They were all sitting there in their stalls, shitting out their expensive lunches and reading the newspaper. Their shaved willies in need of a coat of Bepanthen, the Swiss First Aid cream.

A naked grandpa with a weenie was proclaiming a hymn to Swiss punctuality.

Dianka woke up to a train being announced. She woke up in the train station, but she wasn't going anywhere, although she must have wanted to.

Now Dianka saw the city from the perspective of the junkies in Platzspitz park: boring, rich, arrogant, pretentious. Ugly, basically.

She couldn't stand hearing Swiss German everywhere and seeing those awful, grey-haired old women who never wore any make-up (she called them 'Wilhelminas'!), and those basic Swiss chicks in fancy ski wear talking for the whole street to hear. The blue trams gliding noiselessly on the rails. The tourists, everywhere, flocks of pigeons and tourists snapping photos of old buildings and statues. Buying miniature lions (the symbol of Zurich) and Swiss Army knives made of chocolate, Swiss chocolate cows, Swiss cheese . . . A small city, Zurich, with small, small-minded people living in it. Penny-pinchers, petty penny-pinchers. Tight-arsed tightwads. The awful church spires and bells, those pigeons and shutters!

With them, only time was free. You couldn't go a step without being able to check on the time. On church towers, on train platforms, at art galleries. Maybe because time was money. Maybe that's why they loved it so much, why they hoarded it.

They wouldn't let her back in at Carrousel until she paid back her debt. All she could do now was look in the window at the Creoles, Latinos, Blacks, Poles and Russians sitting inside . . . And then she had to keep walking, walking and walking, because in order to sit you had to pay, you had to pay to have a coffee, and if you weren't sitting you had to keep walking all the time . . . So she walked to the elegant train station that stood at one end of elegant Bahnhofstrasse, where the cafes had original Toulouse-Lautrecs and Mirós on their walls, but they weren't on her floor. She took the escalator to the lower level and walked towards the toilets, where a few junkies were already roaming about. They all looked like that wreck, Renzo's boyfriend. Young carcasses dressed like beggars. In the toilet itself the pine scent was ruptured by the stench of poo. The customers here were completely different—no millionaires, no spruced-up middle-class daddies with their lives figured out: the nine-to-five during the week, then Thank God it's Friday and Happy Hour. What else was there in life? The rest was just that nonsense artists come up with and those hippies from Binz squat. If you did everything in the right order, working and resting at the proper times, you could just relax and switch to autopilot.

She hardly had any customers. When she did, they were just as filthy as she was, their skin ashen like hers, red blotches on their faces, equally untrustworthy, with plastic Migros shopping bags in hand. A lot of times they didn't pay at all, they just ran away. The loudspeaker announced departures to Davos, Milan, Paris,

Brussels, Geneva . . . In the end Dianka gave up the last thing she still had, her shame. Like the other beggars she scrounged up some cardboard and went to sleep by the toilets, where she was supposed to be turning tricks. Relief. She was suddenly released from that life. Now she was seeing Zurich from the lowest level: it was made up of shoes (often made to measure), clacking heels, leather boots, Louis Vuitton suitcases on rollers, floor polishers. Oof. She needed this. Sitting on the ground meant accepting her new status as a beggar. This time she'd have to make herself at home as she'd be staying here a while. The police let her sit there for exactly seven minutes. Then they came with their green berets and dogs and barked at her in Swiss, and she'd had enough, she snarled and screamed at them in Slovak to fuck off, those people and their fucked-up country Switzerland.

A night in jail. Luxury accommodations at last.

The summer had already started, since time never stands still. It was sunny, Zurich was in full bloom. Dianka moved to a bench, to a park, as far as possible from that hellhole of junkies! She sat in the park at the edge of the lake, she swam in it and listened to the conversation of the yachts moored at the pier. They spoke by splashing and dully clanking the cans attached to their masts. Behind them, the snowcapped peaks of the Alps.

Dianka could have gone on living like this on the shore, at least while it was warm, but there was one thing she couldn't tolerate: the lack of food—to be more precise, the lack of junk food, candy, ice cream. Switzerland had annexed chocolate as well, and for years it had waged a never-ending war with Belgium over pre-eminence in the industry, because that was something this country would actually go to war for. That's why during tourist season you couldn't take a step without smelling chocolate or seeing shop windows filled with displays of chocolate, balls of chocolate wrapped in foil. Fine, so they didn't have Mozart on them, but whatever—they stood for the world. The fragrance of white drinking chocolate filled the air, and a river of milk chocolate flowed. Dianka needed sugar. She started walking the city anxiously and got booted out of every shop and cafe. It wasn't easy to shoplift here. In order to start turning tricks again, she would need:

1. Twenty-five francs for the sauna, to wash up.
2. Thirty francs for cosmetics, a disposable razor, toothbrush, etc.
3. At least a hundred francs for new clothes and shoes.

Besides that she needed to trim her nails. Dianka would need a total of one hundred fifty francs to come back to life. They wouldn't let her back into Carrousel, but at least she could make some money at the station and buy a ticket back to Bratislava. Dianka had discovered the bus station behind Zurich Central, and would go there sometimes to look at the buses from Poland, the Czech Republic, Slovakia . . . Peculiar, foreign people would get out, country folk, weighed down with bags, they would look around, curious, smoking smelly cigarettes. Dianka even knew how much the bus fare was: two hundred francs. What she used to make per minute. What she'd give to be able to rob a customer now, but who would hire her, dirtbag that she was?

Later, she fell into a stupor. She was lying on the shore for hours, watching the lake. It was beautiful, clear, the water rippling, reflecting light. Like thousands of tiny diamonds. She could hear distant music in the park. White people with dreadlocks sitting cross-legged on the ground, drumming. Someone was playing a violin. Dianka fell asleep. She dreamt of waste, of seeing all the waste from all the products, the Starbucks to-go cups, the Kinder Surprise wrappers, the used condoms, used needles, used boys, used toilet paper . . . It was all piled up in a huge rubbish tip, a mountain of garbage, an entire Alps of trash! And around this dump her Trashmaster is driving a bulldozer or some fancy orange German garbage truck. He's naked, completely naked. And he's sitting there naked behind the wheel. Covered in tattoos, wearing only an orange helmet. He has a hard-on, like always. Passionately he digs and thrusts and pushes all the Milky Way wrappers and chocolate Swiss Army knife foil, all the empty plastic bottles of silver-hair shampoo for respectable lawyers, all the used condoms with a spoonful of lawyer sperm in the tips, the sanitary pads for low-level bureaucrats, the bottles of dishwashing liquid . . . In a wild frenzy, rutting like a horse, Trashmaster pushes all of it, the entire West, straight over to the East, to the border of the pox, of the shit, of the Gypsies!